Paris Affaire

A Novel
By
Jean-Thomas Cullen

The Love Story of a young Poet and his Angel in the
City of Light. A contemporary romantic novel of Paris.

Clocktower Books, San Diego CA

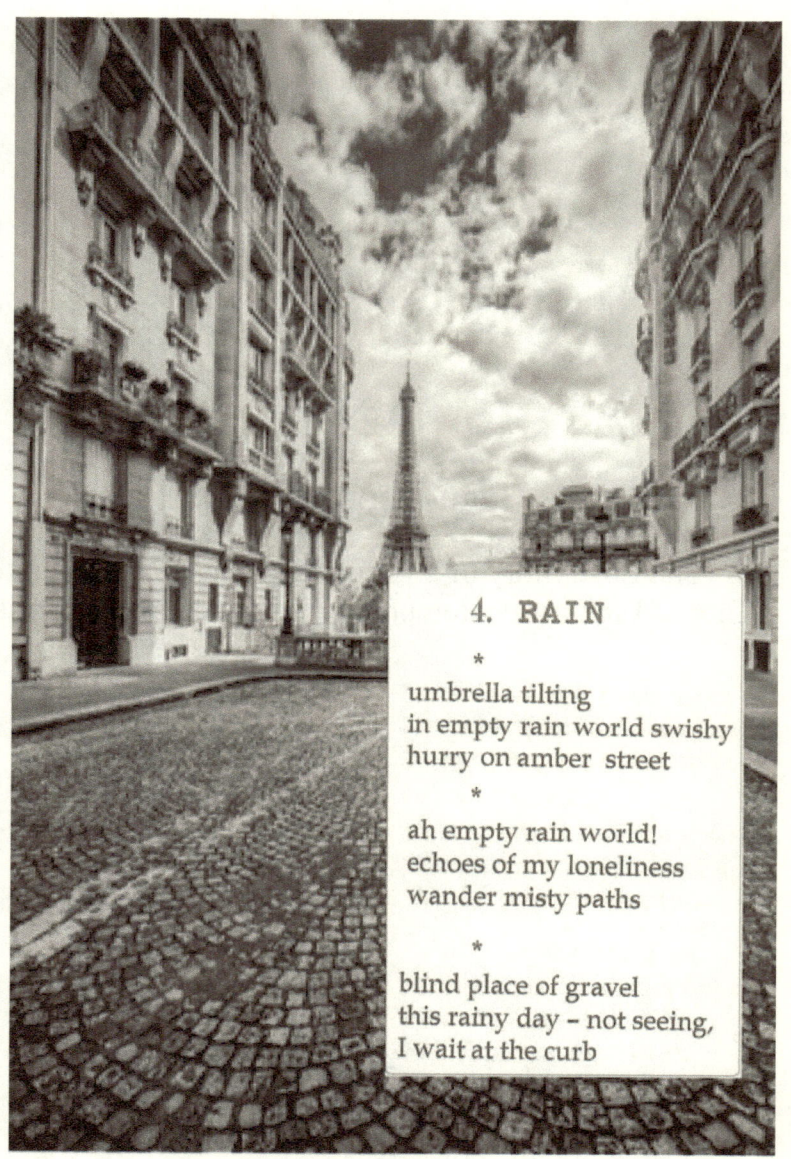

4. RAIN

*

umbrella tilting
in empty rain world swishy
hurry on amber street

*

ah empty rain world!
echoes of my loneliness
wander misty paths

*

blind place of gravel
this rainy day – not seeing,
I wait at the curb

Contents

Author Note: I wrote the original version of this story as a young soldier stationed with the U.S. Army in West Germany. I am a citizen of both Luxembourg and the USA, and have lived many years on both sides of the Atlantic puddle. The original ms was provisionally titled **Jon+Merile** (Copyright © 1974 All Rights Reserved) and remained unpublished for many years. I released a slightly polished first edition in 2016 under the title **On Saint Ronan Street** (Copyright © 2016 All Rights Reserved) by John T. Cullen (my English language name). That edition (which will remain in print as a totally separate literary work) was written with the natural homesickness and longing (ancient Hellenic *nostos* or *nost-algia*, pain for homegoing) of a young soldier far from home. *On Saint Ronan Street* is set in a New England college town rather than in Paris, and may remind some readers of John Updike's work). *On Saint Ronan Street* has a companion volume (which this Paris novel does not) titled *Cymbalist Poems*, by the fictitious hero of the novel, a young poet named Charles Egeny who is in a love affair with a lonely young faculty wife named Merile Dougherty. After seeing the movie *The Umbrellas of Cherbourg* not long ago, I decided that somehow I had struck that same melancholy, almost *laissez-faire* Gallic tone as that of the movie. So I wrote an entirely new novel, based on the plot of *On Saint Ronan Street*, but set entirely in Paris; which, as it happens, is a city I visited many times in my life. I especially enjoyed weekend trips (at the time a four hour drive or train trip; today two hours via TGV) to Paris from my duty station in Kaiserslautern, FRG. I ended up not being so satisfied with the Gallic irony of *On Saint Ronan Street*, and decided to end **Paris Affaire** in a surprising new way that takes nothing away from the *parapluies* atmosphere of *On Saint Ronan Street*, but adds a robust new dimension. Please read **Paris Affaire**, enjoy, and tell your friends. *Merci!*

ONE YEAR AFTER THEY MET

Le Debut au Fin

Begin at the Ending

Chapter 1.

A blue light came steeply from a clear, starry night sky to laugh with Marc Fontbleu and Emma Delors, who were just then (at 3:05 a.m.) having a snowball fight on the slopes of a lake outside of Paris. They laughed and ran around the slopes in their private sharing. Their white teeth gleaming in moonlight, just as the lake surface glittered with ice and water.

Because they laughed and cried out joyfully but softly, nobody heard them. All the swallows had flown south for winter, and the big nasty blackbirds were asleep in their tree forts, so Marc and Emma had the world to themselves—for this precious moment only, but it might as well be a lifetime. The leaves were all down, making the trees look barren and severe.

Marc and Emma were warmly dressed after their steamy adventure. They wore ski suits (hers pink, hers blue) and wool caps and earmuffs that made their red cheeks gleam and their teeth radiant as sugar. She was thirty years old, and looked not a day older than his twenty-three. She was elegant and dramatically pretty (fashion model), while his serious demeanor and intelligently high forehead made him look older. They were a good match in so many ways. And they loved each other. The wide face of a full moon smiled warmly down on them. It was a night for pranks.

* * * *

Half an hour earlier, they were busy making love in a down sleeping bag in the snow on someone's lawn—stealthily, among pine trees and cypress bushes around silent suburban homes—while unsuspecting folks slept all around them in Créteil, Val-de-Marne to the southeast of central Paris.

Marc and Emma snuffled and giggled, writhing in each other's warm, sweaty arms and legs; rubbing feather-soft bellies together, and *ouch*, clacking knee caps.

He started to roll over on her but she pushed him back. Her hand brushed along his side as they wriggled inside a downy sleeping bag for two. "Stay a little while longer—I've never had so much fun."

He laughed and held her tightly as they lay side by side, looking out from their evergreen hideaway among white and sleeping houses.

A blue glow of streetlights stole with accessorial civility among the scotch pines. The air smelled sweet (scoured of its salts and sulfides, which lay buried). Sudden breezes runneled over the virgin snow fields, kicking up spiraling whitewater snow crystals, crossing the buried street to clip snow caps off dazed, beached cars. Marc and Emma sputtered and closed their eyes as cold grit blew freshly into their mouths, eyes, and nostrils.

"Whew. This is like riding in a fast motorboat," said Marc.

"Have you ever done it in a boat?" she whispered.

"No," he said truthfully, thinking of the nearby Lac de Créteil and its Marne River waters and summers.

"You're lying," she accused, slapping his arm.

He lay back with his arms behind his head. "I wish."

"I haven't either," she confessed. He smiled, but she frowned and cuddled close, running her lips and hand over the hair on his chest. Between her cold fingertips, he felt the heat of her breath. She whispered barely audibly, "Let's not delay." They lay hidden in the shadows of pine trees.

He moved in between her long legs, guided by her eager hands; and, rocking on her firm round buttocks, consummated the release of deliciously hoarded energies. Crystal snow enveloped the hair at his neck as his head rose into tingling pine needles and they labored together. Their fingers were intertwined and white. Their groans sounded syncopated and in rapid counterpoint.

After they sank together in exhaustion, she stroked his hair slowly and steadily while he quashed a resting cheek against her shoulder. Sucking in his cheeks thoughtfully, he could see past the horizon of her cheekbone, chiseled and covered with microscopic hairs in bluish light. Her dark, liquid blue eyes, full of calculations, blinked as she looked upward through pine needles. Stars winked high up in the clear sky.

He murmured through a mouthful of inner cheek, "What are you thinking?"

She kept stroking his hair. "We're stark naked, you know that?"

In an exchange of startled looks, they burst out laughing—softly, of course—rolling about in a pummel and writhe of limbs.

"I'm getting chill," he said, burrowing deeper into the sleeping bag. With one long arm, he reached down past his fetally raised knees and icy toes. He sought his underpants among the clothing their trampling feet had compressed far down in the bottom of the sleeping bag.

She huddled down, too, while tightly zipping the mouth of the sleeping back around their brushing necks. "I suppose we'll catch our deaths. What are you reaching for?" She brought her knees up and aside, and added her hand to the search. Their fingertips scrabbled together over the pressed clothing.

"My underpants," he chattered.

"The primal fig leaf," she remarked sympathetically. To the changeless night she added, "This had to end."

"We could do it again," he muttered, knowing it was impossible. Finding the needed undergarment, he sat up and pulled its one large and two smaller apertures over his numb feet. In so doing, he let in a blast of cold air that raked their backs. With a subdued shriek, she flailed through their mingled clothes. "I'm putting on my shirt first," she chattered. Thus together they struggled to clothe themselves as quickly as possible.

He sneezed.

"See?" she said.

Their shoes came last; already their nylon ski parkas enclosed their body heats separately. The sleeping bag lay open and its newly exposed innards were becoming lightly fuzzed with blown snow.

With the heat of motion retained by the airtight parka, he hurried under the impeding pine branches to wrap the sleeping bag into a tight ball while she stood beside him, a figure of innocence. She kept her fingers linked over the opacity of blue parka and ski tag veiling her pleased secret. She remarked, "Say, we melted the snow in a circle."

Wheezing from icy air in his lungs, he swept the downy nylon hull under his arm, feeling it deflate slowly, and looked at the crushed, bare grass which was already covered by platelets of ice.

"Nobody would believe it," she observed.

He straightened up and looked at her. "Would you?"

In the blue light, her teeth were like china as she smiled. "I'm very happy." She was a tall, slim blonde with long smooth hair and an elegant sort of long-faced prettiness, ruddy and radiant as if just from the ski slopes.

He was dark-haired, lean, and muscular, with an angular, narrow head of short-clipped dark hair, a strong jaw covered with twice-a-day shadow, and mournful dark eyes.

"We made one mistake," he said, pointing to the scars their feet had made in the freshly fallen snow. The holes were already filled with snow, but had raised edges like moon craters filled with dust, mysterious in origin.

She shook her head. "It's going to snow some more very soon now." She put her hands in her parka pockets and looked around. "Suppose somebody was watching?"

He touched her elbow and drew her back into the shadows. "Come gaze into my eyes one last time."

"What about the footprints?"

He said, "If anyone comes by, we'll tell them it was a Yeti and we were chasing it."

"I have to get going in a few minutes," she said, staring worriedly at a foot of fresh snow already blanketing the street.

He shrugged. "We'll manage." He looked aside. "I think we've melted the snow in a circle around us."

Laughing brightly, she stuck a snowball down his shirt and he in genuine anguish made jerky motions like one who had been shot, falling finally face-first into the down.

Minutes later, he chased her over the glaciers of snow and ice that oozed from among somnolent houses. Disregarding man-made fences and barriers, Marc and Emma capered under tinkling and ice-laden trees while the moon shone gaily, trapped in the suffusive blue haze of the street lights. The night just sort of floated in a sympathy of winking stars as they held hands atop windy orchards and gazed toward the humming highway, to eternity; and toward the unknowable future for each of them.

ONE YEAR EARLIER, THEY MET...

Part One: Spring

242. Singles Bar

Are you going early, and alone?
Stay.   We
are the driftwood of
conversation, fragments of
ambitions, broken halves,
the late lamp.
       In this
our deep and distant eyes
glanced to agree.
   Stay.   My voice
is inaudible, but my eyes
       are screaming.

Chapter 2.

Marc Fontbleu, secretly alias the poet Léopold Montblé, was mowing lawns one day around the Paris I Sorbonne, more specifically around the College de Navarre off the Rue Descartes. That is in the Pantheon-Sorbonne area on the Left Bank in the 5th Arrondissement, where in recent months he had been crashing nights with some guys he knew from the bar scene. Not to be coy about it, he was a year from having his degree in Literature at the University in Créteil, and he was already a minor published poet if you counted school literary magazines. He had earned the praise of students and professors alike, but they knew nothing of his secret deeds and ambitions.

He had a great fondness for music and poetry, which he combined in the subtle rhythms of his free verse. Or again, that would be the verse of one Léopold Montblé, poet in exile. So he would soon be explaining to a rapt Emma Delors once he met her.

He had qualified to attend Paris XII, and was hoping to finish one day through the prestigious main campus in this area near the Jardin de Luxembourg. He loved the old buildings here, smothered in trees and ornamentation, versus the ostentatious and timeless somewhat-Gothic or wishfully modern glass cubes around his home town of Créteil.

The seasons in the Île-de-France region are extreme and final statements. It was spring—and talk about April showers. Gone were Chaucer's deep snows of February, and the agues of March. Like water dripping in a pot through tendered tea leaves, a gentle April rain sieved itself through the newly bright-green trees. The brown earth was soaked, and the first tender grass sprouted in thin, tall clumps over the tea-like deposits. The very air seemed to glow bright green, and was fragrant with emerging blossoms.

Across the rooftops, high up over the banked tree crowns newly dense with fresh leaves, reared the dome of the Pantheon. Even with the roar of motors and a faint haze of exhaust fumes, the air was redolent with spring. It was a sodden air, silvered with a fine mist of rain that wetted rather than soaked one's clothes.

Marc Fontbleu stopped, turned off his evilly smoking lawnmower, and took off his rain-damp baseball cap to wipe off sweat. He was twenty-three, and employed by the university in this manual capacity. Owing to his ongoing studies in Literature—interrupted by a semester here or there writing poetry, tending bar, or slumming around the Continent's other historic cities—someone in the Sorbonne employment offices had promised him this job as a starter, pending some more important and interesting assignment. Could he put up with the drudgery of mowing lawns for that long? Sure, he told them, what the hell—it was better than no job at all. Besides, being so close to his degree, he relished the thought of some relaxed summer time ahead, innocently spent mowing lawns. He dared not think of his prospects ahead—should he continue to a higher degree, or simply move into (oh God no) the business world and start earning a living? What would become of music and poetry and Léopold Montblé then?

He was tired from years of school, and not sure he wanted to continue in English. Through much of his undergraduate time he had faked it, reading few of the assigned materials, and writing (like running) for his life. He knew there were holes in his understanding of the standard Great Authors. He had preferred to read less well-known but more modern poets and writers of his choice—the cool jazz of writing, blue beats unknown in the bleach of academe; in whose tone and modality he wrote his own verse (free in more senses than one) that could connect with no safe, mediocre publisher. He hoped to have time, living in his rented room in Hamden not far from Lake Whitney—where, a hundred years earlier, the famed inventor had toiled in a small red factory that still stood there on an island amid moss-colored, marbled waters—to read all the authors and works he should have read for courses.

Meanwhile, he wrote poetry under the nom de plume of Léopold Montblé. He'd published a few scattered items. Fame, however, was not yet at hand, and should it come, he would relegate it to the mysterious Léopold Montblé, since he felt he should never succumb to some emboldening and inflated public image of himself. He preferred the freshness and early morning innocence of being forever an outsider; every day was thus a fresh beginning full of idealism and dreams. Confident in the eventual success of Léopold Montblé, Marc Fontbleu wiped his forehead and continued to mow university lawns with his blue-smoking lawn mower in the tinged and tea-dripping green half-light of a spring day in the ancient and medieval Latin Quarter.

He was on his own here, and he relished his independence, which fit him perfectly, even in this menial occupation. In the early mornings, a truck took the members of the lawn-mowing team around to their various work spots. Thus left to himself, Marc Fontbleu took a craftsmanlike, artisan pride in conquering the upstart legions of newly sprouting grass. He had worked his way around a small park in a courtyard this morning, and estimated with simple craftsmanlike satisfaction, that he could report to his supervisor he'd be able to finish the greenery around this building. He paused to wipe sweat from under his cap.

Then and there, that was the moment in his life when he saw Emma Delors for the first time.

Her footsteps, in half-heels, sounded muffled on the drenched and green-covered sidewalk above. Clad in a white dress that reached from her neck down to mid-thigh, she walked airily, innocently, in an elegant swish of slender limbs. She was blonde, and had that fresh, athletic, long face, blue eyes, and pink cheekbones of which advertisements are made. Her skin had a smooth, creamy tan like a flan pudding. She didn't notice him, and perhaps was indeed not conscious of being watched. For this reason, her walk and her facial expression were plain and unassuming, but to Marc Fontbleu she was a goddess, and he frantically resumed his mowing.

Later, he went inside for a soda. Bending down in the wood-paneled darkness of the austere break room, to remove a cola he had just bought, he was startled by the whiteness of her dress as she came in.

"Oh, hi," she said. It was the obligatory greeting between people working for a long time in the same office building, who never get to know each other but eventually learn the contents of one another's clothes closets just from the daily variation among similar themes.

He backed away from the machine, removing the pop top from his cola can. She sidled past and inserted her quarter. He felt awkward, sweaty, and caught a whiff of some subtle perfume, some air of freshness about her.

Her coin slid easily down the innards of the machine, but her pressing of various buttons with a glossy fingernail produced no result. At last, seeing her blush of frustration, he excused himself. "Allow me..." Groaning with effort, he bent down on his knees, inserted a grubby hand into the machine's cool guts, and fished about until he felt a ledge high up in its intestines. On that ledge, his stretching fingers just barely touched the convex, crimped bottom edge of an aluminum can. "I have it now..." he gasped, and with a final effort (his shoulder being in the way) he freed the can and brought it down, balancing in a juggling act on his fingertips.

She smiled at his effort.

He rose, leaving the can for her. It lay in the slot where it should have fallen in the first place. They faced each other briefly before the machine. She was nestled up against the machine, her slender body hunched in a motion of preparing to retrieve the can, and her eyes darted full of pent-in sentiments from a glance at his dirty hands to the dully gleaming can and back to the muscles of his legs.

He stood transfixed as she bent close past him to seize the can. He inhaled deeply the scent of her fresh skin, the disintegration of perfume atoms in the warmth between her roused breasts. He stood back, soaking in the gentle but enveloping ambience of her faint smile. His breath—rattling with heartbeats—caught in his throat.

Around her eyes were the earliest of faint wrinkles, as if caused by the intense and mysterious and subtle melting effect of her smile. She must be about thirty, seven years past his own age.

Rising, she appeared startled by his attentive stare. She seemed utterly surprised, and then a bit cool and disenchanted by his hard, hungry look.

"Excuse me," he stammered, and the smile blossomed out again, crinkling the corners of her mouth and illuminating her skin pores.

They shared that dull, tea-green soaking glow in the gloomy basement room. Perhaps there is some springtime hormone that sets cells ablaze with new hope and yearning.

Their eyes met, engaged, and would not let loose. There arced between them a lightning of emotion. As she once said later, she could have turned away, and as he agreed, that would have been the end of it. He noticed the veiled, dull-faceted diamond, the glimmering platinum ring on her finger in that tea-soaked light—a green ambience flooding the dark wood-paneled basement room.

He yearned to reach out a fingertip and touch her cheek. She looked so open and glowing and helpless in that moment. But his fingers were grimy from the work outside and he hid his hands behind his back because of the proximity of her white dress. She later admitted she would have gone back to her office, where she had a heavy typing assignment. Instead, she sat in one of the Jérômeowy, plush old dark brown easy chairs in the lounge.

Marc Fontbleu—fresh from combat with presumptuous spring grass fed by soaking rains—relinquished his battle and sank into the airy comfort of a parallel chair. She crossed her naked legs, pointing the toe of a white shoe at him. From the first, they laughed easily together. Every time their eyes met, there was that flash of empathy.

She uncrossed her legs and modestly pointed her chiseled knees away.

"Do you mind the rain?" Her voice was plainly tremulous. Her lips quivered as she spoke. Her voice was high and exposed and uncertain, girlish and falsely devoid of strategy.

He knotted his hands around the cola can between his knees. Literary innuendo emerged. "Actually I'm enjoying myself. Every blade of grass is a challenge." He detected a quaver in his own voice. Had he been confronted with a canyon to jump across, his stomach pit could not have been more tense. He sat on the edge of the chair, ready to spring.

He thought, *What am I getting into?* He fought an urge to flee.

"I might enjoy escaping from the office too," she admitted, and in so saying conveyed a sense about her whole life. He sensed this and clutched the can more tightly, smiling nervously.

Her fingers fluttered, trembling, up around the watch she wore on a chain around her neck. "Almost time to go back," she said.

He looked at the floor, feeling a leaden weight of green light upon his back, and said sharply, "Stay a moment longer."

She feigned incredulousness. "Whatever for?"

He stared at the floor, noting the pale outline of her legs in the periphery of his vision. "Because I enjoy talking to you." Scared of what he'd said, he stared at her, and she sat back (imprisoned but willingly) by his look. She said: "You don't want to hurt me." It was a wish and a question.

"No, of course not," he said, swigging at the cola. "I saw you on the sidewalk before."

"I saw you too," she said.

There it is—door open.

He shook his head. "I didn't think so. You shocked me."

Her frown relaxed from worry into an intrigued smile. "Oh? How is that?" Still, her knees pointed away. She hadn't taken a single sip from her cola.

His truthful words, effortfully disgorged, ballooned leadenly around his head in the enclosed atmosphere. "I find you very beautiful."

At this her smile melted away into gratification, while her voice took on a mournful weight. "I don't look thirty and married, do I?"

"You sure don't," he told her. He was glad that her knees remained pointed away. "I would like to meet you." He had never spoken this way to a married woman before.

"A date?" she asked incredulously but not unkindly.

"If you want to call it that." He felt a panic rise inside. What about her husband? What about this job? What about...

She stretched her wrist so the cola can tilted in the direction of her gaze. She stared into the cola can. He watched her nervously as she deliberated. He almost wished he could run from the room.

She wriggled the cola can in her hand and regarded him thoughtfully. "You have nothing to do with the university, do you? I mean, aside from your summer job or whatever?"

He shook his head.

She looked again at her cola can. "My husband is on the faculty. He's an assistant professor of archeology. We aren't doing too well. You aren't married, are you?"

He shook his head.

"Wouldn't help much to cry on your shoulder."

He started out of his chair, approached hers, and put his hand on her wrist, which rested on the armrest. "I'm afraid I only know about marriage in theory. I can't do much to help you." He'd only had one long-term girlfriend during his recent college years, along with a string of flirtations and a confetti storm of gratifications with young women. He was no stranger to the delights of intimacy. He was tall, slender, dark-haired, and intensely handsome. Or so Danielle, his best friend's sister, had once told him; only he'd been annoyed because he didn't know if she was teasing him. His friend Jack said it was a trial and a torment having a sister, except when she was nice once in a while. Marc, who'd grown up with two brothers (one younger, the other older, nothing out of the ordinary except one or two fist fights and nosebleeds early on before the rules spelled themselves out), imagined that all brother-sister siblings said that about each other. Having Dani for a sister-in-friend was instructive enough. *Thanks but no thanks*.

He knelt by this adorable woman's chair, as if in prayer, or proposing marriage, or tying his shoelace. He was not sure which, himself. Something in this stranger drew his emotional engine closer to hers, and he could see in her eyes, the hunger in her face, her engine closer to his, one silent, aching ratchet of gear teeth after another.

She gave him an intense look, quickened by impulse. "You don't just mow lawns, do you?" she said, alluding to his stained clothing.

He told her his secret, "Under the name of Léopold Montblé, supposedly a Belgian or Russian émigré, I write poetry. Fits the void left by Nabokov."

"Léopold Mount-Wheat. How strangely intriguing. I suppose wind blows through the wheat, and it is achingly romantic."

"Poetic," he affirmed. "Often a bitter triumph, a strong drink."

She put down her cola and put her hand on his. "You'll be famous yet."

"You promise?"

She laughed. "Oh you puppy. Yes, I promise." She cupped his face in her palms. "Are you for real?"

"I am only half serious all the time. It's a survival mechanism."

She put her fingertips to her lips and laughed again, in amazement. "Wow. That is so cool. I want to be like you."

"We could write poetry together."

"I can't write anything more than a sympathy card. Maybe you could read your poems to me. I listen well."

He talked jive, while snapping his fingers. "I read the Beats and audit Auden. I compose word-o-phonics like Coltrane or Stan Jets play sax." *Does she get who I am? What Léopold Montblé does? Who those old classics were? What I am saying?*

"You play with language," she said appreciatively. She was thirty but looked younger. The long, elegant cast of her cultured face betrayed a well-trained pursuit of social directions, including tennis courts, cocktail parties, and lawn club debuts—all of the wealthy. The privileged class. Everything he was not, but felt smarter than, so why bother? He was not as impressed as he should have been. They could not write music like Debussy, or paint like Richter, or compose verse like Montblé.

"I type my manuscripts at night," he confessed while moving to the chair beside hers, lithe as a panther.

She reached out and absently stroked his hair. "You'll have your success," she said encouragingly. He saw, in her look, a habit of being (in his view) associated with intelligent and aggressive but weak men. He stood back, proudly, when he saw men like he imagined her husband probably was. He was a rebel and did not play the game, so he defeated himself often, but it was again that poetic triumph. Such men were shadows of conformity; weak in their consuming need for recognition, the adult form of stupid, juvenile peer pressure. Such powerful arrogant and sweaty men filled her world. He could tell. He radiated his refusal to be like them—now or ever.

"I don't need success!" he protested, rising. Blather poured forth, before he could restrain himself. She did something to him. "I don't care about recognition. All I want to do is write poetry. I want to mow lawns, conquer grass—and find someone like you to adore."

Upon this confession she regarded him with confusion and admiration.

I would write poetry about you in adoration. Light candles before you if I ever went to church.

They bent their faces close together, and their lips brushed. It was the electric connection they both needed at that moment. It was the stray lightning bolt out of nowhere on a darkly cloudy, hot summer wheat field.

He pulled away breathlessly from her moist, cool, soft lips. The directioning of her chiseled knees was in disarray. One pointed to him, the other to the slatted narrow basement window. He noted the cool pliancy of a pale inner thigh, momentarily exposed.

He felt stunned, and she looked shocked.

She reached out to touch his hair, but her hand froze. Then she caught herself. *What had she done?* She shoved herself violently erect with both hands on the armrests, and fled from that undersea cavern.

Poor love, he thought, *what was I thinking?* His heart still beat warmly for her, halfway up his throat.

He wiped his hands on a paper towel, thinking that it would be decent to forget all about her. The right thing to do. He slowly turn to rejoin and restart his blue smoking mower in the soaking green light outside.

There would be much poetry flowing from him that evening on the keyboard. Golden verse, like the Cavalier poet Thomas Carew's precious atoms of the day, gleaming in the darkness before the dark tide of chaos and civil war and regicide in the early 1600s. Marc had indeed studied, and studied well. His emotionally and mentally composed *études* poured richly shaped from a well-instructed *klavier* of all the best schools, ranging from Homer and Ovid, Catullus and Petrarch, to Rimbaud and Verlaine and, oh, all the best in the *Ouest*.

Chapter 3.

Marc and Emma sat by a rainy, runnely leaded-glass window in the rear room of George and Harry's, an English-style pub like you'd find in a university town, Oxford or Cambridge. G&H was about two blocks from the Seine on the Left Bank near the Saint-Michel Bridge leading to the Sainte-Chapelle with its gorgeous, dreamy stained glass nave on the Île-de-la-Cité. That is also not far from the famous Shakespeare & Company bookstore frequented long ago by great expat poets and authors from James Joyce to F. Scott Fitzgerald and Ernest Hemingway, to name just a few.

It was Sunday. So they were here together after all, and this train would rush to its destination. This drama would find its climax one way or another. They were each on board to see what their next stops might be in this metaphor. Already, they were holding hands and holding their foreheads close, all the more easily to whisper endearments, and stare deeply into each other's eyes and souls. Nothing else mattered right how. Time stood still for them, around them.

He thought: *The clock that ticks now ticks all so soft and far away.*

Dribbles drummed on lead gutters outside. The narrow street, framed by high neo-Classical university buildings, glimmered in a greenish half-light. From a music conservatory, nearby, issued complex but neutral piano studies. Some anonymous person was pensive and dreaming over the keyboard. Tentative notes complemented ivied walls and drowning spring blossoms crushed in a film of water covering the street, while more water dribbled obscenely out of high eaves and splattered along rust-stained walls.

Marc Fontbleu felt a bit embarrassed. All week long he had yearned and schemed toward this meeting. Now she sat by him and he had nothing much to say. It was too early to say he loved her, though he did. He'd known love enough already to recognize it when it came swirling around his heart. And in this wonderful city of history and art and culture and love.

Paris, my Heart...

She sat with her back to the window. Her hands retreated to the pockets of her open raincoat. Her blue-jean clad legs extended on sharp high heels under the table. Her head tilted expectantly while her blonde hair hung down into the windowsill behind the bench back. He sat askew in a corner, one finger in the mouth of the beer bottle he'd finished. It was an ale bottle, brown as amber, in which light glowered amid slowly falling foam resembling rain—or sea water. He alternately studied the worn mouth of the bottle and the white buttons spaced in a generous arc on her blue shirt.

"I didn't know if you'd come," she said. Her eyes flicked toward the ceiling beams full of worry and determination.

He leaned forward and soccered the bottle between the palms of his hands. "I was afraid you might not come."

I was afraid I might not come.

She sat tensely but let him move close so he inhaled the essences of her hair, her skin, even her tea breath. His eyes fell to the soft salient which pushed her shirt way out, and what quivered underneath. He was surprised to see her sharp breaths, her trembling breasts.

Her finger felt icy with fear when he touched her hands. They were not those of a young girl. If she were a charcoal drawing, he could have washed her to a glowing blur and she would have passed for the essence of a very equestrian, sapphire twenty-three (his age) or even a preppy, pristine seventeen. Hinted rilles and faint, dry cross-etchings were as yet only a preliminary design or intention of time and the universe, beyond her ability to change anything—over her knuckles, at the corners of her mouth, near the orbits of her eyes.

Seeing his look she did not protest. "You don't always."

"Always what?"

"Older women."

He shoved the bottle away. "My own age and younger."

"Oh. So far."

"I guess." The wrinkles could be from too much sun if she'd tanned too much over the years. She was the type for skiing, sailing, tennis, slender cigarettes if any, and credit cards, all prescribed for Ivy League; none of which he had. "You don't feel older," he said. He corrected, "Seem."

Getting ahead of ourselves. The signal is still red, but the signs ahead are clear to read.

She looked directly in his eyes for the first time. Her eyes were frank and grateful. "You seem like a wise rebel."

"It's relative," he concluded.

"I had nobody to feel older than," she said. "Jérôme's thirty-four. Sometimes. Or sixty-four. Or four. Depending."

"Jérôme." Thinking of this other man made a sweat burn in his collar.

I wish you wouldn't talk about him.

Seeing his look, she pursed her lips and studied the flotsam of lemon seeds and tea shreds in the brown lake at the bottom of her cup, aground on a sand bar of stained sugar. "I won't say anything again. After all, it's not your problem." She looked sharply at him. "I promise to be honest. You must promise me the same at all times."

"I do. I promise." He waited through a silent eternity. It was clear in that long instant, she was deciding whether to flee or stay. She stayed. With a sag of the shoulders, she surrendered to the inevitable. And looked pleased.

"Does he beat you?" *What have I gotten myself into?*

Her glance was sudden and bright blue. "Oh no. No, no. Dear." She laughed out loud. "I would be lucky if he gave me that much attention." Her teeth were unflawed white. "You needn't worry. He's gone to Australia. They're digging near Upskate or something on the North Coast."

"Sounds interesting."

"Doesn't it."

"If you happen to be in Upskate at the time," he said helpfully.

"I'm actually rather Downskate."

"And here we are."

"There you are." She reached for her pocketbook. "That's about the way it is." She touched his arm. "I'll be back in a moment."

He sat alone, listening to water gurgling gently in secretive drains.

Dribble, dribble, went the rain, cleansing and nurturing all things.

Clocks moved slower in this oceanic time, where massive waves of leaves made a rushing in your ears, and your heart beat too hard and too fast. He knew he was free to get up and leave. Silly though— run? From what? Morality? No, a single transgression could not be very expensive. He would be mowing other lawns in this garden of easiness. Léopold Montblé should savor forbidden apples and write firmer beats. So much poetry forthcoming.

He heard her footsteps in the hollow wooden room and turned to watch her approach. She could easily be somewhere close to his age. She was beautiful in the way that some women are dramatic rather than puffy-sweet. She must be athletic, judging by the tight body, strong legs, firm arms and shoulders, narrow but sweet face framed in clipped honey hair. She smiled as she approached, guilelessly. Light makeup, nothing desperate, everything easy. Hands in raincoat, steps sure and direct, chin up...he thought he had the answer for her outlook and behavior; what a poet or pianist might call method (thinking of the piano music cluttering the air with thoughtful nuances and probing riffs that often ended in a sudden cacophany, then silence). So what was it that made her seem rebellious like him, and yet married to some *je ne sais quois*? The answer came to him all at once:

She hasn't been domesticated.

Still wild and coltish, she slid in along the bench, quick to be beside him again. He reached impulsively and put his hand on hers. She laid her other hand on his. Their bones and skins were dry but mortised together in a sensuous tension. In planetary gravity, they were the architecture of circumstance: skillfully engineered canals laced through intricate chambers of cartilage, muscle, and flesh.

She might be complex, but she was not deep. She inclined her head slightly away and gave him a questioning look—a friendly but pained contraction about the mouth and eyes. "What are you thinking?"

We are accomplices now—spies or assassins—or at least thieves in the night, a well-matched pair who can telegraph each other's brain waves; fight or flight.

He took both of her hands in his, taking charge.

She let him hold her hands resting on the table, her fingers pliably relaxed but unhelpful.

How to say or ask this? "You're not troubled by existential questions?"

She made the faintest motion of shaking her head.

No such logo on any sweater at the golf or tennis club gift shop.

Her teeth were still white but the smile was gone, replaced by distance and indifference. She said, "Are we going to discuss what is reality?"

In a Great Gatsby mode: *We're in an East Egg roadster, doing ninety in a forty zone with the top down and our hair flying behind us.*

He released her hands and put his hands in his lap. "I was hoping we wouldn't."

"Then let's not," she said a bit sharply. She gave him a long, beautiful, sexy look. Her eyes darkened, and her wide, glossy lips took on a deeper shade of Merlot, with a smart, cutting laugh. Or was that Harlot? She wrapped her arm through his and pulled him close to her firm, warm side. "We aren't going to, are we?"

"What?" He feigned innocence.

She looked at him mockingly. She was in, and the game was on. *Talk about why the sky is blue and stuff. Who gives a riff?*

She shook her head and said in a throaty voice, "Nothing complicated." She added: "Please."

"Of course. Whatever that means, I don't have it in me." He said ruefully, "You are more experienced." He had to resist moments of class warfare. *You have money. Or, Jérôme has money and he has you—rich bitch.*

She brought her hands together and made a gun of them, aimed at his heart. "I enjoyed what you said back in the break room at the college."

"What did I say?"

Devilment glinted in her eyes. "About success. What a declaration! All I want is to write poetry. I want to mow lawns, conquer grass…"

"And love women like yourself," he finished. "What else could a man say, looking at you?"

"A man," she said, making a fist of her fight hand on the table and reaching with her left to grasp his knee and squeeze under the table. "That's how I like you." She squeezed his knee, shaking it with surprising intensity, and leaned close and said with tea-breath, "I'd like to take you by your grass…and mow you!"

He felt relieved, and they both laughed.

Some bubble had broken, a tension had disintegrated and filtered away in pieces into this greenish air.

"What I want," he said, "is to be honest and open. I have this feeling we can have that. I feel such intensity about you. I can't explain it."

"Maybe Léopold Montblé will write me a poem."

"He did last night," Marc Fontbleu confessed. "He fell asleep though before he could retype it."

"Honest and open. Those qualities are hard to find, unless two people hate each other."

"What I mean is, I have this feeling we don't have to act, know what I mean? We don't have to play games."

"Does it bother you I'm married?"

"You bring me neatly from the general to the particular. Yes."

"Would you love me and leave me, excuse my cliché?"

"Maybe if it was the right thing, or the right time."

She raked the opposite wall, the fireplace, the stained glass windowlets, with a gaze filled with hot and cold computations. "Maybe that's how it should be." She darted a look at him. "Suppose I don't surrender?"

He spread his hands in the air. "I would dip my colors to you in salute, and pass you at a respectful distance. In plain language, I already am so in love with you that I would do nothing to hurt you."

"You would let go of me?" she asked, full of hidden calculations.

"Reluctantly, yes." It already seemed like losing a best friend.

Am I nuts? What am I getting into here? Can I be arrested?

She placed her hands in her lap. "Would you think badly of me if I…had you on board?"

"I'd bring my best manners. Léopold Montblé would rhapsodize you in the third person."

She was resigned to her sensibility. Lying back again with her hands in her pockets, she looked up at the ceiling. "I wouldn't get you get into anything embarrassing, or dangerous. Jérôme won't be back for three months."

"Why doesn't he have you along?"

"He asked me. He asks me every time. I just don't want to. Things won't be any better in Australia. You see, I know something he doesn't. He doesn't want me to come along. He really can't stand being with me. That's marriage. This is passion. This is hunger. Maybe it is baby love being born."

"Upskate."

"Downskate."

"Cheapskate," he said, knowing it was the last thing about the world in which she sailed.

"Ice skate," she said, signaling with her eyes. "I am so cold. Make me warm, Léopold Montblé. Heat me up, Marc Fontbleu."

He took her hands in his, and rubbed them for warmth. "Love is free."

She laughed. "That's a student thing."

"We're not undergraduates."

She gave him a sincere, grateful look. "I'd go anywhere with you."

In a play world, we could orbit the earth or be in a yellow submarine blowing bubbles at smiley fish.

She shuddered. "You make me feel warm and loved."

"You don't have any kids either."

"We tried. Half dozen years ago, when we were first married. One of us can't. Jérôme has a really low sperm count. *Zut!* Why am I telling you this? Because you asked, I suppose. Don't get a headache over it."

He felt lost. "Have you thought about a divorce?"

My freedom means everything to me. Why not you? Are you some sort of harem slave? Poor pampered concubine.

"We've mentioned it. Then Jérôme runs off quickly on another dig."

"So he doesn't like to confront things."

"What man does."

"Try me."

"I'm sitting here, am I not?"

"Are you satisfied with being alone all the time?" He held her precious hands in his, savoring the feel and the color and the scent of her soft skin. *My sweet, lovely odalisque.*

"Yes, in a way. I can do what I want. Not going out, I mean. This is the closest, so far, that I have ever come to infidelity. If we can call it that. I keep busy. There is always something to do. I'm not answerable to anyone. I see Jérôme off on the plane with a feeling of relief. When I drove him to the airport last month, I could sense he feels the same way. So the feeling is mutual. And what's marriage except mutuality? Maybe we have a good marriage."

"By that logic, I suppose." But he shook his head, thinking: *I will never understand. I never imagined someone like you could exist, but I am smitten with you. I have tasted the apple in Eden for the first time, and now I know how Adam must have felt when he would do anything for Eve.* He prodded: "Do you ever feel like a prisoner?"

She arched her eyebrows ironically. "I've never known anything else. That's why I cherish your wild freedom."

"I thought I was just poor, and horny."

"You are." She tickled his ribs. "And creative." She gazed admiringly at him. "I feel so at home with you." Her eyes twinkled. "Maybe we will run away together, eh?"

"Where to?"

"Cross that bridge when and if we get there."

"I feel at home with you too, as with no other woman before." *I have no idea why.*

She made that older face. "I know men. You have a fascination for the older woman. There has to be just one in every young man's life. You'll never mention me again, but you'll think about me for the rest of your life."

He put an arm around her. "And you, chatter-mouth? You'll think about me wherever you go, Upskate, Downskate, or Sideskate."

"You are right, of course." She sighed. "Oh give me a man who is always right."

"I mean well."

"I know you do, baby. Thank you." She cuddled against him. With his fingertips, he touched her ribs; her vertebrae like tender, submissive, vulnerable steps to her soul. He wanted to possess her, and have her, and pour himself into her, and hear her laugh, or listen to her surf-like breathing as she gently snored beside him, full of dreams like the sea. All that was within his reach, and he was too intoxicated to withstand her gravitational pull. She was a planet or even a sun, while he was a moon, and she bathed him in her light and warmth.

She spoke at the ceiling beams. "I like the idea of being married. I'm not sure about actually living it day to day. When I meet a stranger I enjoy saying I'm married so they'll go away. I so enjoy seeing the envy. I'm attractive to men, who mistake that as meaning I'm happily married, whatever that means to them. They look closely, trying to read the truth in my hair, in my hands, in my eyebrows. Don't get me wrong, I don't toy with anyone. I just like to leave them on that note. It's like credit, like protection." She gave him a sudden, violent look. "I have never screwed around with anyone."

"Is this screwing around?"

Ready to walk if need be.

She took his hands in hers, as if to blow on them and heal the sting. "No, baby. I don't know what this is. Maybe it's friendship. God knows I am so alone it scares me."

I hope you don't own a gun.

"You're worried about me." She made a reassuring face. "I won't do anything to hurt myself. I love life too much." She added, "The last thing I want is to hurt you."

He pushed his hands out and wrapped them around hers. "I am not looking for anything hurtful. This is like science."

She laughed. "What?"

"Gravity. Mutual attraction. The moon and the earth. Earth and the sun."

She stroked his wrist slowly and considerately, as if reading his fortune. "Maybe you can shed some light on me."

"We can help each other. Not that I'm in much need."

"Me neither. Or maybe we are and don't know it."

"You're nice to look at," he said. "More nice to sit with, look in your eyes, watch how your lips gleam in this rainy light, and love the warmth in your soul."

She pulled herself close as if they were high school kids on a date. "We can split a banana some time."

He laughed. "A banana split."

"Splat." Her eyes glittered and she looked *gamine*. Her lips glistened.

He knotted his hands together on the table, squeezing her yielding hand close to his chest. "Why you have this thing about you, something young? At twenty feet distance you could pass for twenty-one. You're like"(he groped for words, diplomatically)"not yet domesticated. A girl."

"A girl, always young." She looked grateful. "I'm still filled with impulse."

"Yes."

"A colt."

"Yes."

"I am careful, though."

"Are you sure nobody from the faculty would recognize you here? I mean, after all, we're at the center of the university."

"In a restaurant? Some university—I'm sorry. Like there are spies everywhere."

He detected a brief flare of resentment at the world, her world, her tormentors, who had shaped her, such a fine vessel, and yet just property. "You can be a little cynical."

Biting, maybe, which gives you a cutting edge.

"I'm sorry. Sometimes I get to be a wise guy, a wise ass chick. No, I doubt if anyone would recognize me. Jérôme takes me to parties and shows me off. I don't really mind. Are you shocked? I was brought up that way."

"You told me you are from Chaillot."

"That doesn't mean I'm spoiled. My daddy is a famous surgeon. My older brother is an architect. Groomed for Sorbonne, so naturally he went to Polytech."

"And you?"

"Do you know the Style commercial?"

"You mean that new cigarette." He remembered the ads—always anchored on a smiling, tanned blonde accepting a Style from some curly-haired rascal holding a crisp new red-and-white, candy-striped pack of The Really Thin Cigarillos.

"It's a cigar," she corrected. "I was groomed to smile and hold the cigar. Like Momma. She held the cigar for years. It was the only thing she could train me for. So I hold the cigar for Jérôme when he needs me. My face and a few cocktails too many got the chair in Anthro somewhere in Vienna or London to invite Jérôme to teach for a year. Jérôme turned it down for Sorbonne-Pantheon. But now he's in Upskate, and here we are."

Without you, Marc thought. *He must be such a fool.*

"Here we are," Marc said. "Doesn't he want to feel jealous?"

She shook her head with a rueful smile. "He knows I would never cheat on him, and nobody could take me away from him."

"He assumes a lot."

She took a deep breath and looked at the floor, away from Marc. "We'll see," she whispered.

I don't know either, he thought.

She did not resist when he took her hand in his. It was so warm, and suddenly her gaze turned to him full of gratitude and warmth. Her moment of uncertainty had vanished. Her tone became strong and sure. "My parents trained me for the game. They set me up, and Jérôme found me. Bought me right off the shelf. We were all so happy."

"We?"

"Family. Friends. It all worked out according to program. The wedding was in the newspapers. He has a yacht anchored in Monaco, and we all go sailing at least once a year. Egypt, Morocco, and then a big finale in Spain or France. Balearic Islands, Ibiza, Saint-Tropez."

"Lucky you."

"Lucky me." She gave a sardonic little sniff. "I'd trade it all in to mow lawns and be free. Eat and drink what I like, dance all night, drink wine from the bottle, smoke the damn cigars instead of holding them."

He said: "I don't smoke. I like the wine part," he said. "Keep the bottle though." He sighed. "I'm supposed to envy you. My father sells cars and my mother bakes a helluva cake. My older brother's in the Army. My younger brother Hilaire is still in high school. I'm the first person in the history of my family to finish college. I mow lawns for a living. Everyone thinks it is ironic."

"Do your parents live near here?"

"In Créteil," he told her. "Jimmy's the big hope in the family. He's president of his class, is a real charmer, and he wants to go into politics."

She regarded him minutely, running a speculative tongue tip around inside her lips. "We grew up not far from each other, and yet so far apart."

He thought for a moment. "I was starting high school when you graduated from—where was it?"

"Sainte Sophie. Small private Catholic girls' finishing school near Versailles."

"Finishing school, of course."

She posed with raised shoulders, a cocked head, and batty eyelashes while making airy motions with a fluid hand. "My darling Sophie...o to dream of holding your cigar!"

"You don't have to hold any cigars for me. I'll hold my own cigar."

She slapped his wrist lightly. "And blow smoke in my face."

"If you deserve it."

"I am always such a good girl."

"Nobody is that perfect."

"Especially being from Créteil and all." She pronounced the town's name with faint disdain or class venom.

Mildly annoyed, he peered at her in the watery light. It would take a lot for her to really turn him off.

"I didn't mean it that way," she said quickly. She was so vulnerable, squirming. "I was just imitating... oh hell, bad joke. I don't think that way. Please don't be annoyed. Most of the girls in my class at Vassar went off to hold their own cigars. It just so happened I wasn't endowed with the sense of independence. My role is more to the hearth. I spin and Jérôme goes delving. That whole bag, you know?"

"You keep the fires banked?"

"That's coarse."

"And to the point."

"I get the point." She sighed. "Penelope, spinning and chaste by the hearth in Ithaca."

"You have studied Homer." He was glad they had some unknown amount of Literature in common.

"I'm not a dumb bunny." She crossed her arms, wrapping her elbows in opposite hands. "If I didn't feel so...affectionate...about you I'd be insulted."

He rubbed his stomach. "It's getting late and my stomach tells me it's time for supper."

"What do you usually do for supper?" she asked.

"Burger Barn," he told her candidly. "It's a sort of imitation California truck stop in the heart of the Marais."

She irradiated him with one of those warm smiles he'd come to love. "I could go for a Quick Yack if they have one."

"What the hell is a Quick Yack?"

"Oh I don't know. A Slick Snack. I'm sure they have one. Crazy Americans."

"Will you go with me?" he pleaded honestly.

She slipped her arm around his, and pulled herself close to him. "I told you. I will follow you anywhere."

He laid his hand protectively over hers, pulling her even tighter. "Now I feel such an awesome responsibility."

"I'm high maintenance."

"You are a handful." *I wish.*

She planted a hint of a kiss on his cheek. "I want to be your handful. And I will hold your cigar."

"Do I even have a cigar?"

"Every man has a cigar." She laughed. "We'll beat that metaphor to death."

"Maybe it's time we mercy-killed it."

"It's like fleas on a cat," she said, "or dandruff on some people. It never goes away. We're stuck with it, I'm afraid. I am who I am."

They rose, together, now a couple. They walked out holding hands like a man and woman who belonged together. The verbal ping pong was over. The net was discarded, the table folded. The die was cast. The Rubicon glittered ahead, or actually the rain, which was letting up.

They walked out into glowering twilight and drizzle arm in arm like two twenty-three-year-olds—her blonde hair flying, his shoulders spread proudly like a sailor's. Behind them, bottles made chinking noises. Piano music welled up from the Venetian-style windows of the music school. Dribbles drabbled as they huddled, dashing. Envious looks followed their departure into the dripping and fresh spring and mossy evening. He knew she knew he knew now what it was like to have a woman like her holding your cigar. Not such a bad feeling; like being intoxicated with all that Chaillot money and fire and first-class Scotch. Those smiles, like thrown snowballs. That skin like sweet caramel wanting to be licked.

Better yet, remove the wrapper and stare, but don't spoil by touching.

"Do you have a car?" she asked.

Silly question.

"Yes, in Creteil, parked at my parents' house."

"Oh," she said making wide eyes. *Caught again.* He guessed that she'd have maybe an expensive Porsche parked somewhere at greater expense than his tiny apartment when he could afford one. It would be a dark wine color, with plush interiors, charcoal probably, smelling faintly of brand-new leather gloves and expensive Japanese perfume and new-car smell to boot. "Well," she said diplomatically, "Mine is in the garage. Let's walk. I know where you mean. It's not far."

"The garage? Not a garage?"

"You'll learn what you need to know. My family owns buildings in the area. With or without Jérôme."

"Which one of you is wealthier?" He wanted to know things like this, and he really didn't care much what he asked. "You can always tell me to shut up if you don't like my questions."

"I'll tell you when it's the case. I'm old money. He's a little old money and a lot nouveau riche because his father divorced his mother to run away with a Turkish actress, and his mother took revenge by remarrying into a real estate fortune. Whatever."

"You're not hurting."

"Only my soul." She looked at him sincerely. "Only my aching heart. Remember, I promise you this: I would die before I hurt you "

They walked in silence a minute or two in a gentle drizzle.

"We'll get used to each other," he said with mild, affectionate sarcasm.

"It will take some doing, but *mon plaisir.*" She tugged on his arm, comradely fashion. She wrestled her arm through his, and pulled him tightly close to her.

He felt a wind of stars, of love, of mountain highs, closed his eyes, and pulled her tightly to him as well. If he wanted to say *je t'aime* at that moment, the words would not have gotten past his quivering lip. His eyes burned with tears of passion. A good hard sniff made the momentary emotion go away.

She reached around with her free hand, palmed his face gently, and kissed him on the other cheek closer to her. He inhaled the fragrance of her skin, the fine waxiness of her lipstick, and the oddly ocean-like tang of her hair. Was she a mermaid, a sea-nymph, an angel of some sort come to earth? They walked awkwardly but slowly, so close that they could have been a four-legged mythological chimera—the fabled love centaur or something, which has all four legs in a row opposite of travel direction.

They laughed as their bones banged together. They could have taken the Métro a few stops, but the stations were usually full of a rough crowd, and it was so much nicer to have their first taste of privacy and intimacy, just strolling along the brightly lit streets and over the Seine bridges at the Islands.

Somewhere under a street lamp on the Right Bank, in a faint fog issuing up from the Seine, they gave up and stood in a tight, hungry embrace, deeply kissing. Traffic whispered past—and then an emergency vehicle roared in close, a SAMU ambulance with flashing blue lights, awash with the fierce beauty of its raging Martin's Horn sirens. The ambulance slowed at the corner to ease into traffic. Emma burst into laughter. "They've come for us."

"They understand our urgency."

She laughed in a bright pealing sound. "There is no hope."

He laughed as well saying: "There is hope now. I was about to throw myself under my lawnmower, and then you came along, an angel sent by heaven."

With grasping palms, he treasured the willing curvatures of her behind as she thrust her pelvis against him to take her, to enjoy her, to partake of her, while her hands strayed up and down the length and strength of his back.

"Lawnmower," she whispered, nipping his earlobe with her teeth. "Grass slayer. Let me be your grass."

"I'll be your lawnmower," he intoned while holding her face between his palms and kissing her puckered lips. Her eyes were closed, signaling deep acceptance. "We'll make smoke together," he whispered.

She giggled. Her deeply closed eyes (was it the raise of her face?) signaled the end of a drought, a Provençal sunflower rejoicing at sunshine and a light rain.

Arm in arm, loosely swinging, they strode off to *California*.

Chapter 4.

"Oh listen," she said as they rounded a corner, "The Beach Boys." They came onto a narrow street surrounded by cyclopean 19th Century buildings stained with age and human lives gone by. While dark windows looked down, there were neon lights and cigarette smoke and blasting ancient 20th Century rock music at street level amid throngs of vibrant humanity. You could hear it from a block away in the Marais.

"Yes, Good Vibrations," he said. "We're in a time machine going backwards."

"All of Paris is like that." She said: "Tourists love it, but we love it all the more."

We're part of it, and it's part of us, he thought: ambiance, atmosphere. *Although sometimes it's like too rich food, and you want to get away and wander among trees and nature. But places like the Bois de Vincennes are for that. No need to go far.*

"I have an idea," he said.

"Oh no, now I am getting scared."

"Sometime soon, let me take you to the Bois de Vincennes."

"Oh," she said plaintively, as if he were handing her a cuddly kitten, "a nice walk in the park."

"You light my fire," he said.

"Ah, that one is buried in the Père Lachaise." She meant the cemetery at the eastern edge of Paris, where Jim Morrison lay buried half a century already among so many other long-ago famous people who lived their lives, made their splash, and faded into the shadows of time but left their glow behind.

"I want to hold your hand."

"That is not surfing music."

"That's ancient Beatles."

"Also nice." She took him by the hand and towed him along. Her eyes glowed with joy. "I don't get out much. This is so much fun." Tears briefly sprang into her eyes. "I had forgotten what it's like to be human and free. You'll help me, won't you? Not hurt me?"

"I would die before I caused you any pain." He held her close.

Jérôme , you are such an asshole, Marc thought. He added to himself: *Unless there is something I don't know yet. Like she snores loudly. Or farts a lot. We'll see.* Then he thought: *I can forgive anything, except neglecting her.* He'd forgotten what it felt like to feel protective of a woman about whom he suddenly felt so strongly. Judging by her firm grip on his hand, she felt strong emotions as well.

They entered the crowd of young people, many of them in office dress, standing around holding drinks or smokes and chatting. Many eyes followed them, some hungered up with jealousy.

"We make a nice couple," she whispered to him. "We could run away together."

"Anywhere but Créteil," he said. He'd grown up there, his roots were still there including an unfinished Literature degree, and most of all his loving but tone-deaf, color-blind parents who tried to keep him around age five or whatever.

"I can't wait to get my teeth into some meat," she growled like a cave woman. She could be a hearty soul.

I'll give you some meat, he thought. But he drove the Pleistocene away, and reverted to a 21st Century gentleman. "I'll buy," he said bravely. He had just been paid yesterday. He had the rent money in his wallet, but that would have to wait. He could borrow something; maybe pawn a few treasures.

She made a demure, sensible face, and opened her purse to look inside. Her body language was unspoken: *I'll pay*.

* * * *

"Baa Baa Baa Baa Baaaaa, Barbra AAAAAAnnnn…" Marc and Emma sang softly with the blaring music as they navigated past the waving bouncers, through a narrow Third Republic doorway replete with chipped ancient paint, and into a further crowd of young people. Around them, music blared. The young did not need words but body and eye lingo as they looked each other over to mate or form friendships. Or just tangled soap operas, whatever.

They found a wooden bench at a table crowded with singing men, obviously students in their late teens and early twenties—some with huge medieval-looking beards from another age—who were covering the carved and mutilated oaken surface up with empty bottles.

It was another excuse to jam so closely together that their thighs were fused in one hot telepathic console. Emma slid her hand between his jean-clad thighs and palmed him possessively. He did the same, with his arm around her slender back and his fingers enjoying the soft widening of her little seat.

Emma stretched slowly and deliciously on the bench beside him. Her crook'd arms made brackets above her head, while her palms nearly touched the fluttering rag ceiling of the dark blue car. Her eyes were half-closed and her lips widened in a shuddering sense of satisfaction. The air around them throbbed in rhythm with the music beat. Her coat fell open, revealing a blue shirt budding with promise.

He felt entirely right, having her at his side like this. "Let's play Teeny and the Boppers," he suggested.

"Good Good Good GOOOOOOD Vahbrahtions!" the radio crackled.

The voice of a disk-jockey burbled in a sort of French-British-Nashville *faux* accent: "In case you haven't guessed it, tonight's California night and we have for you the Beach Boys and surfers in a solid hour of oldies but goodies not so moldy and pretty darn goldy and if you're told you're old just grab a hold, be bold, hang ten and you'll be sold..."

"I'll fold," Emma said with a laugh, sliding back on her bench as if offering herself up.

"Anything but cold," he said. "I'll protect you."

"Oh thank you." She laughed, as if many men said that to her, and she ridiculed them all. But she reached over and very precisely, affectionately touched her index fingertip to his lips: the fingertip kiss, *une baise à doigt.*

Then she sat sensibly upright, combing out her long hair with long, thin fingers while she rested and watched the crowd all around.

"Are you having a nice time?"

"Oh, ever so much." She put her purse on the table as a white-aproned, dark-haired young waitress arrived, shoving a tight, skinny butt in among the men to get her business accomplished. The waitress slapped a round tray on the table and yanked out a notepad and pen. "Madame et monsieur?"

Marc realized that, with Emma at his side, so understated and elegant, he was suddenly for real *monsieur*, not just *and what do you want.*

They ordered the San Francisco Special, which was a hamburger, Frisco Fries, onion rings, and a light salad with avocado. To drink they ordered Stella Artois, the Belgian beer.

* * * *

While they waited, Emma chewed a wad of bubble gum pink as her tongue. Her lipstick was now candy-apple red. Where had that come from?

Her arm linked into his, and her hip pressed against his hip. He didn't need to force it. She was giving herself to him if he would take

her. He took her by the waist and pulled her close, claiming her. Her
waist was slender, her figure fluid, her skin sinuous in his hand.

Animal love. Give me everything.

She whispered in his ear, "Our first date. Oh god you drive me
crazy. I want you."

He pulled her close, filled with wonder at how her body molded
into any shape he needed her to assume to please him, and she could
not give him enough of her gyrations. *Good vibrations.* He had a rod
on, torch flaming at the muzzle already. No woman had made him
feel this way in years or ever.

Where was the food? Past the crowd, he stared hungrily toward
the counter. The cash register rattled and chained continuously, and
blue-aproned figures darted about behind the plate glass, scooping
Frisco fries, bagging burgers, tapping colas and beers, squirreling out
spiral deposits of ice cream. White paper hats rode jauntily askew
over teenage eyebrows.

...First gear I'M ALRIGHT, second gear UPTIGHT, third gear,
HANG   ON   TIGHT,   faster,   faster,   faster,
FAAAASSSTTTEEEERRRR... echoed a timeless carollade by the
Beach Boys—or was it the Hondells?

A line snaked in to the counter through a side entrance. "Popular
place," Emma said.

"Must mean the food is good."

Spring air was mild. Rain had stopped. The line moved slowly.
Children bawled. A ruddy pot-bellied duck pin bowler in a red nylon
jacket stared at Emma. A tall, skinny high school boy with spider legs
and pimply face arced high to drop-shoot a plastic bag of trash into a
ditzy dumpster.

"Plebeian," Marc murmured of those in line, into her blonde
hair, which smelled of bubble gum and shampoo and car exhaust and
Parisian perfume.

She avidly chewed, like *une américaine.* He found it quite sexy
and provocative. "Not much different from the patricians in Chaillot
or elsewhere. What's missing is the air of everyone being hipper than
everyone else." She blew a bubble, and popped it with a smacking
sound. "Maybe even hipper than hip."

"Hipper about what?"

"The big cigar, of course," she said. She rolled her eyes up and
smacked her gum loudly. The tip of her tongue flicked out to lick
pink off of her lips. He silenced her gnashing with his mouth. She

succumbed breathlessly; their teeth touched. Their lips worked frantically and savoringly together.

The waitress brought a tray of steaming Friscos, with beer and condiments. "Voilà."

Emma and Marc ate heartily. She nudged him with her elbow, rollicking with puffed cheeks and spread mouth as she happily mauled her meal and the beach boys sang SURFERRRR GURRRRLLLL...

Chapter 5.

"I nearly went deaf," Emma said, "but I loved it."

After leaving the restaurant, they strolled back across the Seine to the Latin Quarter. Fog rolled over the water and rose up over the bridges. Street lights looked like lanterns in fog.

"It's so nice to walk with you," he said.

She sighed and rested her cheek on his shoulder. It was like a movie. He expected her to begin singing any moment. She said: "I never thought I would meet anyone like you. That was so nice—all those young people, all that music, the noise, the smoke."

"You don't get out much," he ventured.

She nodded grimly with her chin. "I have been living in a dream. A bad one. And now you woke me up."

"I feel the same way. Nothing looks the same anymore. Are you sure we aren't dreaming?"

"Pinch me."

"What?"

She stopped and put her arms over his shoulders. She was tall, but half a head shorter than he. "Pinch me."

"Where?"

"Anyplace."

He pinched her gently in a few spots that would get him arrested, anywhere else under normal circumstances.

She closed her eyes and said "Hmmmm" in a dreamy way. "This is a much better dream. A really nice one."

She gave his gluteus a squeeze, and they continued walking. They were on the smaller island, Île Saint-Louis, having crossed from the Marais on the Pont Marie and now to the Left Bank via the Pont de la Tournelle (named for a medieval turret there). As they emerged on the quai, she said: "Come spend the night with me."

"Of course," he said. He wanted to ask: *but what about...?*

She explained, sensing his questions. "Jérôme and I live in a faculty apartment near the Pantheon, actually a very small place. My family owns a building closer to the Boulevard Saint-Germain, and I have an apartment there. Actually, my cousins and I share it whenever someone is in town. It's what you call a real *pied-a-terre*."

Marc understood the concept: A foot on the ground for someone living outside of a city, but working there and needing a crash pad during the week. He joked lightly: "Any cousins there now?"

She shook her head. "All out of town. All over the world, actually. Nobody home."

"So you have the place all to yourself. How nice."

"I only go there when I have done some shopping and want to drop off boxes and things. You know, hats, dresses, maybe a bit of furniture." She looked at him, saw he had no clue, and continued: "There isn't room at our apartment. The faculty one."

As they walked, car doors randomly banged shut, marring the evening stillness. Motors, laughter, a swish of wind under a car, a splash in a puddle, night sounds. He whistled as they walked along the high-priced shops and clean sidewalks of the major boulevard. If women from here held people's cigars, imagine the money the men with those cigars must have. He wanted to ask about Jérôme, but did not want anything to intrude upon the magic of the hour. She led him to a little private courtyard near the Rue des Bernardins. "We own it all," she said matter of factly, meaning the 19th Century stone edifice towering all around in dignified silence. "We rent out apartments to bankers and the like."

"Rich people."

"Oh yes. Nobody else can afford to just casually plop here. So the building pays for itself through thick and thin."

He followed her lurching heels up a wind-flickering, honey-lit concrete path under weeping willow trees. There was something wistful, sad, lost, yet hopeful about her and this property.

Call them weeping widow trees.

Speak of weeping, it began to rain again gently but persistently.

Her keys rattled, and soon the building door stood open—colorful stained glass panels in a sturdy oak frame.

"During the Occupation, a high ranking Nazi general lived here." Seeing his look, she added: "Don't worry, we had it fumigated during the *épuration*." He'd read about the cleansing or purification that took place after the *boches* had been driven out. She said: "Took years to get the smell of Bratwurst and Sauerkraut out of the air. I wasn't born yet, but my grandparents used to raise their eyebrows and look horrified when they told stories of what the swine did." She added: "Of course, not everything that followed was so nice either." Paris had gone through a decade of purges, violence, poverty, and dislocation. Marc's lower middle-class family in Créteil had been far enough from the chaos to be spared the worst. Of course people like Emma's folks usually landed on their feet in the end. *Not her fault,* he quickly added to himself.

"I'm on the second floor," she whispered. She put her finger over her lips for him to be quiet. "We don't want to call attention to ourselves. Don't wake the tenants."

Live in the moment, he reminded himself. *Don't get swallowed up or eaten alive by a bunch of dead history.*

He tiptoed behind her up a creaking, carpeted stairway. He longed to touch that rocking rear, those shapely legs, and the rest of her. He wanted to undress her slowly, enjoying her enjoying every moment of his attentions. It would be a matter of minutes now. He watched her head toward him as in a spinning, unavoidable slow-motion crash on a snowy winter street; both drivers are helpless and see each other coming, bracing silently for impact, dreading injury, and calculating fender repair costs.

On a shadowy second-story landing, she fumbled with more keys. The smell of her hair and skin drove away a musty carpet odor. Someone had a cat. The rain-dribbled window crawled with plant shadows. A door creaked, a shaft of light fell out, her sharp heels pounded over polished wood floors. Quickly she kicked her shoes off. For the first time that day she was a lot shorter than he. She swung the door shut. "Here we are. Make yourself at home. I'll get some tea water boiling."

He was on his own. It was a spacious apartment. The doorway led into a small vestibule crowded with coats and umbrellas. A door led to a bathroom, another door to the bedroom, another door to the kitchen. Beyond the kitchen, Marc found himself in the living room. Plants hung from the ceilings, a poster glowered in black and white on the wall, low and fluffy furniture glowered in the light from the kitchen. Books, a stereo, posters, plants, a chandelier, scattered rugs, a pile of record albums, a casually flung nylon stocking, his first impression. Multiple identical windows in a row looked black and curtainless, dappled with raindrops. A clockwork encased in brass chimed. It was ten o'clock.

"Don't turn on any more lights," Emma said.

"You haven't needed curtains," he commented.

She regarded the black windows, "No, not until now."

You've been a modest girl, but that could change.

He sat on a black leather ottoman and brushed the stereo with his fingertips.

"How do you like your tea?" she asked.

He turned. Sitting before the stereo, he could reach out and touch her ankles. Which he did, feeling nylon over skin and bone.

She sank down and embraced him on the shaggy rug.

He kissed her while his hand explored the exact shape of her. He started to touch a button on her shirt.

She pulled away. "I'd better turn off the tea water and shut off the kitchen light."

She looked tall, walking into the halo of kitchen light while he lay on the thick carpet while someone else's (the other man's?) stereo glowed, and he pressed the off-switch. *Be gone, Jérôme.*

Her shoes clattered on the hardwood floors until she kicked them off. Her footfalls were as quiet and pattersome on bare planks as raindrops outside.

The lights out, he heard the swish of clothes being removed. When a woman has long legs it takes longer for her to remove her underclothes—so he guessed.

She pattered on bare feet, closer. He watched her figure undulate in gloom for him.

"Do you like me?" she asked, echoing her own unanswered question about tea.

"Turn around slowly," he said.

Silvery moonlight burnished the glossy wood floor. Her pale figure, singed with a bluish light from street light strained by budding tree branches, turned in a white archway.

She turned slowly on long, naked legs and the moonlight was egg-pale on oval buttocks, round breasts, her smile…

Chapter 6.

He awoke because a sunbeam dazzled the orbits of his eyes, because a hand brushed against his shoulder, because a droplet fell on his bare chest.

He opened his eyes and sat up but she had left the room in a rustle of skirts. "I have breakfast for you," she said in the kitchen. The apartment was endowed with the aroma of coffee, the essence of a light perfume, the stirring of a fresh breeze from some half-open window amid the stale odors of sleep.

Twisting aside to get out of the direct sunlight, he remembered that he must get off to work. He buried his head in the pillow. Bird twitter and consciousness that it was Monday made him swing upright into a sitting position. He awoke fully when his soles touched the cool wood floor and he heard the crackling of ham in a pan.

The bedroom where he had intruded and borrowed time and love was a study in white. Even inside, it was evident the house was very old and had been remodeled, but it was solid as the centuries and as money.

He saw the source of the breeze. While he was asleep, Emma had slightly opened a glass-paned door leading to a wood porch palisaded with flower boxes. White and red blossoms stirred in sun and wind. A delivery truck hummed through the quiet street outside; cowboyed to an impatient stop at the corner with crashing contents.

A broad picture window overlooked the porch. Yellow curtains hung pinned back by heavy brocade cord, revealing banked and newly green elm trees outside. Marc Fontbleu rose, belching, and staggered, stretching and rubbing his head, yawning, past a wall covered in books (rousing creative jazz in Léopold Montblé)—into the living room.

His clothes lay neatly folded and stacked on an armrest of the couch. Daylight filtered in through a sea of tree crowns outside, in a rich and golden stream through a three-sided bay window overlooking a long, narrow backyard. Cross-streams of light from the bedroom and a window at the side of the house stirred millions of dust molecules dancing in a faint breeze. The days of sifting spring tea were over, he thought, sitting beside his clothes.

He thought of home. Soon, spring rains would turn into drifting clouds of gray humidity. Colorful pleasure boat sails would criss-cross the Lac de Créteil.

Emma poked her hand and face around the doorway in which she'd twirled nakedly the night before. "Do you want to take a shower?"

He looked at her and nodded. It was then he learned something about her. Her long, elegant face fluttered with a white smile. Her cheekbones glistened and a tear fell from her chin. "You'll have to make it quick because I still have to finish drying my hair," she told him.

Puzzled, he gingerly entered the kitchen.

She handed him a towel but turned away. "Hurry, your eggs will be ready in five or ten minutes."

He would normally have steamed up the bathroom, but he did not want to cloud the mirror.

Anyway, it was spring, finally, and he half-opened the window and stepped shivering into the cold tub behind plastic curtains fragrant with hundreds of past shampoos. He showered quickly, lathering himself, his hair, then rinsing away the sweat and sticky dried sediment of the night's exploration. He marveled that a person could smile and cry at the same time.

What is it about you?

"Your eggs and ham are ready," she said, opening but not closing the door and then fumbling in the sink.

"I'll be right out." He turned off the water and dried himself behind the shower curtains.

It was a small, ancient bathroom with tall ceiling, tiled walls, and separate sink spigots for hot and cold. Its milky-rippled window set in warped wood were rarely opened. She bent over, washing her face, as he sidled past wrapped in his damp towel. It was 7:15.

"I'll drive you to work if you'd like," he said.

She groped blindly for a towel. "No, thanks. I'd rather walk. Thanks anyway."

Not to be seen. Not to have betrayed yourself. Or Jérôme.

Marc stood awkwardly as she dried her face and smiled at him with gleaming red cheeks.

I have never met this guy but I'm calling him Jérôme.

Her eyes radiated a glimmer of defeat or shame or something nuanced. He reached out to embrace her. She came a bit stiffly but unresistant into his arms.

"I slept well," he said.

She pushed gently. Her brief glance told him she had not slept well. Her eyes glistened. "Your eggs are getting cold."

Your eggs too.

He ate silently, and had to swallow every mouthful with difficulty. He relished only the electrically perked coffee which was aromatic, strong, and yet delicate.

Like her precious bush.

She hurried from the bathroom with her hair in a turban and a bath towel wrapped around her slender body.

"You could be in commercials, Emma."

"Oh please, sweetie." She came close and pecked him on the cheek. "You know how to flatter a girl."

"Cigar girl," he said

"I'm all about the cigar. I know. I can't escape." She added: "I have been in commercials."

"Really." It wouldn't surprise him.

"A company from Brazil needed blondes to advertise how nice it is to visit Rio. It went well. I swayed around and they added samba music. Then you know who got jealous."

Jérôme.

"And that was the end of it. I could go back into it maybe. Who knows. If I ever get free." She dressed quickly, bouncing with hurried motions on the living room couch. She emerged from the bedroom, restored to that formal, gamine, almost wounded, sultry prettiness as he'd first seen her. A delicately flowered skirt reached from her neck to her knees. High heels made the calf muscles of her long legs tense in an accentuated stalkiness. Her carefully trimmed blonde mane bounced about her shoulders and forehead as if she were trapped in a TV commercial landscape without time or cares.

She sat down beside him as he tied his shoelaces. She folded her hands in her lap. She had drawn fine mascara lines through the pale hairs on her eyelids. The mascara on both lower eyelids was faintly smudged.

She asked, "Do you have everything you need?" It was a preamble to saying goodbye.

He did not want to say anything glib, noting that could be mistaken for bluster or flattery. "I'm very content, and a little guilty," he said.

She nodded, staring down into her tightly welded hands. "I am too." She said quickly, "Look, I want to say thanks. It was swell, yesterday, the Beach Boys."

"It was fun," he agreed.

She laughed directly. "Guilt sort of adds spice."

He finished tying his shoes and folded his hands between his knees. "I wasn't looking for the guilt part. I supposed I deserve it."

She leaned over, folding her arms so her elbows rested on her thighs. "It was a long time coming. It's my fault, I'm sorry."

He said, "How can you laugh and cry at the same time?"

She fumbled for a tissue. "Talent. I'm kind of silly."

He laid his hand on her leg. "Do I cause that?"

She shook her head, dabbing her eyes. "We make our own circus."

He rose, feeling sweat break out at the back of his collar. "Look, Emma. Can we sort of…just treasure what happened? Can we sort of…say it was swell?"

She grinned. "I realize now that I really want you to love and leave. Go on, Lothario. Split, will you?" she nudged him. "Abandon ship."

He stared at the telephone by the couch—a mistake, he suspected dimly then, and would later realize.

She put her hands on his shoulder and kissed him briefly but warmly behind the ear, a friendship gesture.

"Go, Léopold Montblé, split. Write something in remembrance of me. A lovely silly and ultimately pointless poem in which you charge around in your little cabriolet with flags flying and Beach Boys playing…"

He turned away. "Should Léopold Montblé write that you were in distress? Did you hang your hair from the window? Did he slip in the ivy and sprain his ankle? Was there a pointlessness clause contractual and in writing? And what, pray, was the essence of this dragon you say you heard flying around your *tournelle*, dear lady?"

"Let's say the lady was undecided about the rescue."

He tried to take her in his arms. She wriggled away. She smiled broadly. "Time ran out and the lady was still clueless. The call for help was premature. Léopold Montblé rode off vowing to help—whenever, if ever, requested."

Marc made a wry face, feeling pained. He remembered, "Léopold Montblé had a pressing commitment which caused him to ride away without helping the lady. It was a prior commitment not to become committed."

At the door she framed his cheeks between her hands. "Léopold Montblé helped the lady very, very much by his mild manner and…oh, go will you? You'll be late for lawn mowing."

He bounded down the stairs, into the green blossoming of true spring, unburdened, freed from the sudden tangle.

Putting the top down, he rode off hurriedly into the sunshine and stray dew droplets. The last tea leaves were gathered around street drains, waiting to be swept from their gravel and asphalt beaches down into the pipes and the Seine and ultimately the distant North Atlantic Ocean.

* * * *

A week passed, and spring rolled into an unusually hot summer that year. He debated if he should call again. He didn't want to hurt her in any way, and this seemed dangerous. He didn't want to get into sauce either. But then he couldn't stand the abstinence from that warmth of her soul together with his, and called her.

Chapter 7.

A telephone waited by a couch. Once a week, a duster held in long, slender fingers descended to brush away the effluvium of time, that weightless dust of motes, some of them raining to earth out of the sum and essence of spent meteorites, others rasped off mountain tops by the wind and after airborne months seeking shelter behind white and remodeled walls; some, more prosaic, raised out of the pores of the sun-baked sidewalks of the Fifth Arrondissement around the Pantheon-Sorbonne on the Left Bank, part of the ancient Latin Quarter. Sunlight and heat pressed through the old walls after a brief flight to tumble microscopically over the fields of wood and rug and couch. Sometimes the stereo glowed in dusty warmth with throbbing music. More usually it was quiet, a silence filled with the rustle of cellulose crackling in growing house plants, the rustle of a stray breeze in yellow curtains, the padding of bare feet on sticky wood floors, the sigh of a comb through long blonde hair, and once in a great while, the murmur of a voice speaking alone. From the gardens below, ghostly children's voices rose when sunlight flooded the room, echoing generation after timeless generation in their playful conflicts and conspiracies.

* * * *

Nightfall.

It had been a hot, sunny day and now night steeped the room with inky-blue-black promise. The telephone slept, cut off by the weight of its receiver from the million-fold electronic babble washing the city in conversations. A fan hummed, oscillating under a rubber palm on a teak table. A gadzillion of crispy leaves crinkled directly outside. It was the earliest summer heat. That rare, brief moment of year was at hand when one would be comfortable with the temperature of evening, when inside and outside falsely promised never again to be irreconcilable, when moths brushed blindly against window screens, when a lemon ice could pierce the palate with citric relief, when streetlights outside were yellow and friendly.

A distant and electric urge startled the sleeping telephone, but did not yet cause it to ring.

The apartment was bathed in a cool blue light. The dry, warm voice of a TV announcer, the rustle of thousands of football fans, the stirring march of a razor blade manufacturer made the dim apartment come alive. A pair of long, slender pale legs were draped carelessly over the armrests of an easy chair. Long fingers crunched in a bag of cheddar puffs. The air smelled of salt and butter. Ice tinkled in a cola glass. A taxi tooted outside. The phone rang. A jet whistled high up in the night sky amid thinly banked clouds under some constellation. The phone burred under the rubber palm. The taxi tooted impatiently. The phone burred. A car passed in the night. A door slammed in the rambling, turreted house.

"Hello?"

"Emma."

"Yes?"

"Marc Fontbleu." A car door closed, a taxi radio crackled, a motor revved, tires rustled on the dry street speeding away.

"How are you?" She sounded vague, or absent, or something.

"I'm okay," he said.

"How are you?" she repeated senselessly, feeling an unexpected surge in her stomach.

"Okay, how are you?" he insisted.

She dropped an uneaten handful of cheddar puffs into its bag and settled on the couch, her long bare legs shimmering in the TV light as the million fans shouted, footballers ran on the field dribbling the ball with their cleated shoes, and the leaves crinkled outside, bringing in a fresh and sweet-smelling breeze. "I didn't think I'd hear from you again," she said.

"Maybe you were right," he said.

"Where are you?" She heard the unmistakable sound of a tractor-trailer rig passing on a busy street, and realized not quite immediately that it wasn't outside but on his end. How close they were, so far yet in one head together like a pair of earphones, a left and a right, a male and a female.

He sounded bored. "Oh, one of these bars. A regular meat rack. I want to leave. I'm so sick of that whole scene."

"It's ten o'clock," she told him. "It's early for bars, as I recall."

"I hope I'm not calling too late."

She rolled over on her stomach. "It's not too late." Her breath somehow was short. "It's never too late or too early in Upskate, Downskate."

It's never too late. I'm always open for you.

"Just thought I'd call," he said. "Let's not talk about skating."

"It's been a while," she said. She added teasingly, "What about your date?"

"No date," he protested.

"It's Friday night," she said. "A date night."

"It's springtime too," he reminded her.

"I know!" she agreed, accentuating the "know." Her fingers were somehow aflutter around the receiver.

Fig night. Fog night, she thought. Come over here.

His voice sounded abashed and sweaty. "I'd made up my mind not to call you."

She laughed incriminatingly. "I thought I saw you staring at the telephone when you were here, right as you left."

"You don't miss much."

"You were standing too close. You must learn to be discreet."

"I thought I was discreet."

"Not discreet enough." Her heart was pounding and the pulse in her throat threatened to cut off her voice. Indeed, her throat tightened, so she involuntarily emitted a faint cry of desire. Embarrassed, she hoped he didn't notice. "I saw you, Marc. You lingered. Actually, you sort of swayed to one side so you could get a good look at the phone number on the switchhook."

"I should be descreet when instead I'm concrete," he said.

She pressed her elbows together, as her nipples tingled just hearing his voice. "I thought you'd be off mowing other lawns."

"I was," he said truthfully.

"Don't sound so enthused," she said.

"The grass is greener on the other side."

"That's original."

"I miss you."

"I know," she said full of sorrow and hope, yearning and soap. "Stop by when you feel like it."

Come now. Please, I need you so much.

Crack! another hard kick. The fans rustled in Milan or Rome, wherever it was, Borussia Dortmund or Manchester, she wasn't paying enough attention. Oh yes, Madrid and Warsaw. The announcer said, "Samy Krakow just kicked another goal home for his team..."

"Someone there?" Marc Fontbleu asked.

"Not a soul," she said brightly. "I got a card from Jérôme today. They found some bones."

"Over in Australia?"

"Where else?"

"Upskate."

"You remembered. Yeah, Downskate."

"I hope I'm not bothering you."

"I was hoping you'd call. Don't drop the receiver in shock now."

"You are so saucy."

"You talk too long on the telephone."

"I can hang up."

"No don't."

"Shall I drop by?"

"What about your commitment?"

"What commitment?"

"To remain uncommitted."

He paused amid grass and crickets and exhaust fumes. Feigning casualness, he said, "You're on my way home."

"Do you like cheddar puffs? Do you follow football?"

"Who is ahead?"

"Madrid over Warsaw. Six aught," she said, feeling a warmth creeping into her stomach as she ran a toying fingernail over the crushed velvet material of the couch's arm rest.

"Sounds like an interesting game."

"If you like I'll warm some more cheddar puffs."

He said, "I'm crossing the Rubicon as we speak."

"Are you walking or driving?"

"I have my old Renault, with the cloth top and raised tail end."

"I can't wait to ride in it." She added, when he was silent: "Honest."

"I'll be right over."

"Hurry." She hung up and went into the bedroom. In the stillness and darkness there, she found some silk briefs into which she slipped her long legs. After a brief deliberation, she decided to leave her breasts bare, and pulled on a mid-thigh summer dress. In the mingled light of moon and street lights, she turned slowly before the bedroom mirror and regarded herself. She would act nonchalant at the door.

Or, anyway, I'll try my best not to seem eager.

In the mild cross-lights, the puckering of her nipples in the flimsy flowered cotton shift did not show at all, but it made a magic glowing lantern to entice him with her figure.

The telephone glowered righteously under its palm tree. She stepped into high-heeled open pumps which accentuated the length of her legs.

"The die is cast," she said to the telephone, breezing past the TV to make some more cheddar puffs.

"The Madrid takes the lead again and this looks like a take-away game, folks," said the announcer.

"De dice is trone," she intimated airily to the mute black telephone.

Minutes later, as popping sounds ensued from the kitchen, she stood behind the window overlooking the Boul' Saint-Germain. She'd had curtains installed—like a fig leaf, a sort of an expulsion from Eden theme—and pulled them apart for a peek. Any moment now a dusty Renault would come careening around the corner. She heard the sound of a car engine revving not far away. She raised her eyes, gripping the window sill with sweaty hands.

What am I doing?

His boxy little dark blue Renault, top down, crawled around the corner.

With fluttering hands, she let the curtain fall shut. And waited hungrily by the door, counting the seconds until she heard his footsteps, until she could tear the door open.

Chapter 8.

On a day not longer after, by the Rue des Bernardins, trees glowed brightly and the buds on the trees were even brighter golden-green as Marc Fontbleu and Emma Delors sat on the little *balcon* outside her bedroom sipping iced tea and lazily regarding Saturday morning tree tops.

"This looks like a day to drive somewhere," he said.

She sat back contentedly, hands folded in her lap, a restful smile turning her cheeks solar. "What did you have in mind?"

He lifted the tea glass and studied its fresh sediment in the morning sunlight. In some spirit of mutuality they had invented this small gesture, They shared a glass. They drank from this glass in turns, refilling it often from a plastic pitcher full of clacking ice cubes. "Where would you like to go?" he asked.

She pursed her lips and arched her back. Her bare ankles wriggled on the porch palisade. The late June breeze ruffled her fine yellow hair. "When was the last time you were in Versailles?"

He shrugged in some embarrassment. "I haven't been to Versailles in five years."

"It's only a few kilometers away, but another world."

"I know. Isn't it sad? I live here, and don't get around as much as I should."

She sat back, giving him a sedate and reasonable look. "We could take my car."

"We could spend the weekend!" he enthused. *Anything to get her out of here.*

She shook her head. "I keep thinking Jérôme might call."

Marc set the glass down, careful to avoid any show of jealousy. What right did he have? He'd resolved not to question her commitments. Somehow he always returned with a faint bitter taste to these reminders that their relationship was bounded, that there were limits. A thunder clap, a landing Airbus, a few bones from Australia, and Marc must run. She was by now the only thing keeping him contented with his lawns and flower gardens. He wondered if he'd have quit by now—perhaps find some coat-and-tie job or maybe bury himself a few more years at some graduate school, only to end up mowing more lawns because he had no inkling of the practical row nor would he then. Sadly, the Jérômes of the world were born with this kind of street savvy. They had this boardroom, mahogany-row

deep pile carpet smell in their blood from birth. Marc Fontbleu, first
in his family to rise above trucking or mucking, had cruised into the
sky but was lost, flying blindly in dense cumulus clouds of poetry,
artfulness, and sincerity.

Emma bit her lower lip speculatively and looked at him. "I have
a week's vacation I can take this summer. That's nine days, if you
count weekends. If you want, maybe I and my imaginary girlfriend
Mimi could take a week's ride up out of town to visit her sick
mother."

He frowned, more for her than himself.

She held out her hand for him. "You care about me, don't you?"

He took her hand in his. "I love you."

"No."

"What else could this be? Am I sick?"

She smiled. "That's Shakespeare. This is reality. Marc, I love
you too, like a—"

"—Husband?"

"Like a lover. You are my lover. I am your—"

"Wife?"

"Silly man. I am your girl, your dream, your *pute*, your bitch,
anything you want me to be."

He wanted to be in love. She wasn't playing along.

She pawed at him. "What do you want, Marc?"

I want you to love me like I love you.

She read the look in his eyes and stared. "You should leave if
you are going to hurt yourself." She reconsidered the legalese in that
look. "I don't want to hurt you." Then she made faces as if seeing him
for the first time. "Oh, baby. I do love you. I am just—stuck like this.
A beetle trapped in amber. You are a poet, Léopold Montblé, free as
the wind. I am a prisoner, and you brought me a loaf of bread with a
file baked in it, but I am too weak and foolish to saw my way out or
even see my way out. What would I do? I keep busy typing and filing
at my day job where you met me, a little light reception work. I
couldn't possibly support myself." She paused. "I never finished
college. I wanted to take singing lessons, but I can't hold a tune. I was
going to major in communications, but I can't write. I was going to be
a history major, but I can't remember the difference between Julius
Caesar and Caesar Salad." She stroked him as if he were a pet
chinchilla. "Baby."

"You are beautiful," he said. "You have a doctorate in being
perfect. I am a lawnmower. I know, one day I'll teach Literature or

something. My creative juice drained away. Just freeze-dried lettuce that's safe to talk about, usually dead poets like in that American movie with Robin Williams. Nothing new, fresh, daring, or original. To a real poet, it's like being forced to squat on the floor and lick someone else's plate clean. I don't even want to think about it."

She laid her head on his lap, the girl from the cigarillo ad, this samba chick who had never been to Rio, whose husband was that craggy handsome cowboy riding away into orange mesas in the remote provinces of Upskate and Downskate. She would never age, nor want for money, nor fail to speak in symbols (money this, institute that, *prix des champignons bleus* or *blahs* or whatever, Lah-di-Dah).

You are not leaving Jérôme to run away with me.

He rose, took her hand in his, and sat on the armrest by her legs. She breathed in deeply, a gesture of sadness, "Marc, this trip to Versailles might be the only few days we ever have together. I mean real days together, where we can be alone and without any thought of being seen or being wondered about." With the corner of her eye she indicated the dense tree crowns all around. "I'm pretty sure nobody can see us, and even if they do, they don't know Jérôme, and nobody would wonder about you being here..." As she spoke, her eyes evinced a deep and sincere thirst to drink from his cup. Their age difference was, after all, slight. She looked younger, and he could pass for older. He bent his head to kiss her hand. He half-lifted her willing, elegant paw, but stopped—instead, more gallantly, he lowered his crown to honor her.

"Maybe a weekend in Versailles would be overdoing it. Maybe there is someplace around here where we can have a picnic," she pressed. "Oh, you mentioned the Bois de Vincennes."

"Yes, that's doable. We could take the Métro."

"*Ça va.* There we go."

He rose and lifted their communal tea glass. The liquid tasted sweet and bitter. Her hand fell onto the thin cotton of her dress, and he noted its early, faint patterning amid the late-hour tennis tan. She saw her hands too, and said, "I just wanted to see you again. I was wondering if you're all right."

"You care. That's lovely."

"I do."

"I care also. It's just—limitations. You don't have to think there's a trap. Only whatever is in your head."

He looked doubtfully out into the tree crowns, where a darting squirrel zigged and zagged evasion patterns across warped dark-gray bark. He remembered a certain young woman (now what was her name even?) a few years ago in a situation that hadn't worked out. What had she said? *Nothing complicated, okay?* Meaning, just a few hours and I don't care if I ever see you again. He'd lost her telephone number. She'd never called to inquire, so she (what was her name? no matter) really didn't care. It was just as well—what was meant to be. Like this relationship, this relativity, with Emma.

Chapter 9.

They enjoyed weekends together, when she wasn't busy at her little secretarial job in Pantheon-Sorbonne, and he wasn't mowing lawns.

For the first time, he had her up in his garret on the Rue Monge. It was just a pied-a-terre, so to speak, except he had no tierre other than this unless one brought into play his parents' house in Créteil (rather not).

"I hope you don't mind it's so small." He sat in the only chair, which was at his desk a meter away from her if that.

She sprawled on the bed with her arms up and her legs parted as if she'd just fallen a great distance. "I'm so happy here. I am away from me and him, and this is so totally you."

"I did the dishes and the laundry so it would be clean." He pointed with his chin to the little sink at one end, and the laundry basket on the other side of his little desk from the trashcan, under the window.

"You did a heroic job." She squirmed. "Oh I love it here. It smells like you. Something so different for me."

"The bed is almost big enough for both of us."

She bounced up and down, listening to the music of the springs. "Listen, it's big enough if one of us is on top and the other on the bottom. Or we can squeeze really close. Would you like to cuddle?"

"I would love to." He rose and clambered onto the mattress. She opened her arms to receive him.

* * * *

They sipped red wine and nibbled on pretzels about two hours later.

The window was open, and it had grown gray out—that long evening in summer, when the sun takes forever to set even though it's not really daylight anymore.

"So what kind of poetry does Léopold Montblé write?"

He shrugged. "It's like composing and playing music. All kinds. Light stuff, heavy stuff. Imagist, surrealist, classical, whatever mood strikes me."

"So it's like playing piano or guitar?"

"Very much. Only the music is from the eye to the ear, as it's been described, not from the fingers to the strings or keys or horn to the ear."

"Do you feel music inside?"

"Usually. A sort of subtle low-down cool jazz best describes it most of the time."

"Can I see some? Can you give me a reading?"

"I'd love to."

He rose and searched in his little filing cabinet for something nice.

"I can be a little slow," she said. "Maybe you can explain. Teach me."

"Whatever makes you happy."

"Put on your pants."

They were both naked.

"Okay. But I like seeing you that way."

She flipped a corner of his bedsheet over her bush. "No distractions."

He pointed. "They are small and delicious, like pears."

She pulled the sheet further up. "I don't want to be distracted by your cigar, mon cher. I want to focus on you poetry, your music, your painting with words and rhythms."

He snapped the elastic on his shorts for a comfortable fit, and slipped a loose-fitting moss-green tunic-shirt over his bare torso. "Very well, so here I have a nice one. I'll explain it to you when I've read it. I think we have to pause for a moment and clear our minds."

They reposed in stillness, while the magnificent city whispered outside like a great park fountain in its ceaseless hiss of human life. Like a radio on no particular station, just static.

"Here is one that I placed in a university literary magazine. It's called Philosopher King." He saw the pained look on her face, and said: "Don't worry. Just float along with it. Imagine that I'm taking out my saxophone and I am just toodling away for you. Nothing special, just some impromptu music." He added: "While I am reading just words, you might try to picture something in your mind. A painting, a sculpture, a scene."

He read the short poem titled The Philosopher King.

Afterwards, she was rapt and as curious as she was pleased. "It bursts on me sort of out of nowhere, the way a horn starts playing at the start of a sinfonia. That's the opening little symphony of an opera, or the overture. I like how your voice is clear, and steady, and focused."

Oh my god she appreciates me.

"I'm thrilled that you like it."

"I have a feeling that you are saying you are a king of solitude."

"That's about it, I think. Whatever inspires a poem deep inside of me, ultimately it has to be about what happens when someone reads it or hears it."

"It evokes something in me." She laughed. "I'm not sure what."

"Maybe we can't put words to it. That's why we have poetry, which is as much music as it is words."

She continued: "I feel like a philosopher queen myself. Alone, and marbled with aching sunshine or moonlight."

"Don't make fun.

"I'm not, my love. I am relating as best I can. You really are a king, and you are filled with wisdom. You are a rebel, and your truth is self-contained. I can appreciate that. You're not holding anyone's cigar."

"I'll take that as a compliment." He ruffled through his stack of papers. "I type them after I write them."

"How do you work?"

"I always carry a pen and paper, or my tablette, and I compose on the spot wherever I am. The short ones. At night, when I am up too late, I crank out the longer ones that run for more than a page. One of these days, I might write an epic poem, but I'm not sure I have that in me. One day, I will probably stop writing poetry and turn to long prose forms.

37. Philosopher King

I am the philosopher king.

I sit on my beach throne
        marbled with
                Achaean sunshine

I am alone
my kingdom is within me.

"You mean like novels?"

"You are so smart," he said. "I want you for my audience forever."

"I would love to be your audience forever. Read something else for me."

"How about this?"

"Number something," she read over his shoulder.

"Yes, I am compiling a manuscript that I am starting to show to publishers."

"Any nibbles yet?"

He made a sad face. "Not yet." He'd already tried all the publishers in Paris, and gotten nowhere. Now he must look out of town, like the one he'd found in Strasbourg near the German border. "I number them in sequence. No special meaning. Just my personal little catalog. One day maybe I'll have enough that I can sort them into groups."

"Any love poems?" she asked.

"I have never really been in love."

"Yet."

"Yet," he agreed. "With you it's like a new world. I don't know what to make of it. My feelings are all over the place."

"Mine too."

"Very deep."

"I could cry sometimes, but I have already cried a lot before I met you."

"I don't want to make you cry."

She placed both hands on his lap, devotedly. "Just let's be two souls together, heart to heart. Mind to mind. Feelings flowing together like neon light in rain puddles."

"You are a poet," he said. "I do have a rain puddle neon thing here." He rifled through loose sheets he had printed out with their catalog numbers.

He read to her No. 4: Rain and No. 20: Umbrellas/Reflections.

"That is so cute," she said. "So you look into a puddle on a rainy day."

"And I see you and me staring back."

"Was that a prophecy?"

He shook his head. "That was my heart, being hopeful. I wrote this as a teenager one day, daydreaming in class. And now you have made my dream come true."

She pulled herself close, hugging his arm tightly as he sat on the bed beside her. "I love you, Marc. I will look at you from your puddle always."

"And I will look for you in the best of puddles."

She laughed. "Only the finest of puddles."

"The ones reflecting beautiful neon lights." He shoved his papers aside and kissed her passionately. She was ready for him. And so they made arduous, wet love again, filling the dark little room with their groans and cries of joy.

* * * *

"Why do you write?" she asked later as they dined on cheese, dry bread, and red wine. Once again, they sat on the bed, or she lay at his side as they had before.

"Because I feel a longing inside. Same reason a musician will never be separated from his or her instrument. Sometimes we pluck nonsense, and other times big symphonies, and sometimes just idle daydreams, or aches full of longings."

"Longings about what?"

"I can't always explain. It just aches inside, and the only way to soothe it is to write."

"I go shopping," she said, realized how dumb that sounded, and buried her forehead in his lap.

He loved her for it. He loved her for being light and airy and different from him. "I'm not sure I could stand being around another poet," he said reassuringly. "Thick air, you know?" He stroked her silky hair, enjoying the shape of her skull underneath, and the warmth of her skin. He bent down to inhale her fragrance. "A guy like me needs a girl like you to pull me out out of my moods."

She dabbed her fingertip against his cheek. "I like when you call me a girl. I am a girl, really. A woman who is a girl, or a girl who is a woman. I'll be your girl if you want me."

"I want you."

She snuggled. "I like when you tell me that."

"I'll tell you every day at least once. My girl."

She rested her cheek against his torso and sighed the deepest sigh he had ever heard anyone make. He stroked her back to comfort her. It was almost a huge sob. "Read me another poem."

And he did. "This is from the singles scene."

"Do you pick up girls much? Tell me you do. I want to imagine how sexy you are, and how they come on to you."

It wasn't quite like that, but she wanted fantasy. "All right." In reality, he and Jack spent many hours hanging out, and often the best that came of it was a nice buzz from beer or wine. Sometimes there was a thing with a female. Whichever of the two scored would fade away into the night with Mademoiselle this or that, to report with a shrug a day or two later when they met again. The other would take the Métro home alone. Most of his meaningful conquests had come at school, or driving a taxi last year, or at all sorts of odd moments. They were generally all younger or his own age. The older women in bars were often putes or barflies, looking with hard, mercenary eyes and sharp, knife-like red lips for a one-night wallet with a man attached. Or woman. Whatever worked. You had to take the cruising scene lightly and not get lost in it. Then you learned to stay away from certain types of places, and ultimately it was just you and Jack and Pierre and a few of the guys hanging out over beers in a place without women. *Whatever.* Not much fantasy there.

"I have a few here about singles bars," he said.

He read one titled Café Macho #1.

"That's sort of sad," Emma said as she lay back in bed.

"I observe people. That's what poets do. We wander around the landscape and write about what people do, what they dream of, the pain they feel…"

"Stop. Read me something happier."

"Very well. I have a Café Macho #2."

"Still sad," Emma said, "but glorious. A lot of grand passion."

"All of literature is the love story," Marc said. "I've thought about that, and further realized that all of life is the love story. We are born, we live, and we die, all of it in hope that we will have that grand, life-altering love story."

"With children," she said faintly, looking at the ceiling.

"I haven't gotten there yet."

"Neither have I."

"Are you sad?"

"Numb." She switched back. "Was that really a girl you saw in a bar?"

"It is a thousand I have seen in bars.

"Do I have a tan and tennis face?"

"Honestly?"

"Lie to me or tell the truth. I don't care, as long as I am with you."

242. Cafe Macho #1

Man of great deeds, o violent life!
He sees his story as one of drink and smoke:
precipitous, with red nights and lightning days;
painful encounters with careless or
                impulsive women;
friends with guns - he is of battlements,
    sailing ships, and cannonades!
        Women (when they see him lingering
                with his Marlboro
                over an expensive drink)
think: there
sits a gentle and unsuccessful man.

245. Cafe Macho 2

Your string has fallen,
pharaonic dancing girl,
I see your tan skin
in the flute music;
    in the liquor,
the dusky lounge,
the airconditioned dance place
with women to pick from,
pastiche of loves
that might have been
were it not for…
    What tender celebration
if you were you
and I were I
but here we are all
the should be,
the would be, and may be…

She walks out to accept this dance,
her eyes are black and fierce,
her beauty is terrible, ringing,
like an army with banners flying. ⇨

She deigns to accept this embrace
from the ninety-ninth shadow
of the man she gave her soul.
    O essential grace,
the jazz of your dry skin
is beige and angled in motions.
    You evoke, essential grace,
music; it was I, once,
who took your soul.
    For the space of a dance,
the embrace of a trance,
quite by chance,
we relive my long ago night
and some evening of yours
        before you had your hair cut
            and styled,
    when you possessed your
            youngest beauty.
Your smile is a white feather
                    floating in my
            air-conditioned eyeballs.
        Your tan and tennis face
is full of invitations,
reasons, address cards.

"You have everything in that poem, and more if that's possible. I love you because maybe, for the first time, Emma, I'm not just a lonely dude glued to a wall, watching such drama playing out in other people's lives. I've loved and been loved, had and lost, but nothing like this affair with you. I worship you, my pharaonic dancing girl. Your beauty is powerful beyond words. You are the gravity of planets, the light of stars, the reflection in moonlight."

She smiled. "The face in a puddle."

"Yes." He stroked her cheek. "My face."

She touched his cheek in turn, looking up warm-eyed, with a little smile. "Only yours, my love. This face is yours to love and kiss."

They grew tired and slipped under the covers, resolving that there would be another poetry lesson some time soon.

Chapter 10.

A week, ten days, time passed. They spent every waking moment together, mostly at her secret family apartment on the Boulevard Saint-Germain near the Rue des Bernardins.

They ate together, slept together, went walking together, and even started bickering together.

"A sure sign of love," Emma assured him at one point, as they sat by the window of her apartment. "I love it when we walk together, hand in hand, like boy and girl."

"I love it too," he assured her. "I don't know how I ever lived without you, my beautiful sweet wife."

She took it in good humor, in a swirl of startled and fond emotions. "So you have married me now?"

"In my dreams."

She ran a finger down his cheek. They were eyeball to eyeball, so close they breathed each other's exhalations. "Wet dreams," she said.

* * * *

They took the Métro all over Paris, just commuters like a million or more other Parisians. They would sit close together, a common enough sight. She wore fun, understate clothes most of the time, jeans and summer blouses, no socks or vaguely pinkish cotton socks, in nut-brown loafers. She had a purse for every occasion, preferring the almost compact, hard-cotton type with subdued patterns (flowers, fruits), that you swung on a round handle; and this purse she would set on her lap in the Métro with the loop over one wrist and her other hand always anchored fast onto Marc, never to let him go. He enjoyed watching the fast play of light and dark as the train shot along on city streets, overhead, or down in tunnels. It was always fun to ride with her.

They walked through the Louvre, enjoying the Mona Lisa and other famous paintings and sculptures.

When they came to the Egyptian relics, he said: "I wrote a poem on this theme once. A short one. I imagined myself thousands of years ago, doing exactly the sorts of things people do now or will do in a thousand years, only with different gods and spirits, but always the same prayers."

"Read it to me when we get home."

"Home."

"To our apartment."

He did that evening, read it to her as they sat by the window and he sifted through his pile of manuscript sheets, while they savored globes of cognac that glowed in the late air penetrating along with traffic noise.

"I don't know what it's about, but I understand. The ibis keeps flying and the grass never stops rustling, no matter what we think we're praying about."

* * * *

In another part of the Louvre, they looked at a sensuous painting of a smiling nymph imagined by some 18th Century Classicist painter, before the Revolution of 1789.

"That's funny," Marc said as they stood close together, each with an arm around the other's back. "I once had a picture on my wall from a girlie magazine. She was so young and delicate, no matter the porn, that her beauty shone through. I loved her smile, which was true and dazzling."

Emma said: "I didn't know men worship nudes."

"We worship the sun at the Nile, and a girl's pretty mooning in a magazine. It's all the same overwhelming beauty like I have with you. I am the world's happiest, richest man."

She pressed close. "I am a very happy woman."

"Girl."

"Your girl. Your moon, your buttocks, your breasts... you did say they remind you of pears, didn't you? You use that comparison with everyone?"

"Be calm. Very few women have perfect knobs like you."

"You get ten free squeezes later." She squealed as he raised a mockingly threatening hand. "Not here!"

"What do you take me for, madam?"

"A very horny boy."

"And you love it."

76. Did The Sun Hear?

If the eye saw me
it didn't blink.

  Near the Nile
  I cast a prayer to the Sun.

If the ibis saw me
he didn't miss a wingbeat.

  If the reeds knew it
  they never stopped rustling.

She shuddered. "You make me so wet just looking at you. We cannot just make love morning noon and night. We have to see the Louvre and the Arc de Triomphe and the Eiffel Tower and a hundred other great things."

"And we shall," he promised.

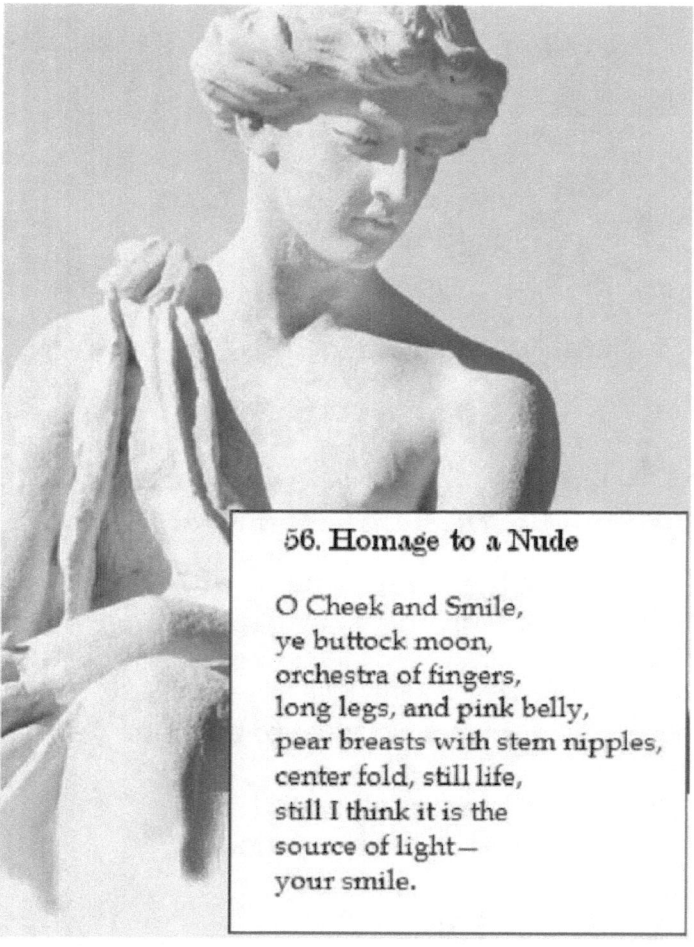

56. Homage to a Nude

O Cheek and Smile,
ye buttock moon,
orchestra of fingers,
long legs, and pink belly,
pear breasts with stem nipples,
center fold, still life,
still I think it is the
source of light—
your smile.

Everywhere they went, every moment together, they touched and spoke in the language of lovers. It was intoxicating.

* * * *

They spent half a day at the Champs de Mars, riding up the Eiffel Tower for a view of the city. "It's different when I am holding you," she said as they looked out over the cityscape.

He nuzzled her neck as they clung together like vines. "It's different when I can inhale you like this. I have fallen in love with your smell."

"I hope I smell nice."

"Bedroom smell. Can't get enough."

"Your nose on my back tickles."

"Mmh." He tried to gnaw on her collarbone.

"People are looking."

He pulled away. "Sorry. I can't help myself."

She growled under her breath: "The reason I don't do that is because I can't restrain myself. I'd rip your shirt off right here, in front of all these people, so I have to restrain myself."

"We'll store it up for later."

"I can't wait."

* * * *

A day or so later, she asked him in a restaurant on the Champs Elysees, as they were eating a fine lunch of game hens roasted with endives in a brothy celery root puree washed down with white wine: "Do you ever write about loneliness, I mean the real thing alone, not in singles bars?"

"What makes you ask?" He was just about to cut into the meat.

She had a dreamy look. "I've forgotten what it's like to be alone. I am so happy and contented with you. I can't believe I've treasured loneliness all these years rather than spend time with Jérôme."

"Well, yes," he said, meaning both his poems about solitude and his thoughts about whether her husband was a fool or just resting.

"Can you remember one?"

"I like trains," he said. "I could stand for hours on an overpass by the Gare de l'Est or the Gare du Nord, anywhere, and just gaze at those long strings of light whizzing out of the station in all directions of the compass."

"And you wonder who is in them, where they are going, and what persons await them. Lovers, parents, children, employers, friends, the whole network of our lives."

"Ah yes. I think I made this one up while walking alone across the Pont Alexandre III." That is one of Paris's best known bridges, named for one of the last Russian Tsars. It was built in the 1890s as part of the enormous preparations for the 1900 World Exposition or world fair in Paris. The bridge connects the Champs Elysees quarter on the Right Bank (north side of the Seine, best known for the Arc de Triomphe) with the Invalides or Champs de Mars quarter on the Left Bank (south side, best known for the Eiffel Tower).

Marc found the manuscript page (226: Lonely) with its catalog number, and read it to her slowly as befitted such a short poem packed with nuance and emotion.

"Such a nice little vignette," she said. Being his biggest (and perhaps almost only) fan, she poured all of her love into the good thoughts she had. "Honestly, you have enriched my life so much, sweet poet."

226. LONELY

Sometimes I think
when you can't be
lonely with your friends

it's better to be lonely
by yourself

than to be lonely
among strangers.

* * * *

That evening, they spent some time in his garret. She reclined on her side on the bed, holding a glass of Perrier water. He sat at the desk with a cold tea with lemon. They had little English ladyfinger cookies for a snack.

He commented while enjoying the cookies, and wiping fine dry cookie dust from his lips: "Hard to imagine that London is barely over two hours by TGV train from here."

"And vice-versa," she said. "All of life has two sides, like a coin."

"You will be a philosopher one day. Or a philosopherette."

"I love hearing your poems when you read them in your own world here. I can imagine you sitting here, a bit sloshed, typing by moonlight. I'd love to be in your head for a few minutes, just seeing all those magnificent trains of thought going in and out of the station."

He grinned. "Like that overpass I was telling you about." He waved a sheet of paper. "Here's one I wrote about a train that made my skin crawl with pleasure, pain, whatever you want to call it."

"Longing."

"Yes, for I don't know what. Longing for you."

"I love to be longed for."

"I live to long for you. Now be quiet and let me read this before I jump on you."

"I love being jumped on by you. But it can wait. Go on."

He read to her #114: Rain, Traffic, Open Window.

"That was at a bridge on the Seine. I forget which one. Here's another from the same time period and place. I think I was just getting over a girl named Madelaine, a waitress over in Montparnasse. I had a crush on her, and she crushe me."

Now he read to her his poem #77: Night Time, Star time.

She lay quietly thinking after he had finished reading in a slow, even voice. Then she said: "You have a nice reading voice. I hate it when someone reads poetry in a high, keening voice."

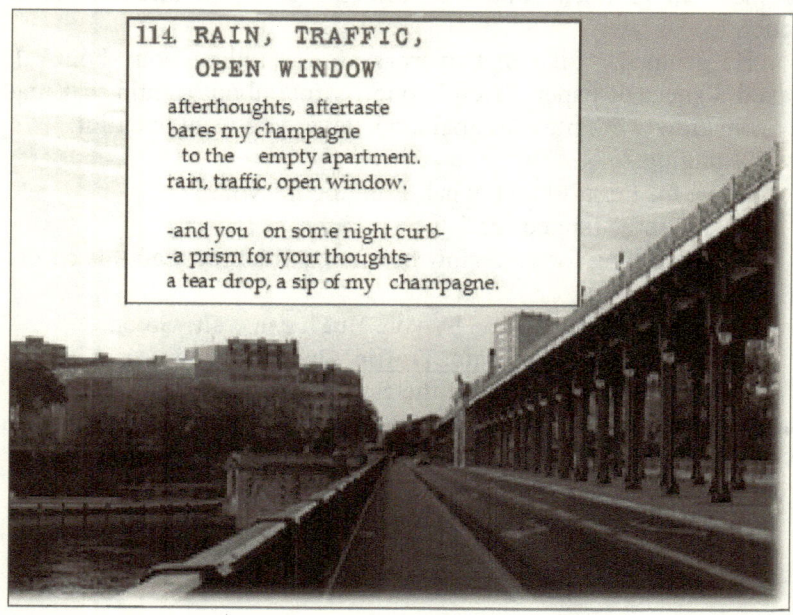

114. RAIN, TRAFFIC,
     OPEN WINDOW

afterthoughts, aftertaste
bares my champagne
    to the   empty apartment.
rain, traffic, open window.

-and you on some night curb-
-a prism for your thoughts-
a tear drop, a sip of my champagne.

"I know, that's weird, huh?"

"I can hear that quiet music inside of you, now that you have read so many of your poems to me."

"Thank you," he said sincerely. "Nobody has ever taken an interest like you have."

"Too bad I have no publisher connections. Real estate, yes. Paleontology, yes. Restaurants, yes. Poetry not so much. Not any. Does anyone read poetry anymore these days?"

He gesticulated. "It's all around us every moment. I don't mean like abstract things like metaphors, electricity and all that. I mean we listen to pop music that is sung verse."

"A lot of it really bad."

"Admittedly, but most poetry is very banal and affected. There may be feeling but no compositional skill."

Ruefully, she said: "If it were a common talent, everyone would do it."

"Yes. I always like to think about people who fancy they are writers of fine art: would you walk into a symphony, pick up a violin with no training, and start scratching and squeaking away?"

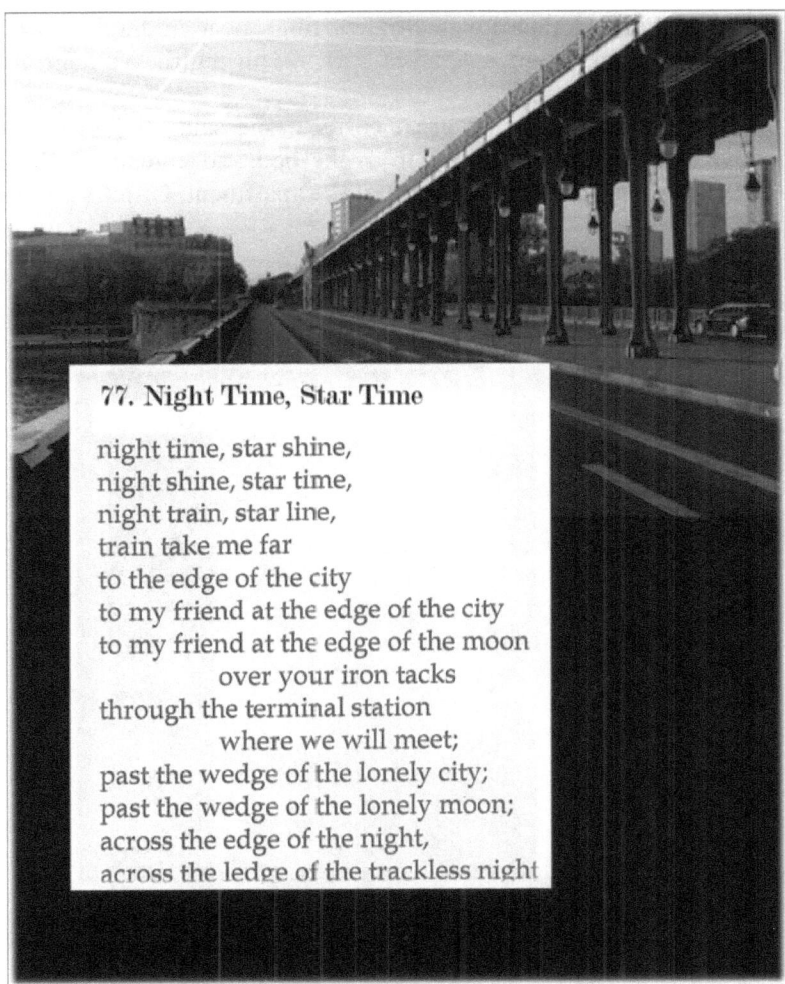

77. Night Time, Star Time

night time, star shine,
night shine, star time,
night train, star line,
train take me far
to the edge of the city
to my friend at the edge of the city
to my friend at the edge of the moon
          over your iron tacks
through the terminal station
          where we will meet;
past the wedge of the lonely city;
past the wedge of the lonely moon;
across the edge of the night,
across the ledge of the trackless night

She laughed. "Oh my god, I tried it once in a friend's apartment. I couldn't even make the violin squeak."

"Imagine what I feel like when some talentless shmoe is babbling. You know, they think poetry is just prose folded into equal but shorter lines."

She made a snuggy face. "We know better, don't we?"

"Honey," she asked, "do you have anything lighter? And then we'll head on over to our apartment for a good hard sleep."

"Sure. Here's one. This is a happy one. I was in the Montmartre one afternoon, having coffee at a bistro. I felt so good and warm inside, and I jotted this down. Strange time, near midnight, to talk about coffee but here goes. Oh yes, I was with a girl. We split up a week later but whatever."

"Must have been some great coffee," she said. "I feel a glow already," Emma said. She rose from the bed and extended a hand. "Come, let's put our thighs together at the apartment. Or let's part our thighs."

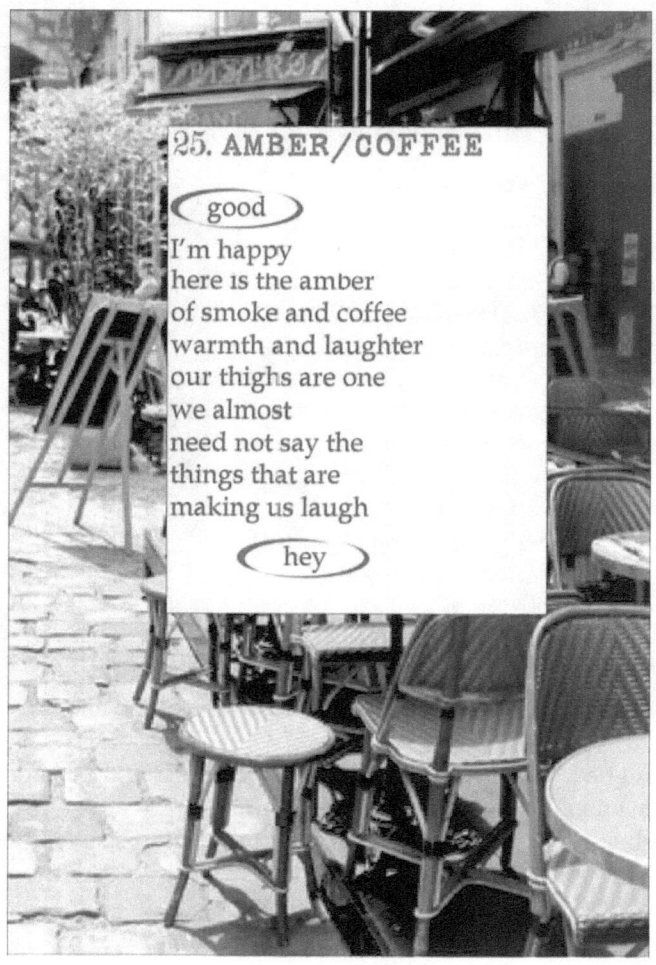

25. AMBER/COFFEE

good

I'm happy
here is the amber
of smoke and coffee
warmth and laughter
our thighs are one
we almost
need not say the
things that are
making us laugh

hey

Chapter 11.

A few weeks later, they had quarreled and kissed and made up, as lovers will. They had proven they could be tempestuous together, and get over it as quickly as the passing of a summer rain squall. Outside the bubble of their happiness and isolation, certain realities pressed home.

The two lovers continued their daily job routines, fitting passion and companionship around those distracted and impatient hours. Marc had been out of touch with his friend Jack, and Jacks's sister Danielle, not to mention both their families and other friends.

One day, they planned a trip to the park.

* * * *

Marc and Emma drove in the Renault, planning to park by the Vincennes Park on the eastern side of the city. It was either that or take the Metro, and they wanted to try their luck despite heavy traffic. It was a very familiar route for Marc, since a few minutes further east would take him to his home town of Créteil in the Marne River Valley.

He put the cloth top up because of the heat and bright sunshine. He wore blue jeans, crew socks, loafers, a maroon football shirt. She wore white deck shoes, pink socks, and a simple skirt of light blue denim. A halter top freed her long caramel arms and slender hands.

"I keep wishing you weren't married," he said along the way, regarding a stubborn red light with frustration.

She budged slightly in her relaxed position, legs extended under the dashboard, one hand in her lap while she watched her other hand toying idly around the mirror outside the car. "I'm older than you. The age difference would bother you soon enough."

He shrugged, shifting gears and slowly releasing the clutch as the light turned green and summer holiday traffic edged along.

"Ultimately it will," she prophesied. "That's why it doesn't matter that I'm married. Although who knows how long that will last. I am so sick of it."

Puzzled, he glanced at her, seeing a grim face. Then concentrated on the street ahead. Suddenly he wished he were far away, tipping beer or chasing girls with one of his male friends. A feeling of futility overcame him, making his hands doubly sweaty.

She smiled wanly. "I supposed one day Jérôme will find the right bones and come back to settle down with me and spend a lifetime writing important papers about his discoveries. Maybe that's the reason I stay put like I do. We're okay together when he's here. He's so busy all the time I never see him."

Marc said in a sickly voice, "Please..."

She sidled across the seat and laid her hand gently on his thigh. "I'm sorry. I was just thinking out loud." She reached up and stroked his hair. "I want us to have a good time today. Don't be sad or angry. It is what it is."

He gritted his teeth, full of frustration and futility. What was he doing getting himself emotionally involved with a married woman? One or two of his friends had boasted about such things. They obviously were not poets and did not fall in love with a goddess like this.

She sat close to him and said softly, so close that he could feel the warmth of her breath in his ear and inside his collar, "You wouldn't marry me or anything. I know Léopold Montblé, maybe better than you think. I know you're not about to tie yourself down, but I also know you're in the back of your mind always searching for that perfect young girl who is going to make you happy. Someone ten years younger than me."

He pulled his ear and collar away. Tears threatened to blind him. He actually heard himself sob, as if he were someone else.

She however pressed—"Please listen. I know how you feel about me. I feel it too. We are crazy about each other. But it's unrealistic to suppose anything is going to come of our relationship. Even if I were to divorce Jérôme, I really don't believe you would marry me. I don't believe you would tie yourself to me. And I know it frustrates you to feel your emotions going down a dead end. But it doesn't have to be a dead end. Maybe just a...brief stop. You can spare me a few hours here and there, can't you? I won't stand in your way."

He looked at her, and saw tears streaming down her face.

"You liar," he said. She only made a wry face. He laughed and brushed the wetness from his eyes. "I suppose you're right. So here I am with you. I have nothing better to do. What would I do now, anyway? Drive around? Drink beer? Buddy up with my old friends and talk about how we'd like to get laid if only we found some ripe young chicks or maybe..."

"...Maybe pick ripe fruit from the married tree?"

He nodded. "I guess that's sort of what I'd be doing." He sat upright and put his hand on her knee. "You're right. This feels like— say, remember that night, with the Beach Boys?" A hard rock tune resounded in the dashboard speaker, and abruptly the mood was broken as they rolled along happily making pretend.

"We're just on a date," she said. She blew her nose in a tissue she found in her purse, wiped her eyes, and pathetically clutched the damp, crumpled tissue in her hand. "It's all a game. Nothing more."

We're just kids playing house.

"Yes, and I haven't dared yet to touch your boobs."

She sighed. "It's such a light, fun fantasy story. It's a *pet.*"

They laughed. *Pet* is the name for a very light pastry, almost nothing but air. *Pet* means fart. It's a common name for this light pastry. Emma laughed out loud, relieved, and couldn't stop laughing.

"No, you haven't even gotten as far as to put your arm around my waist."

"I'm going to try it, you know."

"I see that look in your eyes. I'll fight you off with a chair and a whip, you lion."

"I may be a lion, but you are a pussy."

It's fun to pretend, to play, to fight like this.

"I am open for business anytime you want to get your whip wet."

"I'm ready to pull over and take you right here."

"I wish we could. Too bad you don't have a van. We could make love in the back and nobody would see us."

"I'm going to love you in the back, in the front, in the bush."

"You make me all wet when you talk dirty to me."

I will never find another woman like you in my life.

As he drove, she gently massaged the back of his neck. "I cried about us."

"What?"

"We are a tragedy, baby."

This really hurts—but it's such a love-hurt.

"Oh god now I am getting all wet again—in the eyes."

"Don't, sweetheart." She nuzzled his ear, nibbled his lobe, snuggled her cheek against his shoulder. "My poor baby. And I am so wet for you."

He bit his lip, put his arm around her back, and drove along as life must be driven, one stoplight at a time, staying with the flow.

She stroked his chest with feather-light fingertips. "I will never forget you and you will never forget me. I love you, Marc Fontbleu,

Léopold Montblé, free spirit. You will always remember me, because that is our fate. Neither of us can help who we are or where we are or what we are."

Stupid Jérôme. If you were a man, you'd be here in this car, driving this beautiful angel, telling her how much you love her. It would be you in tears over her, not me.

"I love you very much," he said.

She did not answer, .

* * * *

They stopped at a petrol station for fuel. There, they went to separate bathrooms and washed their faces.

A while later, feeling empty and in love and in the moment and strangely composed (as in the eye of a storm), he turned the corner into Vincennes Park. Traffic was relatively light today, and they found a parking spot on the outskirts.

The park was full of people. Emma sat glued to him, with one arm over his shoulder, and her other hand on his thigh. Her body pressed against his at every possible spot. This short time was theirs and she was his. Nothing else mattered.

"Looks pretty crowded," she said, peering past the back of his head at the picnic area filled with cars and people in Bermuda shorts, billed hats, and colorful summer shirts. The cool, dark woodsy air was filled with char smoke and the sounds of barking dogs and squalling children. Joggers, bicyclists, and skaters abounded on the roads.

Marc and Emma had brought only a canvas beach sack with a picnic lunch and some drinks. They started hiking into the woods on narrow paths. After a time, they came to a secluded corner where the ground rose up in a circle, then dropped into a watery pond a few meters wide. It was scummy-looking (healthy, life-sustaining) water, several shades of green and thriving with insect life. Crickets and cicadas chirped somewhere nearby.

"How's this?" he said, looking up all around at great shady trees.

"It's lovely," she said. "So secluded for a big city."

"Let's enjoy it while we can." His hand sought hers, and her fingers eagerly entwined with his.

They stood between high walls of pine and gray, split rock, looking over an expanse about thirty feet in diameter and oval shaped. A shallow pond of still and moss-green water lay with mirror surface on a depression worn by eons on the rock shelf. Water from high rocks, fed from the highest land, trickled in a steady waist-thick stream down into the edges of the pool. The smooth stone around the pool was covered with old leaves and blooming moss in thick patches.

"I wonder if anyone knows about this place?" she said.

He shook his head. "I've never heard of it."

"Maybe it is a mirage," she ventured.

"More likely it's a well-kept secret of the people living near here. Look." He pointed to a cache of empty beer cans tucked under a rock ledge. The cans were filled with tobacco-brown rainwater and had been there for some time.

"We should have brought our picnic along," she said.

"Do you think I'm going to climb down to get it?" he said watching her sit down, take off her shoe, and shake twigs and dirt out.

She squinted in the half-light between the pines and the tall stones. "I wonder if anyone will blunder up here."

"We'll hear them coming for a mile." He walked in fascination around the rock pool. Water dribbled loudly down into the edge of the wide pond. Green surface scum pushed away by dropping water maintained a thick pressing circle around the waterfall.

"It trickles away through a split in the rocks at this other end," he told her, watching the overflow gurgle away.

"Until the owners of those beer cans return," she said, finished tying her shoelaces and sitting with her arms wrapped around her knees.

"Emma?"

"Ummh?"

"What you said back there. About us, I mean. It's true."

"I know," she said, glancing at him briefly, then continuing her study of the tree tops and sky. As she did so, she unpacked the lunch she'd made. They had cold coffee, eggsalad on rolls with lettuce and tomato, and for desert a couple of eclairs.

They ate slowly, amid this unexpected privacy.

He looked in the same direction, squinting in the sunlight and chewing on a grass blade. "I'm not trying to use you."

She shook her head. "I know that." She paused. "What dopes you men are, with your fifteen-pound egos inside three-ounce brains."

"What do you mean?"

She grinned and rubbed her hand along his neck. "I didn't mean anything nasty. It's just...well, did it ever occur to you I might be using you?"

He shrugged. "It occurred to me in one way or another." The panic from before threatened inside again.

She lay down on her side and elbow facing him. "Silly, we're both using each other. So what? People always use each other. It's not always malicious. People need each other."

He looked out over the still pond. "Why do I feel this desire for you? It's like fire. You know what scares me? That I may not be able to control it."

"That scares me too sometimes. Not being able to walk away smiling."

"You at least seem to be able to laugh and cry at the same time."

"Not an easy trick for me," she said, undoing her bracelet. "This is from a ritzy store near the Place Vendôme," she said, throwing it. Green slime absorbed it without a splash as it sank, a golden, twirling treasure in clear water underneath.

"Why did you do that?"

She crawled close on her elbows and wrapped her hands around his shoulders. "Something of us together has to stay someplace deep inside."

He took her hands, squeezing them between his, and she gently reclined on the mossy stone under him. "I don't understand. Every pore of your skin makes me dizzy. Why is it when I don't have any right to you that I feel I could squeeze you close and never let you go?"

She smiled, her blue eyes sparking in the mossy half-light. The laugh welling up from her diaphragm was a husky, mature one. "Do you think I don't feel the same way? But would you let me own you?"

He made a wry face. Inside, though, he thought, *You already own me, Emma. My woman. My girl. My love. My sweet hot pussy. My eternity.* "Then again, we could get married."

She didn't laugh, but looked as if it were a possibility to consider. "I love you enough. I would marry you if I were free." She grasped the hairs peering over his shirt top and pulled him close. "I could devour you. I could hold you in the palms of my hands like a butterfly. But eventually I know I'll have to let you go. Did you ever have a pet like that?"

He rolled back laughing. "You're sending me back farther than I'd suspected. I've loved and lost but...oh God, who knows, maybe once a long time ago I think it was an ant farm, and the neighbor came home weaving drunkenly in his car and ran over it where I'd left it in the driveway. I never looked him in the eye again. I was heartbroken for weeks."

She nodded seriously. "You are a sensitive type."

"Aren't you?" he asked.

She shook her head. "Uh-uh. Not like you."

"You have probed my weaknesses?"

She broke into a sunburst smile. "And found them very, very appealing. Oh Marc, can't you see, I wasn't looking for an affair, but I'm happy I met you. You're no Valentino...but then I think usually those men gamble and drink. They are vain, something you're not. Oh sure, Léopold Montblé is the best poet this side of...this side of...Montparnasse, but that's different. That's a righteous kind of pride, has to do with paying witness to your talent, I do so respect and honor your talent and you are so sincere..." She finished by sweeping him into a kiss that brought them down together onto the moss.

He pulled up harshly. "Don't make me feel you think I'm so perfect and sincere."

Eyes half-closed, she sought him with weak fingertips. He took the fingertips of her left hand in the palm of his hand and squeezed.

"Ouch!" she exclaimed and looked at him terrified. "Let go!"

He released her fingers and threw himself on his back.

She hovered by him, her elegant features pale. "I was just...I wanted to possess you for a moment."

"Was that it?" He spoke sharply, then closed his eyes and placed his arms behind his head, hating himself for whatever she stirred in him.

Her fingertips played at a patch of moss on a rock, like picking a scab. "I think someday you are going to hate me."

"Sometimes I think you babble bullyshilly from that nutso colony in Fairfield."

She stared. So it was class warfare now.

He rose onto one elbow. "Look, I'm sorry. I don't care what those hyenas do or say. As a teenager I remember we used to pass through the rich town...whenever they had a block dance for you spoiled brats...they used to throw us out on sight. Créteil kids. Blauugghh!"

"What's gotten into you?"

"Poetry! That's what! Can't you see? I'm not sure Léopold Montblé is going to make it out of the slum. He'll write poetry, yes, and maybe publish a few things in tiny editions without pay, just to see his name in a byline, but ten years from now will he still be picking his nose while you and Mr. Kangaroo Bones are sipping cocktails in some high falootin congress of archeologists?"

She jumped to her feet. "Goddammit, that's about all I'm going to take! You're trying to typecast me because you're an insecure bastard! I haven't pulled any airs with you! You...you...lawn-mower!" She whirled and ran past the motionless green pond water toward the cleft between pines and cliffs where an overview of gray and white rooftops hid.

He rose to his feet, cursing, and stood looking into the glowing emerald pond. Balling his fists, he grimaced and uttered a bellowing scream that echoed among the rocks. Then he sat down, nervously pulling out tufts of grass from between his legs and throwing them over the water. The first mosquitoes, bumbling, small, and blind, hovered over the surface. The emerald mirror stench rose into his sinuses. He looked over and saw Emma sobbing, overlooking the houses.

"Can I say or do anything?"

She turned. "It doesn't matter."

He threw more moss onto the water. He kept his mouth shut, remembering her bracelet.

She walked to him. "Did I say something I shouldn't have?"

He threw up his arms. "God no. I'm sorry. It was my stupid thinking, that's all. My emotions. I'm fighting this battle, you see, about losing you. The more I want to hold you, the more I know I'll lose you."

She knelt beside him "Maybe we should just call it quits. We can divvy up the picnic lunch down there and say it was a day."

He crushed his eyes shut. "No."

Her hand stole along his ear. In a very soft voice she whispered, "Will you stay a while?"

He reached up and pulled her down so she rolled over him and came to rest with reaching arms on his left. He pelted her with kisses and she sought his lips with her teeth. He reached down and his hand stole under her panties to grasp her round soft buttock. "I'm going to spread your legs and shove inside you."

"Yes." She whacked him on the back alternately with each of her palms. "Keep an eye out."

"Nobody coming."

"Risky sex. I never thought I'd get off on it."

He felt her kick her ankles asprawl, felt her muscles and flesh quiver as she did so.

As he took her, he knew she was taking him, and he delved between her long sprawling legs oblivious of all commitments to the contrary.

She bawled again, with her pink mouth wide open but no tears this time from her eyes squeezed shut. "I want you in me, I love you, forever, Léopold Montblé Poetry Fuck, I don't want anyone to take you away from me, I love you so much."

I am going to lose myself in you, the orgasm of life and death, as if I throw myself into that pond and drown, and you will be my last thought in this universe, I want you so much.

They clawed at one another, relishing the moment and the glory, turning anger into sexual energy while the afternoon sun began to glare straight down and irradiate the pond so its fronds and slimy surface became dimly visible. That sun was the driver of all life, the engine of existence for carbon-based DNA complexity, replicative and iterative processes of complex organic reaction chains and other explosive realities, like the intersection of Marc and Emma.

This is life: a love affair; something beautiful growing in a place it isn't meant to, a doomed lovely flower we could cry over as it's meant to wilt and die just when it is so beautiful and filled with life.

Crickets shrilled in the prickly bushes. Flies and other insects began a milling flight pattern more complex than that of an international airport. Bubbles fermented to the surface of the pond, and spider-legged insects walked on the surface in search of prey. A bullfrog chirruped mournfully in some shady glen of leaves.

Marc and Emma sagged sweatily at the exhaustion of their sex. Their skin stuck together in the heat. They rolled apart to let air between their steamy bodies.

Some brief thrashing noise in the forest startled her. He had not heard it, but she sat up, pulling her dress down to her knees. "You'd better put on your clothes," she whispered.

He rolled lazily into a sitting position, listening into the forest, but could hear nothing. Clothing was scattered around them on the warm rocks.

She reached far to retrieve her panties, which she used to dry herself. He dried himself with his own and then dressed, feeling drained and finished and lethargic. The tension was not gone between them. Like the unmoving air, it hung between them. On a far ledge, he spotted a copperhead snake sleeping in noon sunlight.

I could start again, and take you, and again, and you would welcome me with open arms and legs. I would lose myself in you and never regret it for a moment. Except this is not ours to give or take. We are playthings as fate decrees.

He led her back downhill and into civilization amid the shadowy but hot woods, holding out a hand which she accepted wordlessly to help her down. As they approached the car, she stuffed her damp panties into his backpack. The secret of her nakedness under the skirt still excited him as it had during their ascent.

"Maybe they had the same idea," she said listlessly, pointing to a small white car pulled in among the woods some distance up the road. "Anything left to eat?"

"You're hungry again?" he asked.

"Sex makes me ravenous."

They shared the last of the sandwiches, and savored the vanilla-filled, chocolate-drizzled eclairs. Cold coffee hit the spot.

"You don't miss your bracelet?"

She shook her head. "It is a piece of us that will live in the slime of creation for a million years."

"Good idea you had to come here." She shrugged and grinned. "I went along with it, though. See, that's part of holding a man's cigar."

"Live and learn," he agreed. "I would like to spend the night with you if that's all right."

"Really? What an original idea."

She could be sarcastic. He grinned ruefully, looking at that vulnerable, sultry, wounded face. He saw that distant look, and imagined her gaze was directed far away at Mr. Cigar (that fool, Jérôme) and what she must endure. "I'll make it better."

She looked up, suddenly all sunshine, as if he had promised to be a better husband. She said: "Maybe we are married already."

That would be so cool. Did he dare hope? To think of such a thing?

Summer heat softened slightly in its intensity as he pulled the car out onto the oozing tarry road surface. A breeze bringing with it smells of hot tar and lukewarm leaf juice rattled softly under the tattered cloth top of the faltering car. The car seemed to find its own way back toward central Paris. They rode in an engorged silence. "Shall we go to a movie?" he offered, but his voice sounded unconvincing even to him.

She shook her head and said "I'd rather not, I think. I'm sort of tired and in a mood to take a long soak in the tub."

After heavy traffic, a half hour later they entered the 5th Arrondissement.

She touched his arm. "Marc, I don't want you to be mad, but I don't want to see you for a while. I'm not saying never again, though maybe I should. I don't want our lives to get any more tangled."

He submitted with a mix of reluctance and relief. "We get too dramatic together."

If nothing else, suddenly life is very simple again.

She shook him by the shoulders. "It's all okay. We've known each other for such a short time, and it's been so intense—I've been wondering when we'd have some sort of blow-up."

He frowned in sunlight. "Léopold Montblé hasn't written a really powerful poem in weeks."

"All this happiness makes you soft." She looked out over the passing green lawns and elm trees. "You can't let your own things go, you know." She grinned and added, "Can't let your friend the poet down."

He turned the corner slowly onto her street. "I really need some time to take care of things I've neglected."

"Like your buddies," she said sympathetically and sensibly. "Your poetry. Your dreams."

As he pulled up at the curb, she reached over the seat to gather her bag with picnic remains and various books and extra clothing. They were at her married apartment, rather than the family hotel near the Rue des Bernardins.

He manfully removed the cooler and carried it to the house for her. They ascended the dark, cool stairway in silence. He waited for her familiar fumbling with keys.

Then the apartment door opened and he followed her into the dwelling. He'd only glimpsed this place once, when picking her up for a date. This was Jérôme's territory, if he were ever home. Marc felt guilty and ungainly, an intruder, relishing the freshly painted and book-filled quiet and neatly ordered young/oldness of the apartment. Setting the canvas carryall aside on a kitchen counter, he walked into the living room with his hands in his pockets.

She emerged from the bedroom where she'd gone to put her unused sweater and book. She walked slowly, hands in the pockets of her skirt, kicking off her white deck shoes as she walked.

He was pointedly aware that she had nothing on underneath. "I'll go home and take a shower," he said.

"I hope Léopold Montblé will write some poetry soon." Her smile was pointed and wistful. Her eyes were not without tenderness, yet an unconditional something hovered in her gaze, directing what must be done.

He felt relieved that he'd be leaving her. "I think it's long overdue."

"I'm expecting a phone call from Jérôme," she said. He called her every Saturday evening at five. As if she'd suddenly remembered, she sat dutifully on the couch beside the phone. She became insular and withdrawn.

Marc sat down on the couch about two feet away. "Look, I'm not going to kiss you goodbye, okay?"

She cast a minute glance in his direction. It was a dull, veiled, hurt look.

He said, "I'm realizing that I have no business kissing you goodbye. I mean we've shared our time. And all. I just. Oh, well, maybe you understand what I'm trying to say." She was someone else's wife into whose life he had briefly and ludicrously intruded.

Should he seal their dead-end relationship with a kiss or just turn his back? Somehow, it seemed, any gesture now would be to sanction a thing that should not have happened. A gesture would take away the thinly worn accidentalness with which they had both approached their liaison. It had been little more than a flirtation, a licentious thought, until that angry moment by the pond. Somehow things had gotten complicated at that very moment.

He started to rise, but with a swish of clothing she moved suddenly, putting her arms around his waist and resting her head in his lap...only briefly.

She sat up and took his hands between hers. "It's meant something." She whispered rapidly and her smile was only a half-smile, torn between emotions. "I wanted to push you out the door, but somehow I can't do it alone. When you leave I'll be glad you're out. I know what you're trying to say. I had a little forest pond to myself, before you plopped in like a big old rock and disturbed everything. Now the water is full of ripples and I'm almost dreading this phone call today. I think it would be best if you don't come anymore. But I would like it if you would give me a kiss before you go."

He kissed her cheek, but it wasn't enough. Smelling her hair, seeing her eyes flutter shut and her lips open, breath bated, he hovered on the brink of sinking down on the couch with her. In that moment he respected her weakness and rose, pulling her to her feet. She moved readily as he directed, eyes still closed, hair tangled and fuzzy, lips slightly parted in an expression of exquisite want and hurt.

He took her hand as if she were a doll and led her to the door. She padded along, unknowing and confused. Her bare feet padded quietly on the cool, glossy wood floor.

At the door, she clung to him. He embraced her tightly, kissing her, and he ran his hand along her waist, down to her buttocks, feeling the material of her dress slide loosely over bare, electric skin.

She stiffened and pulled away.

He unlocked the door and started into the hallway.

Her hands reached for his arm, caught it briefly, then released it.

He plunged into the dark stairwell on wing-borne feet, giving a last spastic wave to her shocked and indistinct face hovering around a closing door, and then he was out on the porch, feet pounding on the hot wood, down on the concrete, in the car, struggling with a whining starter, and off in a screech of tires which he knew he shouldn't as he pulled away down the sleeping street, turning the corner sharply to get away from its crinkling elm leaves and sad, knowing, owl-windowed buildings.

Chapter 12.

The night of his departure from the owl-eyed street, he would have a battle all alone with moths high in his garret room. But first— it was still daylight before then, and he was filled with the purpose of picking up dropped threads.

For the first time in several weeks, he drove out to his parents' house in Créteil, arriving just as streetlights came on in the inky-blue evening. Crickets chirped in the squirrel and frog-filled tidal swamps around the nearby lake as he knocked. The door was as always radiant with a friendly amber light. Good old milk box, good old dog house, good old trees, good old door handle, good old moths ticking blindly against the brick wall and the milky lamp cover.

He and his parents ate in the den while the TV flickered and the potatoes looked blue. His father, wearing Madras shorts and a crinkled white shirt whose buttons were laden with the weight of his belly hairs, sat enthroned in the easy chair with a seven-and-seven at hand. His mother, a small, wiry woman with her jet-black (obviously dyed) hair in curlers, sat beside Marc on the couch as they ate calmly.

"How about school in the fall?" his father asked after dinner, kneading his fingers and peering at Marc with discomfitingly direct, gleaming eyes while a handsome male talkshow host sat back laughing on the TV, and a circle of appreciative, gossipy looking young women in casually dressy clothing joked with each other.

Marc shrugged. "I've thought about it. I'm making a little money and I may put it off for a year. Save some money, you know, get a bigger apartment." It was a lie, sadly; he knew Léopold Montblé would demand periods of dissolute artistry in which no money could be saved.

His mother said, "Are you going to continue in your major?" It was a reproving question requiring a negative answer. Her dream was for him to be a teacher, preferably a college professor.

He shook his head. "There is a good business program at one of the Unis."

"How about some other city, maybe Poitiers?" father asked.

Marc shook his head. "I need a total change."

"Do you think you can handle business and accounting?" his mother asked.

"I'll have to take the entrance exams first, of course." Marc Fontbleu, if not Léopold Montblé, was practical minded. He had no idea if he could do well in those highly competitive exams against people who were far less loose and creative, but so structured and ambitious.

"That sounds a little more like it," said his father, a smart fellow, lately working as a mill foreman supervising the extrusion of stinking rubber at a nearby tire factory. His father hadn't had the chance to go to college. His good mind and sound body had been carefully harnessed over the years to the task of raising a family and providing a comfortable, if small, home in a middle-class suburb which forty years earlier had been swamp land and a country of gravel pits.

"We just wish you the best," his mother said.

They were easy-going, understanding parents. They understood struggle, though they little realized it could exist in the form of poetry. He could attach no formula of rebellion to his departure from their enclosed world. They had married when his father was nineteen, his mother sixteen. Perhaps the one benefit of this premature liaison was that today they were still young enough to enjoy the relative calm as their children moved beyond adolescence.

It was too quiet around the house, and he rose, saying he was going out. "Try to stop by or call a little more often," his father told him as they saw him to the door.

"And remember there's always a room here for you if you need a place to sleep," his mother added anxiously.

"Mom!" he admonished. After kissing her, he re-entered the night and dove back into his own life.

Chapter 13.

He drove reasonably and calmly through the narrow avenues and white houses among wind-swept trees he'd known all his life. Lac de Créteil glittered under a field of stars. On a distant highway intersection, a beacon swirled across galaxies—as if sailors from distant Aldebaran or Fomalhaut were in danger of running aground off—like—the Seine islands or the hills and buttes to the north and south.

The ultimate destination right now was his desk far away in the Rue Monge, where at the moment he was subletting a tiny fifth-floor garret from a couple of graduate students. He resisted the thrill of sitting at his computer screen and clicking the keyboard to create sheets of music in his head, which would pour out as fountains, flower-spills, and ivy-overhangs of free verse; not flowery, nor needless, but each word chosen lapidary and polished like the single jeweled notes in a careful saxophone solo.

Instead, he drove paused along the way in a familiar neighborhood. He parked before a hedge-hidden house. Leaving his car at the curb, he rang the doorbell and stood waiting on a porch of laid brick, with amber light and moths, not unlike that of his parents.

As he waited, a passenger jet thundered in the sky over nearby Orly International, the only thing that marred the peacefulness of the area.

The door opened, revealing a tall, slender figure in a dark burgundy robe. She looked like the shadow of an angel for a second. Long black hair dangled glossy around a pale face with delicate pink lips and dark eyes. "Hi, Marc, how are you?" said Danielle (Dani) Poncelet. She was the sister of his best friend, Jacques (Jack) Poncelet. The Poncelets had lived in Créteil for many years, where Jack and Marc and Dani had gone to school together. More recently, the Poncelets had moved to a pleasant little street in Thiais, another town in the Val-de-Marne Departement.

He gave her a brotherly wink, to which she responded with familiarity, even a cool fondness. She was his best friend's sister, which made even the thought of her as a woman seem offensive and incestuous. In return, she seemed as stimulated by him as by an old car on blocks.

"Is Jack home?"

She rubbed her hands in concern. "No…" She shouted over her shoulder, "*Mami,* where's Jack?" The distant voice of Mrs. Poncelet answered. Marc could have reached through the screen and hugged her, loving these people and their familiar voices. They were a second family to him, and Jack and his sister felt the same way about the Fontbleus.

Welcome back to a normal existence.

"He's out on a date," Danielle said regretfully, wringing her hands on a dish towel. "Want to come in?"

He felt slightly relieved. He'd done his duty and made this initial gesture of re-establishment of contact with his old high school friend. He shook his head. "I know he's probably mad I haven't called. I'll head on back to my apartment. Can you tell him I called? Ask him to call me? If he calls tomorrow I'll stop by tomorrow night!"

Dani knicksed. "You can go for a beer or two."

"You can come too."

She shook her head. "Got a date."

"Life goes on."

"It does." She touched his cheek with a fingertip, and gently closed the door as he bounded down the stairs backto his car.

* * * *

He drove north on the Avenue de Fontainebleau toward central Paris. He headed through the poorer outskirts of the city. It was tempting: park his car and go bar-hopping? Or go home and write?

He had nothing to lose here and drove through rapidly, thinking of the several phone numbers secreted in his wallet from meetings in meat racks and not-so-meat racks (bars frequented by college students rather than divorcées) in recent months. Satisfied with the evening's picking up of threads, he resolved now to explore the world of Léopold Montblé, which had stood delinquent for weeks.

The city was enchanted with lights, betraying the bitter truth of its mean streets here and there, among the haunts of poets and artists over the centuries. Not to mention the bloodshed of the Revolution and the Commune and the Occupations (post-Napoleon I, post-Napoleon III) and other violent episodes in the city's growth over thousands of years. As he drove by the river and the islands, in light traffic along the Quai de la Tournelle (Turret Quay), those spotlighted gargoyles atop the Notre Dame de Paris seemed to wink and leer while looking down at human foible and folly; what else could a gargoyle do? Besides acting responsibly employed as an efficient rain-spout?

Glad I'm not a gargoyle, Marc thought. *Can't do much with a stone pecker, and what do lady gargoyles have?*

Coursing amid squinting streetlights rubbed by leafy elm branches, he was touched for a moment by the irony of the fact that Emma's apartment was a scant six blocks from his own, separated by layers of wealth, prestige, and social formalities (marriage). He pictured Nazi colonels strutting around in her bedroom, and snickered. Ironically, for the past few years one of the prime renters had been a wonderful professor of architecture from Berlin, his beautiful brunette Turkish wife, and three well-behaved, exemplary little kids. Different world nowadays. As Dani had agreed, life goes on.

Boy am I in the mood to get good fucking stinky drunk tonight. But I'll try writing a stream of emotional jazzy poetry like a trumpet solo somewhere really exotic, like the Art Deco arches atop the Manhattan skyline. Maybe I'll go to New York one day and see what that's all about. But going there pops the bubble of the dream. Then it would just become more of the same. Or more of the Seine.

His street, as leafy and owl-eyed as any, nestled amid the parks and histories of the Latin Quarter, the old Celtic and Roman city of Lutetia. You could still walk through the ancient arena, the Arènes-de-Lutèce, where people could alternate seeing fancy Greek dramas or bawdy plays by Plautus, or watching men kill each other in gory gladiator combats. All gone, all history like everything else. Today it was a place to stroll, maybe sun yourself, or roll *boules* in a friendly game, or at night have a rock concert on the still huge circular expanse that once held over 50,000 seats.

He arrived in the Rue Monge and got lucky, finding a parking spot just two blocks from the apartment. He strode along the sidewalk among old townhouses, hotels, store fronts, and entered the little beat-up brown doorway of his own building (for the moment, his pied-a-terre). He climbed in a gloomy stairwell, up long, creaking steps to the fifth floor of the rambling house in which he shared an apartment with two university students. The two guys were genial fellows who kept to themselves, both working at odd jobs (one a translator, the other a tour guide) while taking classes. Nobody was home, as usual, so it was peaceful and quiet; they made for the best roommates.

He emerged into darkness. He flickered the light switch. Morose illumination spattered a tiny living room, which was no more a living room than their apartment was a home. A century or more ago, this had been the maid quarters of a wealthy family—whose descendants, just as with Emma's family, still owned the building. In the refrigerator in the shared kitchen he found several bottles of inexpensive red wine, left from a party he'd helped co-sponsor, but never showed up at. He brought one to his bedroom along with a plain glass.

He took a steamy shower in the shared bath, reminded of separate, territorial masculinities as he smelled three distinct shaving creams stacked on individual shelves.

Toweling himself dry, he regretted that the place did not have any sort of forced air. The summer night was not yet airless, oppressively sticky, and sweaty. He had a small window fan that only blew hot air from one place to another, but at least the air was moving and not tomb-like.

Here was the poet's world: a small room with a low, steep garret ceiling under a sharply slanting roof. A bed, under the head-bump ceiling; a bureau filled with rumpled underwear and unironed shirts; a steamer trunk filled with manuscripts and untouched books; a chair, a desk, and a typewriter. One poster adorned a limply wallpapered wall: the Manhattan skyline, with a thundering jet moving in an absinthe trail of underwater looking light, superimposed over a verdigrised Statue of Liberty (which the city of Paris had given to the city of New York). Léopold Montblé would one day be famous there. *Or die trying.*

A wall of loneliness engulfed him as he sat at the keyboard and computer screen, which sat on his little desk in front of a narrow, high window. The wooden frame of the window was painted gray, and peeling. The walls around him had been wallpapered maybe before the Second World War, and now had assumed a uniformly hazy, olive-drab fog of lost colors. You could make out dim flower shapes.

Three moths coursed about the open lamp nearby. A fourth moth buzzed in the glowing trough of light, fanning itself into extinction while its fellows danced about. He opened his wine, and poured a tangy few ounces the color of blood.

Growing eager, he read through his most recent files, and opened a fresh, blank (virtual) page.

He tried hard, but only crap came out—no sexy rhythm, no jazz, no undercurrents, nor sensuous entendres. The keys under his fingertips chickled dustily in the night.

Too many distractions.

Somewhere a window clapped shut. He stopped and looked into black night. Stars shone over Paris. A woman with a fishwife voice yelled insults, and a man with a voice like an ox responded in short bellows. A streetlight glowed amid a great conifer. A brilliant diadem of yellow lights crowned a residential building across the skyline. In one apartment, a party with raucous laughter was in progress. Somewhere else, a wistful hand bricked out sequential piano thoughts which rose disconnected through pine sap. A mosquito hawk's shadow bumbled in fast zigzag motions on the tilted ceiling. The wine was tart and cold: stored Bordeaux coastal sunshine (cheap side).

The keys chickled and echoed over the street and he stopped and took another sip of wine.

Nothing. What's missing is my lady's loving eyes.

Léopold Montblé was not here tonight. Where was he? With Emma while he, fool, labored here? No such luck even. He hosed down wine as if putting out a fire. The computer-composter, dark and matte, sucked up his thoughts like a Black Body in space. He exerted sweat beads of force to drive home phrases ringing with irony and contrapuntal inventiveness. From the eye to the ear... Charles Olson had written, tracing the bioelectric flow of poetic music.

This hot machine, resentfully steeping these past weeks in sunshine and driven motes, absorbed all that nurture and belched forth not a spare syllable of meaningful reverie. The seat of his pants grew glued to the unkind, tacky seat of the chair.

In a window obscured by plastic blinds, a feminine form undressed. Not knowing she was on stage, she innocently cast filmy white garments onto a cold bed. He sat frozen at his machine, watching and afraid to tap out another key sound, as pink nipples dangled into/

—and then, as Marc stared hypnotically, her light went out. Whoever she might be, she went to bed alone, or so he fretted. She was unaware that here a man sat listlessly sucking in puckersome quantities of bloody grape ferment, wishing their destinies could be briefly twinned.

The wine bottle was empty, and another half-empty beside it.

He printed out a sheet of vacant speckles, ink stars on space paper, and threw it on the stacks of paper and books surrounding him. He was close to quitting. More useful to mow lawns. Live in the solid world rather than this ephemeral ghostly wine cellar of angel wings and demon eyes, of evil grinning and beards, of virginal hips and pale arms waving in a dance in this crazy place, this hazy space...

No love tonight. That special gift comes only once in an age.

The glass slipped from his fingers, met the desk top hard, but did not break. He weaved, sitting. Like a fish in an ocean of night, he gulped cobwebs. Those moths had multiplied. He gestured feebly to keep them off the blank page, but one great juicy green buck with majestically flapping, dirty-bedsheet wings hovered obsessively, almost angrily. With a crescendo of aimless keystrokes, this noble pilot turned a color like the speckling of sparse black hatchings on the page, where he'd tried to summon Léopold Montblé, conqueror of the skyline and the torch-waving statue. It got late and the party ended; not a single nipple beckoned pinkly nor ironically behind any more slatted windows. He heaved himself out of the glued chair with a rip of sat-on skin and staggered to the bathroom. Flailing drunkenly, he aimed a heavy piss at the porcelain crapper. Alone in the oppressive garret heat, he wended his way into the room again. There, gulping and gasping amid a sea of flailing dirty-white moth wings, he sank sideways into a stupor.

* * * *

The indignant mosquito-like keening of his dirty-white alarm clock, coupled with a damp, cold, greasy wind on his bare back, summoned him into gray dawn, many aching hours later.

Heavy-headed, he swung into a sitting position and enumerated the ways in which a red table wine could taste muffy, fluffy, nauseous, and thirst-burning the morning after.

Marc stumbled on aching feet over the dusty wooden floor into the kitchen where thankfully a pitcher of ice water was in the refrigerator. He quaffed deeply, draining perhaps a quart from its echoic hull. He'd read that most of one's taste comes from smell buds. There it was: he winced in distaste at a rankling descent into ripeness and over-ripeness of variously refrigerated sausage and onions and browned lettuce.

Ahh... thus a bachelor pad, or what say ye?

He was on time for work. As he often did, he treasured the simple security, sought the ordered rhythms of work.

Let there be lawn mowing and hedge trimming.

On brick building walls all around, with their decorative sugar-white and cream-blonde bands of marble or granite, smiling *putti* and laughing angels and delighted cherubs looked down in approval or was it carefree mocking?

The growing day's warmth would dispel the soggy corona of a summer stored in bloody wine—all too briefly a summer's resigned hope.

The city was alive. Its throbbing traffic, exhaust air, squealing brakes and horns and tires on the streets outside the courtyards, pounded on his head. The passage of elegant young women on high heels mocked his yearning eyeballs.

Then came a summons from his superior, whose office was a former hay barn on a side street.

* * * *

Puzzled and apprehensive, and holding a little paper cup of machine coffee, Marc stepped into the tiled and damp interior of the foreman's supply room where Armand Artiglio rested a grim mien and a pudgy thigh upon a worn dark wood desk. "I hate to tell you the bad news, son, but there's no putting it off. There has been a cutback in funds and naturally since you are the lowest on the union list you are affected directly." Armand, wearing checkered pants and a dark blue windbreaker, nervously shuffled papers—which needed no shuffling—on his desk .

"Wait a minute," said Marc, struggling not to drop his cup of acrid and rubbery-smelling coffee.

"I'm sorry," Armand said afraid to meet his eyes. The hard, distanced look, the stanced attitude, in Artiglio's eyes threatened the rest of what had to be said. "You're terminated effective right now."

"Just like that," Marc said. *Zut*. What a *tarte de mierde* this turned out to be. A shit-pie.

"You can pick up your final check at the union office," Armand said, shuffling his papers aimlessly. "Even though you ain't fully one of the union; yet; so now you'll never be."

"I understand," Marc said, leaving his coffee steaming on the hard chipped desk as he rose and started dazed and wonderingly out of the tiled office.

As he left, he saw in the fuzzy environs of Armand Artiglio's office a darkly coiffeured man of indeterminate age, wearing a frown and a dashing gray suit.

This had to be a cute setup.

The union steward, a balding little man with conspiratorial eyes and ever so boyish cynicism, passed him in the parking lot; probably no accident; a gesture of sympathy, "Sorry…"

* * * *

Marc paused under a cloudy skyline and surveyed his ruined thoughts.

What to do now? He must be Marc Fontbleu now. No time for the poet and his precious jazz thoughts. Léopold Montblé once again gone into hiding, to make way for harsh daylight and bitter bread. Hard reality, this. How to scratch enough together to pay the rent? Back to bartending, taxi driving, mierde shoveling, what? Or back to mom and dad's house in Créteil, be a child again, do what you're told, don't track in those muddy feet, *blah blah blah*, back to studying dead poets at the local college factory of vapors...

As he stood on the street, numbly, almost guilty because right about now he should have been sitting on the assignment truck with the rakes and lawnmowers, he saw that silent man leaving the office: tiptoeing on hushed & puppied soles, his suede-patch elbows raised at an indignant angle, shoulders hunched so his school tie dangled, collegiate curly mane scraping his collar, and dark eyes peering poisonously; so Marc glimpsed him. Snapshots are always a glimpse of unintended truthfulness. This man, this creature, was an assassin, a conspirator. More was at work here than just a union list or a lawnmowing budget.

After that fraction of a glance, the man entered a little yellow Renault 5 (Supercinque). Marc stood frozen. Had the guy seen him? He memorized the license plate as the very hip, academic little car tooled away into dense traffic.

What is going on here? What just happened?

Survival before information: Marc had a quick cup of real coffee and sat in a bistro, wrapped around the cup, as he planned a strategy to avoid both starvation and depression. A quick check of the newspaper revealed that *twenty men were needed right away* and all that sort of thing, but unless you had experience in a trade or profession it was clearly an uphill fight to land even a lower-end job these days. He left the paper in a trash can and went to the employment office. Between there and the unemployment office, he wasted precious time well into the afternoon.

Well, there's always the taxi company if all else fails.

The city—emptying of its daytime multitude of suburban working people, but never the crowds of wandering tourists—took on a sleepy, bated empty atmosphere in-between time. It was Happy Hour in the bars. It was nearly five in the afternoon when he walked up to his apartment off the Rue Monge. He had no appetite, but forced himself to eat a cheap salad in a small, stuffy bistro.

Here's proof: there is really an Unhappy Hour.

At night, a totally different sort of traffic coursed through its old veins, but it wasn't dark yet. He escaped the stifling heat and basking streets, relieved that the day's struggle was over, almost happy to say to himself he'd done enough and enter the leafy, sunlit half-world of suppertime in the city's residential and hotel streets.

In the quiet, breezy stairwell of the building in which he lived, Marc opened the communal mail slot for the uppermost apartment. He sifted through envelopes large and small. The mail of his fellow renters aroused in him a mix of resentment, boredom, and joy.

He was resentful because a lot of their mail, related to their job-seeking, came from important-sounding firms eager to draft gray-suited robots with green and red ledge-ink flowing in their veins. No poets need apply.

He was bored by the company names—dry-sounding law firms, conglomerated canners, incorporated shoe design, creative(not) wretches, executive searchers, and the like.

He was downright joyous at times that he wasn't interested in hooking up with Undulant Design, Marketing Associates, cardboard box manufacturers in Brest, a chemical company in Alsace, or anything else redolent of rumpled dark suits.

In the mailbox were several items for him. One was a postcard from Aunt Lorraine, aged sixty-seven, vacationing on the Rhône; she sent love and kisses, and he nodded to her in spirit.

He found two bills to pay, and an offer to join a book club. The Randol R. Dette Poetry Society's current offering was Delphic Zones by one Ziskin Piedkopf. Scoffing, he decided such an esoteric name would properly baffle his roommates, even make them jealous and curious. Maybe Léopold Montblé was too esoteric, or not esoteric enough. Not a good marketing name. Too fresh, original, talented, sincere, and heartbreaking to sell sausage to stupid cattle. He slammed the item back into the common mail box, full of spite.

Ah! Here was a big manila envelope addressed to him by his misspelled name Mark, from   Publishers Inc. They were, at the moment, a keyFrench poetry publisher in Strasbourg. He tore the envelope open with trembling fingers. It had been six months since he'd submitted 25 poems. He sat down on the stair step and read:

Dear MF: You write well and show much promise. However, you should know that publishing is a flihty business. Your poetry is genuine and full of a haunting classical quality and I imagine maybe we could have published. Our editors for the most part wanted to say yes but then came the marketing folks and they tell me we couldn't possibly go ahead with an unknown. So you'll have to keep trying with the magazines until your name becomes famous. If you're still interested by then. My advice is keep trying. Don't quit your day job.

Best wishes, KNG

Léopold Montblé read and re-read the letter with outrage and disbelief.

What in hell is a flihty business?

He tried to read between the lines but there was nothing there which was clear. What did they mean, calling him MF? Did they say things like this in every rejection slip? Probably a form letter.

Should he try them again, or should he simply keep trying every publisher in general and not them in particular?

Is publishing a flighty or a flitty or a filthy business?

The typos annoyed him. Who was KNG? Some sweaty elf in a business suit who was afraid to commit himself even when he thought the writer was 'genuine' and 'haunting' and 'classical.' Finally the Catch-22, namely, they wouldn't publish you if you didn't have a name and you couldn't get a name unless you were published.

"You idiots," he said to himself, walking heavily up the stairs.

Stallion, his black computer, like everything else in his room, sat where Léopold Montblé had left him.

Still wearing his shoes, he threw himself across the bed, rumpled bed sheets only half covering the striped mattress. Somewhere a stereo was throbbing.

He drifted heavily into sleep—the drug of recovery.

Chapter 14.

A telephone waited in fingerprinted, dusty repose under a rubber palm tree in the Delors apartment. Stifling summer air penetrating to its quiet perch took on a hopeful, seeking, delicately probing quality. Having neither lungs nor taste buds nor soul, however, the telephone receiver, rarely ever rung, responded to this organic stimulus by stolidly sitting between the involuted globules of its handset.

When the air had achieved a late-afternoon fullness, the apartment door opened, then closed. A pocketbook sailed rapidly and briefly to a landing in the cotton and dust of an easy chair. Hands struggled with high-heeled shoes that dropped heavily to the wood floor. Bare feet padded on the glossy wood floor (one might have choreographed a dance of liberation from sweltering office routine) and fingers rustled in cotton clothing which swished in being removed over long limbs. Cotton clouds sighed to the floor as bare feet padded onto the linoleum kitchen floor and then the tile bathroom floor and then there was the rattle of water on enamel, made hollow by the acoustics of a bathtub and the snare drum of a shower curtain.

The telephone reposed under the rubber palm, subject to the waxy brushings of the palm's large, gnawed-looking leaves. An electrical impulse quickened as the telephone—receiving hints of a sweaty, nervous, importuning emotion far away—prepared to ring.

Shower water turned off. Dozens of small needle jets stopped striking printed flowers on a snare drum plastic curtain. Nothing followed. Two minutes later, the curtain rattled aside on brass rings. A tile floor whispered with wet footprints and water spatters.

In the living room, the phone shrilled over hardwood, ending a long, cruel stillness.

Bare feet padded quickly on the floor, leaving damp prints on the linoleum and then on the wood. A terrycloth towel made a muffled snapping sound, drawn over a long, slender back. A hand with long fingers still moist under the fingertips picked up the receiver.

A male voice crackled, "Mrs. Delors?"

Emma said, "Yes?"

"Gustave Bouchard from the Paleo Department. You remember the Susskinds' party? My wife wore the orchid?"

"Yes?" Slightly harried, she sat on the armrest of the easy chair, her dangling breasts beaded with stray droplets, as she strove to wrap the towel up around her sopping hair.

"I was just headed home from the office and I thought I might stop by and drop off some mail for your husband."

She laughed to herself in relief, having feared an invitation to another party. At these parties were always a collection of wives, ranging from the orchid-wearing to the mousy or brassy-voiced, engaged in irrelevant but feelingful subterraneous clashes. She'd inevitably just as well see smiling dons in their hushed puppies and carefully unkempt tweeds—worn these days with suede elbow patches—once a plaintive sign of undergraduate poverty, nowadays an understated symbol of overstated status. She recalled seeing maids and servants tendering cocktails; colleagues with tactical smiles and carefully hoarded cleverness; and, amid all that, one or two queer-eyed, suntanned, dirty-fingernailed field workers like Jérôme, briefly back from the actual work.

She said, "Sure, Mr.—ah—Bouchard, when?"

"How about a—haha, right now?"

She frowned. It sounded as though he'd licked his lips.

"Will you be there this evening?" he asked.

She frowned. *Do I detect...?*

"Why yes, if you think it's important," she said. And thought: *A woman can tell; especially a woman who is sweet cheese and has been fighting off rats all her life.*

He (she could feel his moist smile) said, "I'll just stop by in about fifteen minutes."

What's just stopping by versus stopping by?

She hurried to finish drying herself. Left her hair in that turban for drying later, under the fan, combing it, while moths ticked against the window. Slipped on sheer panties and a bra (which she did not care to wear around the house). And left her housecoat by the door like a suit of armor (not of amour).

Chapter 15.

Hey!" Feeling himself being shaken, Marc Fontbleu raised his head groggily and peered. His mangled bed sheets and striped mattress were wet with sweat and unpleasant dreams.

Jack Poncelet pounded on the door until Marc let him in.

Marc threw himself back on the bed. Jack sat beside him and gave him a shove. "Wake up, man. Get with it."

Marc wiped sleep from his eyes. He sat up, suddenly refreshed and happy. "Hey. I'm glad you stopped by."

Jack Poncelet, twenty-three like Marc, was a philosophy graduate and currently bartender by profession, and coincidentally a drily vulgar comedian. "*Pute*. Get out of that crappy bed, you loser. I thought it was going to be another hundred years before I ever heard from you again, you dipshit."

Marc stood and stretched. It was evening. The clock read seven p.m. "I slept for a few hours. I got fired today. Had a rough day."

Jack regarded him with quizzical blue eyes in a round face under reddish-blond hair. "What happened?"

Marc shrugged. "Just laid off, I guess." Groggily he searched for towel and soap. "Hope you don't mind."

"Got anything to read while I wait?"

Marc pointed to a stack of racy magazines.

"What are you giving me these for?"

"Your level of mentality."

"Thanks. Now you see why men have two eyes and women have two tits." He had a very dry, understated sense of humor, served on a heaping plate of common vulgarities and ironies. His degree was in philosophy; his practical application in life (thus far) at the fountain of spiritude (bartending).

"Evolution. So we can detect each other."

"Yes. Survival. Women have two eyes and we have a cock. Makes absolutely no sense."

"That's called a triangle."

"Very complex geometry." Jack's eyes gleamed with a mix of humor and concupiscence as he sifted through the magazines looking for a cover that interested him. "You know that I only read these for the articles."

"I have never actually looked in one," Marc lied, laughing, as he stepped into the bathroom and wrapped himself in the steam and hot water of a rehabilitative shower.

The door opened and shut as Jack came to sit atop the crapper cover with a magazine. "Do women like this really exist?"

Marc Fontbleu soaped himself. "Nah. Not in real life."

I've just been in love and lust with one.

"Hey, are you screwing some married bitch?"

Marc sputtered through soap bubbles, "Where'ju hear that?"

O my god, what now. Who else knows? Mr. LeCinque? Some oily faculty LeFart driving a really preppy Renault 5 trying for a shot at Emma for himself, thinking she must be cheap?

"Simple deduction," Jack said. "I didn't hear from you for the longest time, ergo you were getting laid regularly. You weren't bragging, ergo it's illegal."

Marc rinsed himself. "She'd take your breath away."

"You were seen downtown," Jack said.

"By who?"

"By whom?" Jack corrected. "My sister. She says she saw you pawing each other; some chick out of a fashion magazine."

"It's all over now," Marc said, rinsing. "God am I glad it's over."

"Who is she?" Jack asked.

Marc turned off the water and reached blindly for a towel. "Some Sorbonne professor's wife." He found a towel.

"You have balls like a brass monkey statue."

Marc pulled aside the curtain. "Small town, isn't it?"

Can't keep any secrets here.

Jack shrugged. "It's like a movie. We've all seen it. Umbrellas of Cherbourg. Imbeciles of Paris. Cretins of Créteil. Never ends well."

Marc dried himself and they migrated to the tangled bedroom. He told Jack, "Don't ever get involved with a married woman. It's hell on the emotions."

Jack looked up from the magazine. "Don't I know it?" Jack had the past winter involved himself with a waitress from the Hotel George V where he'd been tending bar. The upshot had been that the waitress, who was resigned to being beaten regularly by her husband, gave Jack a case of clap presumably obtained from her hubby, and that Jack had lost his job after being seen with the guy's wife by another guy in the bricklayer's union or something. "This is your first adventure, isn't it?" Jack asked.

"The first and last," Marc declared, dressing.

"Smart move," said Jack with utter conviction.

"It doesn't lead to anything," Marc said.

"Want to take a drive home?"

"Sure. Get a free meal. Why not?"

They drove in Jack's Citroën past the Notre Dame de Paris, where at the moment the bells clattered in ever so wistful melody. They were anwered by a carillon somewhere near the Jardin des Plantes. Marc thought: Big bells might proclaim boldly, but precious little Emmas like these carillon cups lisped in hesitant, cute phrasings.

I ache for her.

At Marc's request, they passed through a small side street in which Marc knew the department of Archeology was housed. Sure enough, there was a small Renault 5, looking very preppy but like a sharp with teeth, parked beside the curb. "Drive on," Marc said.

Jack said, "What do you say we take a drive down along the lake?"

"Anything," Marc said. It was always nice to see boaters on Lake Créteil on a sunny day.

Jack brought the Citroën into high gear. "I hear the chicks down there are ripe and ready."

"Sounds like the pinkest and ripest thing to do," said Marc without any conviction.

Jack grinned as they headed for the distant, dusky suburb where colorful sails circled around slender bathing bodies, feminine in nature. How complicated everything now seemed.

As motorway wind rattled through Jack's campy little car, Marc tried to put aside feelings of guilt and apprehensiveness. What would this Mr. LeStink do to Emma's husband's career? What would happen when Emma's husband found out? He pictured Emma, and longed to be with her.

I want to hold you, rock you, shelter you in my arms.

Chapter 16.

The doorbell rang, and Emma rose quickly from a flickering TV screen to don her house robe.

When Emma opened the door—knotting the belt of her house coat, conscious of the ungainly turban about her head—she found a short, stocky man with a smile standing before her. He had dark hair, bald on top, curling in an aging preppy style, wannabe, over the collar; and an ingratiating smile. He wore a shirt and tie and hash-guppy shoes; his tweedy jacket bore the unmistakable sign of current collegiate fashion in that its sleeves had leather elbow patches. He held a sheaf of papers and bowed slightly. "Gustave Bouchard."

"Won't you come in?" she said reluctantly.

He swam into the apartment, wearing a mixed halo of academic respectability and lip-licking greed that no woman of class could mistake. But he was an older man, and thus as subtle as he was sneaky. "What a hot day! I am parched."

"I have some cold water," she said and went to the kitchen.

"That would be fine," he allowed.

She served him bottled water in a dripping, raspberry-colored glass. They sat in the living room, he on the couch and she strategically on a backless stool. She thought of herself as England, and Bouchard as Norman France, ready to invade. He held his glass in both hands like a potion tainted, if one cared to explore Shakespeare. "And how are you, Mrs. Delors?" he said.

"Oh I'm fine," she responded vaguely, toweling her hair and careful not to expose more than her ankles. Even at that, he stared at her naked feet as if wishing to lick them.

He carefully suppressed his nervous anxiety. "I came here on a rather sensitive mission," he said.

"I am a sensitive woman," she admonished.

"How true," he said. "What I meant to get at. Well, Mrs. Delors, what I meant to get at. Well, it's certainly a warm day isn't it. Mrs. Delors, what I meant to get at."

She fanned herself. *What did you mean to get at, as if I didn't know?*

He reiterated, holding his glass in both hands, "What I was going to say. Mrs. Delors, we of the university are a small community. That is, we are like a family. All the more so our small department." He paused to let this sentiment of closeness sink in. "We are devoted to

the cause of paleontology." He paused for effect, like a judge
deciding her fate. Prison or death? "Our wives are part of this closely
knit community. Now as you know, often husbands are called to
esoteric corners of the earth by their careers. That is to say, wives are
separated from their husbands for long periods of time. And of course
this is a situation not very dissimilar to that of soldiers. That is, I
mean to say, husbands and wives are separated for long periods of
time. And of course at all the faculty gatherings, when the husband is
gone, it is the wife who is expected to fill in for him. Now this implies
more than just what happens at parties. In any case, it is important to
realize the effect a wife's actions can have upon her husband's career.
Especially, that is, I mean to say, when the husband is far away on
some vital field mission. Do you know what I mean?"

She answered bitterly: "You are not saying as much as you
mean, and I suspect you mean more than you say."

You randy old pervert.

He put his glass aside and moved closer on the couch so that he
was barely two feet from her. "Mrs. Delors, may I call you Emma?"

He pronounced her name as if it were a foul, overripe fruit. She
wanted to go take a shower to get his taint off of her.

She shrugged, meaning more than she said.

No, you asshole.

He continued, "I am a very liberal-minded sort of fellow. In fact,
I am an admirer of the free-minded spirits who have been known to
grace the annals of our university. In short, if there has ever been a
person who, as Assistant Chairman of the Department of
Paleontology, was willing to further the aims of the science, it is I.
However, there are certain social restraints which are always
important to the advancement of a talented individual within our field.
I refer to well—how should I put it—the strenuous efforts of your
husband in the field while of course all of us wait with bated breath to
learn of his results. Emma, a small indiscretion on the part of the wife
of such an individual could have a very negative effect on the results
of such an individual's rise within the department. That is I mean to
say, oh hell isn't it obvious Emma, your associations of late have not
contributed favorably to your husband's career?"

She stretched languidly. "Oh?"

He smiled wretchedly. "Emma, my sweet dear little Emma, there
is funding involved. As assistant department head, I can only be too
painfully aware of circumstances which could lead to the cessation of

funding and ultimately the suspension of your husband's project due to the indiscretions of his loved one."

She curled her wrists dangerously in the cotton of her turban. "So?"

"We can remedy that." He nudged her knee. "You are a very attractive woman."

She shrugged. "What's that mean?" she seemed to survey flocks of shit birds passing over the ceiling on a migration south—literally and figuratively.

He nudged anxiously, "You are a passionate and needful woman like any, aren't you?"

"You'll have to speak clear French if you know how."

He gestured secretively, "Your husband is going to be a famous man in our field someday. You wouldn't want his name brought low by any allegations, would you?"

"What sorts of allegations?" she asked.

Are you accusing me of murder, because I'm about to beat you to death with an aluminum mixing bowl?

He inched closer and closer, physically and verbally. She could begin to smell his breath—an unbearable essence of toe jam. "Darling, you are a woman alone. I know you have been seeing a certain individual who mows lawns around the university."

"Serious allegation," she said.

You sick fuck.

He said, "Said individual has been terminated."

"I'm glad," she said.

Poor baby. My fault.

He shook his head, denying any gesture of denial. "I don't think you appreciate the seriousness of the situation."

She stared at him directly. "What exactly do you want?"

He broke down and the game was over. "You."

"Me."

If I could shut my sagging mouth, I could still not talk.

"Yes. I'd give anything." His eyes implored. He tweedled and dummed his little pudgy fingers in a ball together.

Will I be able to breathe again after he leaves?

She surveyed him. "Have you had your temperature taken lately?"

Will there still be oxygen?

He buried his face in his hands. "Emma," he slobbered. "The first time I saw you…"

We fumigated after the Nazis, and we can fumigate after this lizard.

She rose. "Get out of here."

He threw himself around her knees. "Please."

"Get out of here!" she bellowed. "One more word, and I will call the police."

"What will your husband say?" It was his final, feeble threat before he walked dazedly out the door. She listened to him on the stairs, fighting her tears of rage, humiliation, and terror. She watched him out the window as he went to his car down on the street.

She tore open a window and hollered out the worst curse she could think of, "Go try to screw your wife if she'll have you!" She added: "With your one-inch dick, you marionette!" Before slamming the two window panes together, she shouted: "My husband will stuff you and exhibit you at the zoo!"

Slam! Went the window.

Ohh! Cried Emma, putting a hand to her forehead.

Then she did go shower, a pink shadow of fury amid pelting droplets inside the steamed up glass.

When she finally started to calm down an hour later, with turban and wine glass, sitting on the couch, she realized it was the first time in weeks she had not thought of Marc Fontbleu every minute of the day. Her gaze flicked sideways, to the telephone. Would Marc call?

Chapter 17.

Feeling bad about Mr. LeStink, Marc sat beside Jack in the Seven Winds Bar by the sandy shore in Créteil as they sipped beer. They had trawled the little streets of neighboring towns through the early evening hours, until word filtered somehow among the gray houses that the girls might have all gone to the Seven Winds Bar. So Marc and Jack went there.

It didn't take long. As Marc and Jack sat at a table littered with empty bottles, couples danced to pounding Euro-Rock nearby. Like all watering holes around the world, the darkness was full of searching eyes—some needy, some sincere, and plenty of them predatory.

Two young girls attached themselves. Jack went off to dance with Jeanne, the taller of the two. The bar thundered with loud rock music and the slap of ice being thrown into glasses by busy bartenders. It wasn't the sort of place where you ordered something fancy to drink.

Jeanne's friend Alice was a slender young chick in blue corduroys pants and a double-knit sleeveless pink jersey that left her brown arms and shoulders exposed and barely veiled her heroically forward-pointing breasts. She was Liberty Leading the Masses in the famous painting of revolutionary France by Eugène Delacroix.

Alice and Jeanne were from Sartrouville, on the west flank of Paris, out for a lark. "What are you doing in this neck of the woods?" Marc asked.

Alice, with long auburn hair carefully washed and falling in a frilly tease over her brown shoulders, was all smiles and white teeth. "We just happened drive this way." Her attitude was guarded; her smile hovering very white against dark velvet skin in a black light glowing around the bar. "Out for a wild ride, looking for wild guys."

"Are we wild?"

"Not sure you are wild enough," she said a bit coldly.

Marc felt a chill. Maybe they were call girls out fishing for a nicely padded trout? Very subtle, if so.

Marc saw that Jack, on the dance floor, was having a struggle getting his arms fully around bodacious Jeanne. He wondered if they could each be much over twenty.

"Do you often drive east this way?" Marc asked, conscious of the hundred jealous looks fastened upon Alice, who preened with adolescent queenliness.

"I just happened to get the Mercedes from my dad to go shopping," Alice said, smiling through braces.

"You don't get the Mercedes very often?" Marc asked indirectly, unprepared for a long, vague exchange of credentials.

A tall, muscular fellow hefting a beer bottle and wearing a stylish BVD shirt elbowed in close, casting lingering looks over the pale skin of young Alice.

Marc sipped intently at the beer on the bar before him, ignoring the guy's wiry arms that rippled discreet warnings in his direction.

You can have her. No need to flex your jail muscles.

Alice turned glowing eyes upward. *Sans* apology, she left in the sinuous embrace of one Gary, or was it Scary? Seeing under ever-attentive brows the departure of Alice, and catching signals, Jeanne untangled herself from Jack's embrace and swooned in the direction taken by Jailflex and Alice.

"Bitches!" Jack remarked under his breath, rediscovering his abandoned beer bottle and gripping it with clenched fingers.

Marc was thinking about Léopold Montblé. "Say," he said, "I think I'll hand-carry my manuscript to a publisher."

"What are you talking about?" grumbled Jack.

"Nothing," Marc said. "Just talking to myself."

The music inside the Seven Winds grew louder. The *air-climatisé* atmosphere, filled with sweat and beer, grew more intense at the dance performed by Scary and Alice in a corner. Her milk-coffee skin and glowing face.

Someday, somewhere, someone, breasts like those…

"Let's split, Marc."

Chapter 18.

The letter, just received from a Paris publisher, was a rejection but it read something like this:

Your voice has a power unrivaled in recent poetry. We like the elegant flow of your haunting and classical lines pertaining to the boredom of a faun in a garden filled with flowers and fountains. Unfortunately, we cannot accept your work because you are not a known poet.

Marc reread those words in his attic apartment on the Rue Monge in Paris. He savored every word. It was time to do something desperate and grandiose. Something almost Napoleonic. He would invade and conquer the east. Well, Strasbourg, capital of the *Grand Est Region* of France, the Great East.

An hour later, without a job, unable to afford the TGV train, he was in his worn but trusty old car on the N4 motorway, heading east into ancient Burgundy. The Burgundians had given the French a run for their money centuries ago. In the opinion of some, just as Bavaria or the Rhineland were not Berlin, so Burgundy was not Parisian. It was a distinction argued among some historians, who sought to break history into its puzzle pieces like cookies on a table, bite into each, and taste their varying flavors. Hitler in 1915 had not joined a German army but had signed up as an infantryman in the Royal Bavarian Army, seconded like millions of others to the empire of the Prussians centered in Berlin. Marc had studied history. He knew there was always room for the bold stroke, the daring ride, the pointed sword and galloping charge with bugles and drums, with bayonets glinting and banners like beautiful women fierce in beauty, as Scripture spoke from thousands of years ago.

Haunting and classical lines, the form letter (or was it?) from read.

Maybe we can rediscover a little of that old-time spirit.

Lying beside him on the passenger seat (where Emma should have been) lay that letter open to the sky, like a heart holding its arms out to the sun. Underneath it lay the stapled, thesis-bound (in fine little fleurs-de-lis) manuscript of his poetry.

Was it not time that Léopold Montblé (secretly the Parisian *apache* Marc Fontbleu) pulled a coup?

He had this letter from a prominent publisher and wasn't it time he pressed the point, pushed the issue, tried to make his mark? Time to strike while the iron was glowing red-hot.

Genuine and classical and sincere.

* * * *

As he drove the over four hours from Paris to Strasbourg, he often glanced at the letter and the manuscript sitting silently on the seat beside him. And he thought:

If only Emma were there instead.

I would sacrifice everything, even my life, to have her beside me.

I would give up my poetry, my identity, my very soul to her.

On the drive to Strasbourg he realized that he loved her with all of his heart. He nearly turned around to go back and tell her, but it would be better if this mad journey turned out to be fruitful. Then he could bring her wonderful news, and she would be happy.

* * * *

Wasn't it time for the poet to find his audience?

He arrived in Strasbourg a little after noon. He found parking on a little side street downtown, among strip joints and check cashing stores. Apparently, the work day in this part of town had not yet begun.

On the streets of Strasbourg, he felt small and burdened; men in gray suits hurried about, as well as women with briefcases. He'd studied his maps, almanacs, and fact books. This was France's seventh largest city, with over a quarter million souls inside, and nearly a million in the great metro area. It lay almost at the tip of that nose of France that projects into a fold of Germany; some might call it a finger or a foot. Marc had no appetite for metaphors today. He was on a mission.

Walking a short distance in the heat and sunlight to the railway station, the Gare de Strasbourg, he let lukewarm water run over his hands in a restroom. This station was an older building of the Belle Epoque style, before innocence was once again shattered by two world wars. Of late, the city had built a sort of *passage* in front, to use the antique term, a sun hall made of glass and iron to let the light in but keep rain and snow out.

Summoning up his courage, he carried his letter and manuscript in search of Publishers. So many of the place names here were German, a testament to the region's interlocking heritages. From the Gare, he walked on the Avenue Kuss, across the Canal of the Outer Ramparts, and into the old city itself. He found the great old Gothic cathedral and lots of other ancient and medieval structures. A very rich city, he thought. In ancient times it was called Argentina, the Silver City, or Oppidum Argentoratum.

* * * *

Tired of the walk, of gaping at sights, he found the publishers' offices.

They were in a reddish sandstone building, four stories tall, with ornate Belle Epoque windows. This was near a central tram station, called Homme de Fer, Iron Man, because in centuries past, many blacksmith shops here made armor for soldiers. Now the square was, by Paris standards, a modest outdoor rondel of tracks with a circular glass roof.

Marcel entered the building, inquired at a receptionist desk, and made his way up an elevator, to the fourth floor. This had its own little lobby and two young receptionists. A plain but attractive sign read Livres . He had come unannounced, and was in luck. Monsieur Mézières was in and would see him.

And what was the young author's name? The clerk, a pretty young brunette, raised her eyebrows and asked him to spell it. Then she pressed an intercom button, spoke briefly, and gestured for him to enter the greenish, frosted-glass portal behind her.

Léopold Montblé stepped into the paradise (or hell?) of his fate, sweating and now slightly trembling. He was filled with marveling, and sweaty from his long walk on summertime streets.

The hall smelled of shoe polish, artificial carpeting, and books. So this was where poetry received its official blessing and became a business product to be adored and worshiped in schools and libraries, to be pawed over in bookstores, and ultimately to sit on shelves in the offices of admirals, presidents, school teachers, and sometimes of prisoners in jails. This was a hurdle he could and would get past—he must. He believed in his destiny.

Unlikely looking fellow poesans nodded politely to him as he stood outside the elevator wiping sweat from under his collar and soaking in the cooled air: An old lady in jogging shorts; a tall, gangling, balding man in a gray suit; a frail-looking white-haired priest who looked about eighty years old...

This then was the literary fountain in paradise of Livres , publisher and adept.

Marc entered an office labeled M. Mezieres and walked on thickly carpeted floors to an impressive mahogany desk, where a chubbyish-pretty young secretary typed.

"Hello," he said.

"*Bonjour*," she said readily, turning clean white sclera and teeth up at him above a purple dress matching her violet irises. Her name tag read 'Jess.'

"I've come from Créteil and I was hoping to be able to speak with somebody."

"Well, who did you want to speak with?" she gushed.

He laid his letter and Léopold Montblé's collected poems on the desk. "I brought some poems...I really would appreciate..." He'd come to the brusque city prepared to climb in the editor's window if necessary. He would explain that, although the poems had already been seen, he must really find a way to reach potential readers. The readers would understand and appreciate if nobody else quite did. The words echoed in his mind:

Genuine and classical and sincere.

The commonly human nine-to-five air at Charleville surprised him. These people were as human as he was. Where was the band with the 101 Trombones and all the sacred music?

She folded her arms together, regarding him with tolerant eyes. "Who in particular did you want to talk to?"

With whom did you want to speak? Jack, philosopher and transubstantiator of wine into the divine, would be all over this with ironic, mocking rhetoric.

He smiled uncertainly. Personally, he found her and how she talked cute—live jive, real people, real time. He wasn't prepared for her question. "Well, I...anyone, I guess, who reads poetry. I've published a few of my poems in various magazines, and I have the clippings with me."

She tisked. "Clippings! You shouldn't have cut your poems out!"

"I put them together in a thesis-binding," he reassured her. "It was the best I could do."

"Poor guy, you are sweating. The water fountain is over there." She pointed, and Marc desperately dove to irrigate and cool the desert that his mouth had become. Were those cannon shots or heartbeats shaking the dunes?

She pressed a button at her side. "Mr. Mézières, there is a young man with a manuscript—do you have a minute to speak with him?"

An answering noise crackled, sounding indistinct to Marc's anxious ears. The woman nodded encouragingly and pointed down the hallway.

John went down a corridor that smelled of ashes and rosewood, as in a funeral parlor. He walked in on a tall, thin-looking man of about forty. Mézières, just then stretching, tilted back in a black leather easy chair. He saw in a corner, window office behind a desk covered with manuscripts, newspapers, and galley proofs.

"Come on in and have a seat."

Marc laid his manila envelope on the desk; or rather, on a foot-tall pile of assorted hardbound books. He and Mézières shook hands and Marc sat down in an easy chair facing Arthur Mézières. The easy chair seemed to want to fling him into a semi-reclining attitude of relaxation. This wasn't suited to his elevated adrenal count in this emotional state. He sat on the edge of his chair while Mézières picked up the bindfer (a life's work in those surgically clean, lightly haired fingers!) and peered inside.

"I see...clippings...poems...nice..." Mézières sat back and crossed his arms behind his head. The phone rang and he answered, "No, not yet... yes... maybe in five minutes... sure... no, make mine a brioche with ham and cheese, no capers. Okay, see you in five." Mézières again sat back.

Five minutes? That's all I get?

"Well, uh, Mr. Fontainebleu...hot outside, isn't it?"

"Fontbleu. Yes, it is."

Marc sank slowly back in the chair, realizing just how tiring had been his journey here—from Créteil, from a lifetime. Here he was, and the most pressing topic was a brioche without capers, no less. He'd made this pilgrimage through dangerous, unfamiliar streets, through the pressing crowds of hundreds of thousands of people...

"Nice little city you have here"

Mézières chided gently, "Oh come on now."

Wrong start. I've already blown it. He hates me.

Mézières was obviously just killing time until he could leave to eat his bagel. "It's one of the great cities of the region. I kind of enjoy it. My wife and I have a nice little apartment over by the Roman Road."

Marc thought of quiet Créteil neighborhoods where you could soak in the leafy, sunny solitude and write—poetry, the thing he'd come to peddle here, to fill the emptiness left by an absence of capers.

Mézières grinned. "I see you are from Créteil. Must be nice there this time of year. I spent two years at Sorbonne, then dropped out and went to England. The only thing I used to miss about Paris when I was at Oxford were those bookstores along the Seine."

"Filled with poetry," Marc said.

"Yes, sure," Mézières remembered fondly. "I've never actually lived in Paris. I think it's too big, too dirty, to full of foreigners." Mézières, apparently unaware of Marc's desperate urgency, sat back, closed his eyes, and ruminated. "Yep. Maybe one of these days I'll get tired of northern living and retire to the Mediterranean."

Marc looked at the clock. Two minutes to brioche time. He gnawed at his lip. "About the poems, Mr. Mézières... I was hoping you'd like them."

A frown briefly crossed the orbits of Mézières' closed eyes. Then he smiled sadly. "I'm sorry," he said, sitting up. His blue eyes crinkled tiredly under bushy brown eyebrows and he ran a hand through his mussy, curly hair. "Sometimes I need to lean back and get in touch with myself. I do it at the oddest moments."

Marc said, "Of course. I understand." But did Mézières understand his life and death urgency?

"That's okay," Mézières said. "I know you've come a long way and you're anxious to present your work. So are a million others." He suddenly became quizzical. "What are the chances of a new man like yourself getting into books? Slim, I'm afraid to say. Very slim."

Marc breathed, "Even if I'm very good?"

"Even if you are brilliantly gifted, which you might just be. Who knows. It's all about marketing." He regarded the pain on Marc's face. It didn't rattle him to see a man disintegrate emotionally— clearly, this was a common occurrence here. "It's supply and demand," Mézières said. "We have too much supply and not enough demand."

Marc's head reeled, and his chair seemed to sink into the floor.

So I'm dead.

Mézières said generously, "It's all about product and packaging. Yet, there's always a chance. You have to stick with it. If you're lucky, you might just make it."

Luck. What the fuck?

"There is hope, then?" Marc asked. He'd forgotten all his carefully nurtured questions. He'd wanted to point out certain aspects of his syllabification and metrics, the breath, as Olson would have written, direct, *ex* Pound: He'd intended to prove that he had a theory. All his Literature classes failed him, even the many he hadn't bothered to attend because he was busy writing or thinking.

The atmosphere in Mr. Mézières' office was less conducive to theory and more to sleep or to tepid tea.

"There is always hope," Mézières reported with oracular mien. "Who are your favorite football players?"

"I don't know." Marc couldn't think of any. He didn't care. He tried to calculate: five hours here, two or three hours futzing around, five hours back to Paris. With luck, by nine or ten he could be sitting at his computer with a beer, composing poetry and pretending this had all not happened.

An immense weight sank inside Marc. He looked past Mézières' shoulder through a window at neon street signs. Traffic noise rose in muted concert, including the busy hum of a passing tram. It was a long, slow falling gaze, as if he were dropping through time and space and would eventually go splat on the sidewalk below. He glimpsed distant throngs of tiny people.

Marc stared at that brightly clothed ant heap and wondered, What am I trying to prove here? On whom am I trying to lay the freight and the weight of my poems? The weight that I'm alive that there are pretty young girls in Paris, that I feel a union of heart and soul with the city, in all of its seasons and wondrous geography, from the baking Mark Zero at Notre Dame to the pale orb of the Pantheon to the phallic spiderweb of Eiffel's iron tower. Prematurely, he felt the aching gray collapse of summer, an echo of bright spring, a melancholy harbinger of leafy autumn and dead winter... He thought of his precious verse: *why should I export those precious wines to these sweaty spear carriers, money counters, and wearers of leather elbow patches who sit counting their money in green glass towers?*

"So you like poetry?" Mézières asked patiently, a new hint of curiosity or alarm in his eyes as he stared close at Marc, who struggled to speak.

Like? It is my life's passion. That, and Emma.

The clock has nearly run out. Brioches ahoy—a joy.

The feeling was momentary, however. Here he was, after all—finally—in the halls of a publisher, given an opportunity to speak. He saw now why they were all relaxed. This was everyday stuff to them; to him, Marc Fontbleu, briefly escaped from the cliffed coral that was his life in Paris, these were heady waters in which to swim. "Yes, I am finishing my degree in Literature, and read a lot of poetry," he said. *Traitor*, he thought of himself. *Say anything to get this guy's attention.*

And of course just then Mézières glanced at his watch.

"I like..." and he enumerated until Mézières laughed and held up a hand for peace. Mézières said, "It's clear to me that you're well-read and I'm sure I'll enjoy reading your work. Can you give me a few weeks? I'll have a look." He pointed to the poems neatly assembled in their modest folder.

"Sure." Marc was prepared to give him months if need be, even years, as long as maybe a slender volume for the ages found its way into bookstores and classrooms and libraries. His dream was to walk along the Seine and see his book hanging there for sale in the stalls.

Was it possible that this man—whose single word could spell the difference between fame and namelessness for him—had just lowered himself to inquire of him, Marc Léopold Montblé Fontbleu, if he could have some time to read his poetry?

Yes, a thousand times yes. A real live publisher cares!

Mézières rose, smiling, and stepped to the door, which he held open. *Invitation to leave.*

Marc took the hint, rose, and started out. Mézières extended a broad, dry hand. He winked and said, "Good luck."

Good luck? What do you mean? It's in your hands.

Mézières vanished into his office and Marc left as if carrying concrete blocks, or his own headstone.

At the desk, the young woman smiled with white teeth, cherub skin, dangling bracelet, round breasts, violet eyes...

Life goes on. C'est la vie.

Feeling a thousand times lighter, Marc descended into the sweltering heat of the city. The thesis binder with his hopes and theories and crafted phrases now lay in Mr. Mézières' perceptive and sensitive hands, ready for a sympathetic reading.

Or whatever. Nothing more I can do at this point.

* * * *

It was, he suddenly realized as if a car had hit him, a learning moment. He cared so much about his art, and the world did not care in the least. That bitter realization swept him nearly off his feet as he staggered out, made his way down in the elevator, and walked blindly until he found his car and sat down in it. It took him a few minutes to get the courage up to care enough to drive home.

The long summer evening faded into an endless bleak reverie as he drove kilometer after kilometer on autopilot. He was like a man facing death. What did you think about? Your next sandwich. Your next poem. Your next raindrop. Your next kiss (Emma).

If only...

Paris eventually crept up on the horizon, a city of lights. He knew in his heart that he would never hear from Mézières or

Charleville. His poetry would wind up in the trash. Or maybe someone would clean the office and throw it out the window to scare pigeons. He could picture myriad pages fluttering and twirling in the wind as they drifted to earth like snowfall.

All he wanted to do was be home in his garret, be typing, be out drinking and horsing around with Jack, or be on the phone with *her*.

Chapter 19.

On a hot Saturday afternoon in early July, the telephone slumbered electronically under the rubber palm.

Emma, feeling feverish and cold despite the heat, lay on the couch wrapped in a sheet. The end table was sticky with spilt juice and crowded with the remains of conflicting drinks: stale coffee in a stained cup; flat cola in a warm glass; curdling milk in a small pitcher. She'd been having cramps all day and couldn't hold anything down. She'd been dozing fitfully and every noise—the children outside, the doors in the hallway, a radio next door—jabbed her like a knife. She'd turned on the TV and the oscillating fan, and thus shrouded herself in a veil of familiar noise. She woke only whenever one of the contestants on a prize show shrieked or a commercial babbled too loudly.

She awoke and it was dark. Startled, she sat up to see what time it was. It was eight and Jérôme hadn't called yet. Why? Groaning, she resolved to pass more time sleeping. The night air was chilly, and the humming fan bothered her. The television set resounded with the fanfare of some ponderous biblical bromide. Annoyed, she threw the sheet aside and turned fan and TV off. In the ensuing calm, she tried to nestle back into sleep. But she couldn't because she was sick and angry and disappointed. A dog barked someplace. An ice cream truck patrolled the dark streets with ringing bells under the moth-dancing lights. Somewhere, the stereo appropriate to a party blared cheap, pointless rock music.

She tossed her sheet aside, held her head in both hands, and forced herself to sit up. Dazed, she stared at the blank TV screen, realizing that the noise was not going to abate and that she might as well get up. Perhaps fix herself something to eat.

At nine-thirty the phone rang.

She was watching the last half of *Trumpets in Galilee* (English with French subtitles) where an actor resembling Charlton Heston, as a captured renegade slave, sweated mightily from a long, handsome face (he even groaned huskily) while a huge, bald-headed overseer weighing 300 pounds whipped him, and a curly-haired man in a papier-mâché helmet laughed cruelly.

She answered the phone in a quiet, nerveless voice.

"Long distance, station to station from Australia. A Mr. Jérôme Delors. Will you accept the charges?"

"Yes." She clenched her fist.

"Go ahead," said the operator, and in the same moment she heard Jérôme's voice. "Emma?"

"Yes. Are you all right?"

His voice was slightly slurry. He said brightly, "I'm sorry I'm calling late tonight. We're in Sydney at a party. Got caught in traffic and didn't make it here until half an hour ago."

"I was worried when you didn't call. I'm not feeling well today."

"Anything the matter?" As he spoke, she heard men and women laughing, music, a distant car horn.

"Just my period, I imagine. What are you doing there in Sidney? Or with Sidney?"

He sounded perhaps a shade too jocose. "Oh, we drifted up this way for the weekend. Brought along a crate of bones, potsherds, some ten-thousand-year-old egg shells. We're going to get some expert opinions."

We? Is Sidney a woman?

Going to get laid, she thought to her herself, but oh well what I don't know won't hurt me. "How's the party?" She tried to couch her question in *ennui* rather than reveal a sharp edge of momentary jealousy.

He laughed, probably swaying slightly, for the phone rustled with some small struggle. "Oh...after all these weeks up on the coast, it's hellacious seeing civilization again—you know, streets, street lights, cars other than muddy Land Rovers—you know, things we take for granted back there."

She added, "I bet the girls are pretty too."

He said, "They are always pretty." He finished the sentence with a sigh, suddenly switching to sounding uncomfortable.

She resolved not to probe any further. She had feared it would be like this. She felt ill at ease.

He said after a pause, "I wish you were here." He didn't sound sincere. He amended, "I wish I were there." That sounded fully sincere.

I'm glad I am here and you are there.

She said, "Your parents are fine. They say hello."

With a spark of familiar interest suddenly kindled, he asked, "Do you get over to Chaillot much?"

"Just about every Sunday," she said. She tried to find points of particular interest to relate out of the every day. She randomly enumerated, "Your father's gained a little weight. Your mother made an appointment for your brother's kids at a photographer's studio…"

"What's Maurice up to?" he inquired fondly of his older brother, who owned a well-to-do real estate firm. He was married to Sabine, with whom he had three children.

She started to reply, "He's doing very well. Why only two weeks ago he and Sabine were…" She broke off when she heard a muffled, sinuous giggle; the phone rustled again. Emma felt distracted and found herself saying sharply, "Well, so much for expert opinion."

Her meaning was clear. He understood the accusation. "Really, Emma, it's nothing. You know how people at parties get. Everyone's been drinking…"

She overrode him with chatter designed to drown out the unpleasantness. Her voice, though pleasant, had a direct and purposeful edge to it. "So as I was saying, Maurice and Sabine were over at the Pitié-Salpêtrière Hospital because Sabine is having that trouble again, you know, with the veins in her legs, and they stopped by for a few hours with little Marco. He's quite a little rascal. He pulled all your ties down out of the closet. And a friend of yours stopped by, a Mister whatsisname, Gustave Bouchard from the Department."

Jérôme interrupted, "I don't…oh, yeah, I remember him, sort of a mealy-mouthed fellow…"

"I threw him out," she told him, smiling closely, almost giggling. The idea of Jérôme wondering about a little creep like this Bouchard assuaged her sense of justice.

"What did he do?" Jérôme asked sharply.

"Nothing at all," she told him, settling back on the couch with purposeful, cat-like enjoyment as she toyed with him. She hesitated to tell him the truth about Bouchard's visit.

He never had a chance with me.

Then she decided *hell why not?*

"He stopped off with some papers—he regularly drops off all sorts of mail sent to you at your office—this time he decided to come personally and bring all the information—and—well, I began to feel a bit funny about having him right here in the living room, you know…he got a little bit fresh, and I landed him on his ear."

Jérôme's voice was close and angry. "You keep that bum out of there. Besides, I told you not to have any strangers in the house."

You like to control things. For my safety, you said.

Enjoying herself, she turned on her back and crossed her left ankle over her right knee, swinging the phone cord by the side of the couch. She said, "I didn't want to be too hard on him. After all, he's assistant department chair."

Jérôme could be heard slurping quickly at a drink. He said even before he was done gulping it down, "Never mind. I don't care if he's the Pope. I…" Bright, drunken, cascading, malicious feminine laughter interrupted from thousands of miles away. In the background, a canned orchestra played *Strangers in the Night*. She smiled grimly and thought: *Stranglers in the Night*.

She goaded purposefully, looking for a reaction. Mainly, did Jérôme know about her lover? She said, "He was concerned about us. You and me."

She heard Jérôme curse.

She added, "About me. And about your career, since I'm such a loose strumpet here in this apartment."

He said, "We'll talk again. I've got to go. I don't like the atmosphere here. Keep that crawling crud out of the apartment. And ah… well… take care of yourself, and—dammit!"

Emma, abruptly losing interest in goading him, sat up. With a wry face, she said in her best voice, "Don't let me get between you and your party."

He sounded harried. "Oh for heaven's sake, Emma, goodbye. I love you. Goodbye."

She sensed that he was waiting impatiently for her to let him sign off from his obligatory call. Still, she felt shocked. This wasn't real. She whispered, "Love you. Goodbye," and let the receiver fall gently onto its cradle.

Alone again, she whirled, crossed her arms, and buried her face into the pillow under the rubber palm. Her shoulders heaved.

Chapter 20.

It was nighttime, but heat still moved in muggy sheets over the lake in Créteil. Fog horns in all sorts of high and low tones moaned in the night as ships talked to one another on the shipping lanes, to avoid colliding or running aground.

Jack, toweling his curly hair and sputtering with his round face, entered the screened-in back porch where Marc sat reading. Marc looked up and said, "I've been counting the moths hitting the window."

"We'll go dig up some excitement," Jack promised, sitting down heavily at the card table. He threw the towel down. "What a hot night!"

Marc tossed the magazine aside and reclined on the couch. They'd been swimming that afternoon. Marc had gone to his parents' house to shower and eat supper, then he'd come to Jack's parents' house. Dani and their parents had gone to a movie. Marc said, "I don't know if I could ever live in Créteil again. I remember when we were in high school and had to hitchhike everywhere."

Jack rubbed his shaven cheeks thoughtfully, staring vacantly in the yellowish porch light. "Can't go back," he said. He quickened, "Besides, we're not in school anymore. We have cars now, and no one tells us when to be home."

The tang of Jack's aftershave reminded Marc of the manly impulse to go hunting for female companionship (and did the women not hunt back?), a primordial preoccupation of young men from the suburbs. He rose and tapped out a two-handed tom-tom on his navel. "Ready to go?"

Ten minutes later, Jack had locked up the house and left a note. They chose to drive in Marc's car.

Half an hour later as they parked on a side street in downtown Créteil, Jack said, "I'm getting so I could walk this stretch blindfolded."

"The routine does grow on one," Marc observed as they strode into the air-conditioned coolness of their favorite student bar, Café Kino .

They sat crowded in a corner at a windowsill. The place swarmed with a blue-jeans and long-hair crowd. Rock music blared from speakers in each corner. "Not too many girls," Jack said, looking hungrily about.

"I must be getting old," Marc said, shaking his head at the sight of a pair of pert young things holding brews. College girls, they wore mechanics' overalls over preppy pink T-shirts. They had glowing baby cheeks and carefully silken hair, and engaged in admiring conversation with a ratty-looking group of local musician heroes.

"We just don't suit the image," Jack agreed.

"Where do we fit in?" Marc questioned. He held up his newly arrived, pearly-beaded bottle of Black Horse Ale. They clicked bottles and quaffed thirstily.

"Ah! That hits the spot!" Jack gasped, wiping foam from his nose.

Marc grinned. "Another night on the prowl."

Jack shrugged lightly. "The hunt is sort of fun in itself as long as there's cold ale to be had, if no hot babes."

Feeling out of place, being neither nineteen nor ratty-looking musicians, they sat quietly and observed the welter of human activity.

"It's the pairing instinct," Jack remarked.

"The mating drive," Marc agreed.

"Desperation. It's the first week in August."

"Yes," Marc said, "and summer is almost over."

Jack looked startled and briefly glum at this realization. Then he brightened, "If we were orangutans at the zoo we'd have it made."

Marc laughed. "Unless we were twenty-four year-old orangutans . That's probably old for an ape."

Jack said, "After zillions of years of evolution, if we were orangutans , we'd probably be hanging around just like we are now, but on a tree, looking for orangutan babes."

"Or picking fleas off each other."

"You keep your fleas, I'll keep mine." Jack looked fated. "I think we were made for this."

They were silent, reflecting on the annual convergence of swimmers and boaters for a final summer blowout.

Jack drained his bottle with a definitive gasp, clapping it down on the table. "We won't find any bikini babes here."

"Let's go."

It seemed every soul who could had found an air conditioner to sit by. The streets were empty. Signal lights changed colors in lone and steady rhythm.

They walked aimlessly around the fringes of the lake and the narrow streets downtown. "Dead," Jack judged. "Another dead night in Créteil."

Marc said nothing of his tiring foray into Strasbourg. It was not a night for Léopold Montblé; the hunt itself, vestige of teenage years, those first-car years, prowling the suburbs, promised more excitement. In the coolness after midnight, perhaps, Léopold Montblé might drive his neighbors crazy with his clicking, clattering keyboard once he really got going. But not now. Life was to be lived.

The phone rang, and Jack answered. "Yeah? Yeah? Okay, that sounds good."

"What's that?" Marc asked when Jack hung up.

Jack—professional bartender educated as a philosopher—said, "This friend of mine says things are hopping over in the center of Trocadero, in a place on a Rue Nicolo. We could take a ride down there if you want."

"Sure," Marc said. What more could happen today? Chaillot was a very upscale district with lots of money and fame in Paris' 16th Arrondissement; home of Emma and Jérôme Delors and their banks no less.

Marc shrugged. "No more Alices, thank you."

"And no more Jeannes." Jack snapped his finger. "Let's take my car. I don't feel like hassling with the Métro."

"It's either that or hassling with parking."

"We'll get lucky. I feel it in my bones."

Marc spread his hands. "Why not?" Enthused, they headed outside to his old Citroën.

* * * *

Marc lay back in the passenger seat morosely while Jack drove west on Paris' main streets.

To their right rose the well-lit Eiffel Tower, the world's tallest building a century ago until the New York skyscrapers had been built. The tower was in the Champs de Mars area, named for the ancient Roman god of war.

They crossed the Seine at the Isle des Cygnets, or Swan Island. As always, driving made for air conditioning as a breeze blew through the car. Bright city lights flowed pleasantly and excitingly past on all sides.

Jack commented: "We do this summer after summer."

"Do what?" Marc asked, combing his hair with both hands.

Jack stared out into the darkness. "Maybe if we had real jobs," he muttered.

"Yeah," Marc said. "We might meet real women."

Jack laughed. "We probably wouldn't know what to do if we found some."

Emma, Marc thought. *What is she doing right now?*

Jack broke into a smile. "Let's not give up."

The steady movement of red taillights became swallowed up by the increasing brightness of streetlights as they entered the western districts of Paris. In the distance, the landscape was all lights. "You'd think with all those lights and people, half would be women, and a few among them would be looking for guys like us." So said Jack.

"Look at that," Marc said.

"This street is hopping," Jack said.

"You were saying about parking."

"Oh man, stop being right about everything."

The view was full of party-goers, holding drinks, smoking, and chatting on the sidewalks and in the street. Between neon bar signs and regular spotlights, the place was almost bright as daylight. Blinding, really. Jack managed to find a place to pull onto the sidewalk about six blocks away.

"The walk will do us good," Marc said as they strode along from the Parc de Passy area near the Seine, westward in the direction of the nightlife. It was actually closer to the Rue Chernovitz and the Rue de Passy, a tangle of ancient streets that had later been pave-stoned and then later macadamized over so that in places the older paving stones were still visible on the street surfaces.

Restaurants, boutiques, bars, and arcades beckoned. They were thronged with casually walking people—a come-on for tourists and single men on the prowl. On a wooden railing sat the teenage members of a motorcycle group. They held beer bottles, smoked cigarettes, and engaged in their own mating ritual. Myriad lights glittered along the street.

Clashing energies (but matching rhythms) of rock bands in two separate night spots urgently massaged the night air around Marc and Jack like a giant mating dance. Orangutans indeed, Marc thought. Aromas of *pommes frites* grease and fried fish mingled in the air with perfume and motor oil.

Marc and Jack leaned for a while against a railing by a small pay-parking lot, and watched feminine bodies swaying past. So did two African-French private cops in blue uniforms, unarmed, in the parking lot.

"Not too many single girls," Jack reported after squinting silently up and down the street. Not for the first time, it sounded the death knell to a night of girl hunting.

Marc suggested, "Let's go have a drink."

"How much money do you have?" Jack asked, pulling out his wallet.

"Fifteen Euros," Marc said.

"Twenty Euros," Jack reported. "We'll manage a few."

Marc laughed. "Maybe we'll get invited onto a yacht on the Seine." The river was just a few blocks east, but it was a total joke nonetheless. At least Jack meant it that way. He forgot about Emma and her wealthy family. Marc winced. He must get over it.

"Lotta action here," Jack said as they sidled through the entrance corridor of a nightclub. The throb of rock music and the smells of perfume, carpets, and sweet-sharp liquor greeted them, mellowing the pain of paying a three Euro admission fee to a shadowy figure in a tuxedo.

Marc felt giddy and electrified. Lots of action—if you had money. Deep carpeting under his feet; a refreshing night wind penetrated the air-conditioned interior that glowed red and amber. Glittering bodies gyrated under strobe lights while pounding rock music throbbed through their bones. Ice tinkled in glasses.

Here there be buttocks and pear-breasts, in white deck pants revealing the outlines of (if worn) briefs hulling poignant skin.

Marc stood transfixed at the sight of a young lady with sugary skin and shag-cut black hair and coal Italic eyes and sharp features, dancing with an accountant type guy in a Madras suit, while Jack fetched two drinks. The young lady was skinny, and she held up thin arms while bobbing avid buttocks, and each motion of her bottom caused the loose front of her backless jersey to shift, revealing small, round, bouncing breasts like caramel ice cream scoops.

Jack pushed his way through the onlookers. "Ouch—three Euros apiece," he lamented, while thrusting an icy Scotch-and-water into Marc's hand.

Marc accepted the drink and glared at his friend. "We have enough money to get mildly buzzed, if nothing else."

"You're driving, right?"

"Oh yeah, that. I want to meet a heavenly girl," Jack protested.

"I don't think you will here either," Marc said.

"We could have stayed in the suburbs and drunk a gallon of beer."

"You're gross," Marc told him.

"What's so gross about our favorite ale?"

Marc had to admit wryly, nothing was wrong with their main venues in the Val-de-Marne. To say anything was wrong with the sacramental beer would have been like a lewd comment about, oh well.

Jack inveigled himself toward the end of the bar, where he sought and accepted the charms of a female of the species with frosted hair, who instantly understood his hunger and let Jack put a hand on her rear end. As Marc watched, Jack and the woman danced briefly. Marc turned away to look longingly after a young girl with auburn curls and a smooth body verging on ripeness, who was engaged in a rollicking tango with a smooth, dark-haired young man in a puffy white blouse. Jack and the frosted, aging bar fly parted company. She had mistaken him for having money, and he was disappointed by the sharp, hungry lines around her mouth and eyes. It was a cruel world in this reddish light, this amber sea with its dusky food chain—predators, bottom feeders, and drifting krill.

Marc was summoning his courage to approach a pouting young debutante in a long red gown, when the sight of a group at a far table deflated his courage abruptly. He seized Jack's arm.

"What's the matter with you?" said Jack, new from his disappointment. Marc pointed with his chin. At that far table, which showed evidence of having had a sumptuous dinner upon it, were two men and three women. One of the men was a tall, fiftyish gentleman with a tanned, seamed face and bald head. The second man was short, pudgy, smiling figure with a dark goatee. The two elder women were pressed together, laughing at some joke being told by the tall, bald man. The third woman, tall, blonde, and with a narrow attractive yacht club face, sat in the shadows as if only half there. It was Emma, a ghostly presence who merely smiled downward, alone, staring into some thousand-yard tragic vision. She had not seen Marc.

"That's her," Marc whispered to Jack.

You almost don't even look like you. Is that loving feeling gone, gone, gone already?

"Who?" Jack demanded, prying his arm free.

"The one I was going with," Marc said.

Jack stared across the sweaty, pulsatiously lit dance floor. "Wow, she really is a looker. You had a good thing there."

"Do you mind if we leave?" Marc said.

Jack put aside his glass, whose dross of melting ice slivers and watery scotch he had been nursing. "Anything you say."

Minutes later, they stood inhaling river smells at the Park of Seine Banks. Fragments of laughter and rock music reached them from some nightclub in the direction they had just left. Jack leaned back and inhaled the pretty air deeply. "Ahh...it's good to be alive. Someday, you know, we're both going to have a piece of all this perfume and good looks."

Marc gripped the railing and stared out over the twinkling water, toward a jetty with a distantly winking garnet-red alarm light. It suddenly dawned on him that the Champs de Mars lay almost directly across the river, and the enormous iron-lacework of the Eiffel Tower rose into the night sky festooned with lamp globes and aircraft warning lights. *Wow.* It looked so close you had the illusion of a huge toy that you could reach out and touch.

Jack turned and gripped the railing beside him. His face bore a wistful smile as he stared for a long minute or two at the best-known of all Parisian landmarks. "Maybe not this summer."

Marc shook his head. "I already have."

Léopold Montblé.

Harbor lights.

Chapter 21.

It was far past midnight where the woman slept in her large, lonely bed. It was a summer night but too late for ice cream trucks or children or cruising taxis. An insect, some night predator, hunted in the waxy leaves of the rubber palm. Finding an other insect as victim, it stung deeply and surely, settling with hair-fine legs onto its dying prey.

Cool night air probed through darkness. Snoring fitfully, sprawled under shadowy sheets, she dreamed: bones; desk drawers; gargoyles; floating men smiling; horror grimaces; mud—she searched frantically, paranoically, for a testament sunk in a green pond.

The air was ringing and ringing.

The telephone, startled under its rubber tree, agonized with the endless sound that was meant to be disruptive and get someone's attention. Groans and protests in the night attested to its disturbing effects. Eventually, there was a gasp in the bedroom. With a rustling amid bedsheets, a woman moved, placing sweaty palms on the bed beside her, placing damp soles on the wood floor. The call of the telephone was unrelenting.

"I'm coming..." she mumbled, staggering through the darkness, fumbling with the receiver.

"Night call, station to station from Australia, a Mr. Jérôme Delors, will you accept...?"

"Yes, yes, put him on."

He sounded close by. "Emma, did I wake you? I'm worried."

I was just dreaming that I was diving for you deep in the sea, and you were nowhere to be found.

"I'm sorry," he said. "I'm sorry about everything. I was trying to reach you all evening.

She drew her fingers through her hair and said in a muffled voice, "What—what time is it?"

"It's seven p.m.," he said.

Three a.m. here. Always your time zone, never mine.

"Look, should I call you back in the morning?"

"No," she told him, "go ahead." The pained, distant quality in his voice was unmistakable. They had a good connection and every fibrous rustle, every labor of his breath was distinct.

"Emma...Oh hell, I can't stand it any longer. Look, it's about us. There is nothing for us. Nothing. I just can't go on with this charade. I've been away all this time and..."

She weaved in the darkness, trying to unzip the back of her little black dress. "It's three in the morning," she said.

"You've been out, haven't you?" he accused.

She laughed, smelling lemon and gin on herself. "I've been out, I've been out; yes, I've been out—why should I sit here by myself?"

His voice was cold and distinct. "Why should we pretend anymore? It's all over. I can't stand it any more."

She sing-songed, "It's all over, it's all over, oh so over."

"You're drunk," he said.

She leaned dangerously on the arm of the couch. "I am not," she said. "Walk the line, touch my nose. Don't fall down. One two three four, three two one, I'm wide awake."

His voice was crisp and indignant. "Hear me out. Emma, I've fallen in love. Oh, I wasn't looking for it. I've been out in the sticks too long. Suddenly this angel came along. I saw things clearly. We haven't got a thing going for us over there. I hate to tell you—I feel free for the first time in many years. Her name is Madelaine and..."

"Madelaine!" she said. "What a pretty name. I'll bet she's French. Parlez-vouz a-humma-humma?"

"Go ahead," he told her. "I deserve it, I suppose. Oh, Emma, I've tried, all this time..."

"I've tried, I've tried," she sang tunelessly, swaying on the edge of the couch. That zipper—so important—there; she had it open, and rose. Her dress fell down around her feet.

"Emma, I'm sorry."

She undid her bra and threw it across the room.

"Emma, I do care much about you—but this isn't the same."

She stepped out of her panties and threw them across the room.

"Emma, I'm putting everything on the line. It's over between us. You know all those...problems of mine? I feel like they're a dream. Finally, I feel whole and together. Oh dammit, say something."

She said, "Why because you found some dried up desert—I should—well no, the hell with you—please, tell me, she's American or something, isn't she? Does she do it better..."

"Emma, for the last time. Please."

"Please what? What please?" she parodied. "Say something, Emma, please."

You need me to say it's okay, you spineless, needy bastard. It's not and I won't. You don't deserve that much.

"Emma...I am trying hard here..."

"Master Delors," she said. "Master Delors, I'm drunk and I don't care but I have been waiting—oh I have been waiting. I held your cigar, but I'm afraid your flame has gone out. It's an exploding cigar, a joke, I fear. What do you mean asking me please at three in the morning Huh? Answer me that. At three in the morning. I'm sleeping, you hear? It's early there and you are going out to screw your Madelaine and I am going back to sleep because I've had too many gin and tonics. I am all alone here. My, how time flies. When you're having a good time. What a wonderful way to pass the time."

He rustled uncomfortably. "Emma, I'll call you again. We're always honest with each other, right?"

Ha! Creep!

He said, "I couldn't hold it in any longer."

She sat down hard on the couch, her nakedness tingling against the brushing material. "So long, Master Delors. Fare thee well." She had mastered the art of crying and laughing all at once. Tears dribbled on the receiver, laughing, until she choked with sorrow.

"I'll call you tomorrow," he lied.

"Go to hell." She dropped the receiver rattling into its cradle under the rubber palm. She crouched down and cried loudly, framed by darkness. Her shoulders shook—not from laughing now. Brokenhearted, she wailed like a child amid unimaginably cruel tragedy. She cried for the lost years, and her pretty eyes, and all the times she'd gone to bed alone.

She dared not think of—that sweet boy. The poet. Marc. More than anything, even more than wanting him to hold her, she wanted not to involve him in this, on the rebound, and hurt him in any way because she, yes, she loved him, really, not just saying...

Chapter 22.

It was the day before Mrs. Poncelet's birthday. Jack was working on a project over in La Defense, and could not join the preparations, so he deputized Daniella and Marc to travel to a certain bakery in Montreuil, Seine-Saint-Denis, that made a very special marzipan-filled cake.

Dani drove the family car, a sedan. Marc rode in the passenger seat, glad to get some Poncelet time. Dani was tall, mild-mannered, and direct. "About time we saw a little of you."

"Your brother has reminded me."

She smiled lightly as she concentrated on the road ahead. It was a half hour ride and covered about eleven kilometers north-south each way. "Can you make it tomorrow around noon?"

"I absolutely will."

She was tall and athletic, but with soft caramel skin and gentle hands. She wore pink fingernail polish, very girlish, but it was chipped and her nails never got very long because she was too fond of dribbling a basketball or play rough pickup games at the parish hall. At the moment, she wore a gray plaited skirt, light nylons over her thin but strong legs, and navy blue flats. On top, she wore a white blouse with a rounded collar and a lot of tiny flowerlets embroidered in all colors around the edge of the collar.

"Jack tells me you have a new girlfriend."

Marc felt a bit uncomfortable. Where was she driving with this? "Yes, I met someone over at the Numero XII while I was mowing lawns."

Dani had a way of being diplomatic whereas Jack tended to be blunt and direct. "So she's a wealthy lady?" She meant by that 'older, married, and what the hell are you doing?' but Dani would never present her innermost thoughts that way.

"Her family has the euros," Marc allowed. "They own property all over the place. That's got nothing to do with it. We just get along really well."

"So you're happy." It was a question.

"Happy," Marc said as if he had just heard the word for the first time.

"You know," Dani prodded, "ha ha, make lips like this." She gave him an absolutely grimacing look, pushing the corners of her mouth up with her fingers. She was like Jack, an old friend, someone who could do stuff like that and not offend.

"Better than this," Marc said, leaning forward, toward her, and pushing the corners of his mouth downward. "Wah, Wah, cry all day."

Dani couldn't help herself, but burst out laughing. She had this angularity of motion Marc had seen in athletic women and found intriguing. "How about you?" he countered. "How's your love life, Miss Nosy?"

"I'm doing all right," she said coyly.

"Is there a guy? A Mister Wonderful?"

Dani nodded. "There is a guy, and he is okay."

"Just okay?"

She shrugged, while negotiating a busy traffic zone near the Rue de Rosny on the D-241 motorway. "Not the love of my life but a friend."

Marc sensed not to ask any more.

"Tell me about Miss Twelve," she said with a touch of sarcasm, well intentioned in a buddy sort of way. It was the sort of banter he'd expect from her brother, so he was used to it.

"I'm taking it a day at a time," Marc said.

"Sounds perilous."

"That's a good word for it."

"Jack was saying you should find a girl more suited to your"(she groped for diplomatic words, not 'age' and 'unmarried' and so forth) "lifestyle."

Marc said sharply, as one would with a sister: "Are you my mother?"

"No," she said slowly, "just a concerned friend. You dropped out of college, you're mowing lawns, you write poetry, and you chase married women. And we, your friends, are not supposed to worry."

He sat back, rubbing his face as if she had just washed it with a carwash full of soapy water. He sighed deeply, not knowing what to say. If he were looking at himself from a distance, would this be how he saw things?

"Aw come on," Dani said, giving his thigh a light punch with a caramel fist. "If you need someone to talk with, Jack will always take the call. If I'm able to, I'll do whatever I can do to help out."

"Like what?"

"Oh I don't know. If you need a chick to hang out with, we've known each other for most of our lives. I'm not married, I'm your age, and we can tolerate each other, right?"

He started laughing. "Yeah, I suppose so. You are a funny person."

"I am? Why?"

"Because I don't know. If you weren't Jack's sister, I'd probably have chased you around at some point."

"Jack's sister? What's that got to do with anything?"

"Well, you know, you're practically my own sister. It's different."

"How so? I mean, just for argument's sake."

"Oh for god's sake, do we need an argument?"

"I'm not arguing. That's just a manner of speaking. I'm making a point, Bobo, if you can follow."

"Okay, talk slow and use small words. You know I'm retarded."

She gave his shoulder a light shove. "Now you're going to cry."

"Not if you go first."

"You are like a brother, a nuisance. Well, I was just trying to be helpful and tell you that if you want someone to see a movie with, or go for a milkshake some day, give me a call. Don't be fucking dense, okay?"

"I appreciate the offer to help, Dani. Honestly." He leaned over and gave her a little peck on the cheek. It was a sweet, soft cheek, and she smelled faintly of vanilla. "You've been baking." He admired her pink lipstick on lush little lips.

"How do you know?"

"You smell like a cookie."

"I am a cookie. Want to take a bite?"

"There's vanilla in your hair."

She muttered something to the other side, like *guys are so dense*.

He did, in some chaste corner of his mind, look up and down that long, lean body with those soft places, that cookie-dough skin, those pink cheeks and bright eyes, and wonder just for a moment what it would be like to dance with her, or to hold her, or to make love. It was a fleeting thought, along a track he would not permit himself to go. Jack would kill him.

"Seriously, Dani. I'll cherish your offer. Maybe I'll come by in the taxi sometime and pick you up, take you for a ride."

"I'd like that."

What an odd girl.

"All right," he said after a second's hesitation.

Soon they were in Montreuil, and Dani pulled up at the bakery. Which ended the banter. She went in and paid for the cake. Signaled to him to come help. So he went in and picked up the carton with the cake in it, as if she couldn't carry it herself. *Whatever. Women.*

He walked toward the door but then waited as she stayed to pay a lady in a striped apron, who actually had the marbles to audibly ask Dani, conversationally, while looking at Marc: "Is he your husband?"

He expected from Dani's sharp tongue something like "He's my brother" or whatever.

To which Dani, in her usual unfathomable humor, replied: "He's my fiancé. I haven't broken the news to him yet."

"Men," said the lady in the apron, looking puzzled.

"Yeah," Dani said. She took Marc by the elbow. Marc stood gaping with the carton in both arms, and she guided him out the door. "I had to tell her something, didn't I?"

They returned to the car, and she spent most of the time on the way home totally ignoring Marc while chattering on her *tablette* cell phone with some girlfriend about the latest hockey and basketball schedules in their club over in Thais.

Marc sat with the cake on his lap and thought: *well, blabberbitch, so when are you going to grow up and move out on your own? Or do you intend to live with mommy and daddy all your life and play kid sports?*

It was a momentary pique, which he immediately regretted. She and Jack were the two closest friends he had in this life. Better to treat them gently. So at some point he reached out and patted Dani on the knee. She instantly responded by briefly patting his hand on her knee. She then resumed ignoring him.

Chapter 23.

The stairway smelled of cat. He knocked hesitantly, then stood back in semidarkness, sweating in the heat. The door opened a crack. Blue eyes blinked.

"Taxi," Marc said to no one in particular and everyone in general. Cats can't open doors, so there had to be a human in there.

The door opened wide and there stood Emma, tall and surprised.

Timing and tragedy; that's no strategy; but it makes for beautiful drama.

He said, "Did you call for a taxi?"

She tossed her blonde hair. He saw she had the beginning of lines in the corners of her eyes and mouth, but only if you looked closely. She might look twenty-three, in a blur, if you stayed moving.

They regarded each other frankly.

"Come in."

He trod across the lacquered floor. "Is this the right address? Are you Madame Canary, and did you call for assistance?"

She laughed and closed the door behind him and leaned against it. "How have you been?"

Marc turned and regarded her. "I saw you last night in the Rue Nicolo."

She grinned and wrinkled her nose. "I was out."

He put his hands in his pockets, surveying the apartment. "Just wondering. Thought I might stop by and see how you are."

"Who is Madame Canary?"

"Some blonde who stole my taxi and has the meter running. She took my heart with her as well."

"You're sweet."

"I was trying to get over you."

"Me too you." She looked deeply pleased and amused as she took him by the hand and led him to the couch. "How about a glass of juice?"

"I will if you will."

As she bustled brightly into the kitchen, he helicoptered a hand ambivalently over the couch beside him.

Does she still want me—as much as I want her?

She called from the kitchen, from amid a tinkling of ice cubes and their rattle in a plastic pitcher, "How is Léopold Montblé doing?"

Surprised, he said, "Oh...waiting as always." He was reminded of the publishing house of Charleville. He'd almost forgotten already.

She marched briskly into the living room bearing a tall glass beaded with cold droplets. She sat down directly beside him. "That makes two of us."

He accepted the glass. "Thank you."

Summer was nearly over. Powerful autumn comes pounding at the doors of the heart.

He sipped at the sweet-tart (sweetheart) raspberry liquid. "What have you been up to?"

She gathered her house dress at the knees and breathed back coolly, "Waiting."

"That's it?"

All the money, beauty, power, sunlight trapped in glass tabletops, brutality...

She shrugged helplessly, with her elbows on her knees and her bare, tanned arms wrapped around her elegant body. "What else is there?"

There is nothing if there isn't you.

"I was thinking of you," she said.

Let the dance resume, he thought.

94. SUMMER THICK AIR

What could go wrong
on a day like this,
when the summer air
is thick and sweet
like a heady wine?

What could go wrong
on a summer day
when the sticky road is squeezed
between massed green leaves
and banks of perfumed woods?

Chapter 24.

For three golden-yellow days the heat and haze had beaten down on Créteil. The lake was dotted with blue, white, and red sails nudging through rationed space. But the autumn message penetrated every nook and cranny of hope and desire. As Rilke wrote while wandering the boulevards of his city, *Who by now does not already have a house, he will never build one...*

She called from Paris, said to leave his car home, so he took the regional express network in as far as Chateau de Vicennes in the 12th Arrondissement, and from there, at Nation, hopping on the urban Métro. After crossing the Seine, it was just a few stations before he disembarked at Place d'Italie where she had promised to scoop him up and run for the hills with him. It would be their grand escape, their marriage, their weekend away from all distractions and demands. And deep in his heart, not being a prophet, he could only imagine that it would be a warm, wonderful future together somehow if everything could be made to work, if this thing they had gotten in the mail together could be assembled successfully with all of its moving parts using the mysterious tools that love provided. A sort of Meccano or a Lego construction kit for children.

How to build a life; takes two.

A song for two, a duet with tiny wrenches and birthday cookies. *Innocence and truth of love.*

* * * *

Top down and radio rocking, Emma's dark plum-colored Porsche churned on hot tires as she drove westward on the Boulevard Périphérique toward Boulogne-Billancourt.

"Do you know where you are going?" Marc asked in the passenger seat. He sat back, relaxed, with one arm loosely over the back of her seat so his fingers could dally in her golden hair. He wore a new outfit she had insisted on buying for him—sunny chequed bathing suit, a dark blue T-shirt with happy St. Tropez summer beach theme (sails, bikinis, palm trees, big sun over dark blue ocean), and deck shoes. The footwear was if you owned a yacht, or if you were dating someone whose husband did.

"I have no idea where I am going," Emma said. She wore sunglasses and had her flying blonde hair bound in a silky kerchief with London prints on it. She wore a light pink sun dress—no sleeves and modestly cut, elegant in its simplicity. Her skin was naturally *vanille*, blending into a softly cloudy *caramelle* on the arms and neck that were more often exposed to sun in her daily passages, while down the décolletage the less often exposed attained a more *fraise* light sunburn quality. "I never know anymore who I am or where I am going. Only that you are the joy of my life, living moment by moment."

"It's not the destination but the journey," he offered.

"Old sayings have great truth," she agreed as the wind fluttered her sunny hair. "We'll be in nicer country soon."

"With you, it is all beautiful."

"*Cher*," she said in a low, appreciative tone. "My love."

He leaned close to nuzzle her slender neck. "My precious," he whispered. "Chére."

Looking more like a seasoned husband, or as he imagined he would if he were, Marc sat more loosely back now, with one bare arm draped over the windowsill. He caught looks of envy from other motorists, and tried to look nonchalant. What else could he do? How did she put up with this all her life?

Marc had just found a job driving a taxi around the poorer areas of the northern arrondissements; dangerous work, not for the long term. One needed to think of how to fly one's jet over the horizon where clouds and future years hung, stacked for inevitable and wondrous passage. In some dim way, that included dreams of Emma lookin out the window of a huge airliner, waving and smiling. *Mon Cher.*

"I'm sort of surprised," Emma said, retying the kerchief around her hair. Hot, dying wind blew around her handsomely, tragically beautiful face.

"Why is that?" cried Marc Fontbleu, alias the poet Léopold Montblé, through the rattling wind in the furry-white interior of the wine-dark car.

"You don't fit the image," she said smugly.

"I'm not sure I understand," he cried, extending his right arm out of the car, with the hand moving up and down in sinuous motions like an airplane wing.

She subtly gestured at the traffic around them, while the great city simmered in haze and heat with its baking monuments. "You will be, as these others see you, the owner of this *ménage*—the chick, the wheels, the money…"

"The cigar," he added. "Oh spare us the bullshit." He didn't say it harshly.

"I agree," she said firmly. They were on the same wavelength.

"I like when you talk rebellious!"

She sniggled. "Me too."

"We are going to Versailles, yes?"

"Yes." She laughed out loud and enjoyed her freedom. Her eyes stayed half-closed as she faced into beating sun and wind.

"The signs were back there," he said.

"I'm going to do it my way."

'I'm with you all the way." He settled back, folded his arms, and closed his eyes as if drunk on the wine of her, and the final summer sun blast.

* * * *

They got off the highway for petrol at a station in Issy-les-Moulinaux or Issy-the-Windmills down below by the river quai, just before the highway crossed the Seine. Late summer heat glowered oppressively, and the northern horizon was tinged with blue-black clouds like welts: first autumn storms moving in from the Atlantic far in the west.

Great glass buildings shaped like boats gleamed by the river. Marc felt a thrill, wondering what sorts of jobs you could have in those places—probably good money to be made. One was the Microsoft, another a France Television something, and so on. Once a Roman estate, it had always been an industrial area on the periphery of Paris. Lots of places like that around the ancient Lutetia or Lutèce. *I should be a historian,* he thought; *another useless occupation unless you have connections and play the game. What will I be when I grow up?*

I don't want to play the game, but I am curious: Who will I be when I grow up?

He did the tanking, standing by her window as she found the right credit card on her hand-held mini-tablette. She handed him the small phone, and he leaned down to surprise her with a kiss as he took it. She reached up eagerly with all ten lean, red-glossed fingertips and took his face into her possession. "You are always a surprise, my love. The kisses come from nowhere, like snowflakes."

"Or pigeon feathers."

"You are so irreverent when I am trying to be sincere."

He reached around the pillar holding up the glass roof above, slid her hand-held around an embedded electronic reader, and handed it back to her. A mechanical genderless voice like out of a cartoon informed them that the card had been successfully read, thank you, and come again soon.

Emma laughed as Marc pressed a fingertip under his Adam's apple and, in his own cartoon voice, croaked: "It was nothing."

Marc closed the petrol cap and replaced the (so to speak) receive on the switch hook. Then he jumped back into the car, young and lithe, and she patted his thigh appreciatively.

On the road again, she muttered just within earshot: "That is the problem. No more surprises with Mr. Kangaroo, or only bad ones." She looked at Marc and said clinically: "Every minute is a delight with you, even when we are bickering."

He stroked her arm. "I love bickering with you."

She sighed deeply. "May these moments last forever."

He said philosophically: "They say a million heartbeats is a lifetime. How about a million of these moments?"

She sighed again. "I want them all." She added in a defiant war cry with a throaty voice: "All!"

He whispered in her ear: "I'm impressed. The poet and historian in me pictures you as Athena, with a plumed helmet and a spear. The ancient Greeks named Athens after their goddess. *Athenē promachos*—Athena who fights at the forefront of the warriors."

"You are so smart," she said humbly. "I don't want to fight. I just want to make love and bake cakes and be happy. The wife of a loving man. Even have a child someday. A little baby I can squeeze and rock and softly sing to." She gave him a lingering, soulful look with big dark round eyes that silently said: ...*named after you.*

Smooth sailing so far, but then... Marc sat back, suddenly nervous at the edge of deep ocean waters. *Could I ever be ready for such things?*

* * * *

She took the Péri across the Seine and out in to Boulogne-Billancourt and, again crossing the Seine above its elbow, across the Pont de St. Cloud out of the main city.

"I see where you are heading," Marc said.

"Trust me at all times. I have the map in my head." She pointed to her forehead.

He smiled, appreciating her. As she made that sudden move, pointing to her head, she seemed girlish. All the muscles tightened up and down her athletic (tennis, swimming, bicycling) slender form to make that gesture. At times their age difference bothered him, but at moments like this she might be an athletic girl next door of no particular age. Especially at moments like that, he could brave his uncertainties in the dark forests of his periphery, and dwell with her happily forever on some hilltop in fairyland.

"I believe in you totally."

"You are so romantic."

* * * *

Emma exited from the highway and drove into city streets near the Gare de St.-Cloud, westward into a growing parkland. "I could have taken the faster road, but we have autoroutes enough. This will be a nicer drive." As she spoke, the landscape grew green all aound them on the D-985 autoroute.

"How long?"

"Not quite two hours. A little more if we stop to kiss."

"I don't know if I can let an hour pass without losing myself in you."

"Watch me drive straight into a tree," she said.

They both laughed. It was fun all the way.

They passed through the pleasant town of Ville d'Avray and back into parklands.

Soon the autoroute became the Avenue of the United States, on which they entered the clean, neat town of Versailles. "Everything looks so manicured. So small compared to Paris," Marc said.

"It is," she agreed. "Such a cute little place. No wonder the Louis and Marie-Antoinettes loved it so much that they built the world's most famous palace in Versailles. I went to school near here, so I know the area pretty well."

"What school?"

"Sainte-Sophie."

"Oh yes, you told me once. Catholic finishing school for girls. *Sainte-Sophie des Cigares.*"

"We were trained to handle a cigar the way other girls might twirl batons."

"Everything for the team."

"*Mais oui.*" She feigned absurdly. "*D'accord.*"

"I'll tell you what," Marc said. "I don't smoke, and I particularly hate cigars. They stink like a men's *pissoir* in a dirty train station." He brightened. "I know! You can hold my carrot."

"What? You are a vegetarian tyrant?"

"Not a tyrant at all. A bunny. I will share my carrot with you. We can waggle our fluffy white tails, and hold the carrot together at each end. We'll have a contest to see who nibbles to the middle fastest."

She laughed happily, raising her face to the sun so her goddess-features gleamed.

"I love you," Marc said.

She looked at him sincerely. "Je t'aime aussi." *I love you too.*

"Don't hit a tree, my love."

She slowed, though the road was clear and she drove well. "You make my engine race. I go too fast."

"I'll put some rubber on your brakes."

"You can rub my brakes anytime, just not now." She looked perplexed at an intersection. "I want to get through the town."

"Don't want to visit Ste. Sophie for old times' sake?"

She curled up a corner of her mouth in revulsion. "Like you want to go back and live in Créteil."

"That would be time travel. Sliding backwards down the bannister of years. Oh my god no. I'd be a teenager again."

"So would I. Who wants to go back in time?"

He spoke more gently: "If we could be teenagers together."

"I would so love that," she breathed.

"We can pretend."

"I'm not good at pretending."

"That's one of the many things I love about you. So straight out and true."

"I try." She made a sour face. "Mr. Kangaroo might not agree." Then she looked furious. "Mr. Kangaroo is not true. What am I thinking?"

"Throw that cigar overboard."

She quickly tossed an imaginary incendiary out of her window. "Done."

"Time travel forward," he said. "We move on with life."

"Life moves on with us in it, like a train."

"Our wagons are coupled."

"We are coupled." She dropped the joke and said: "We are a couple."

He felt warm inside. "You mean that?"

She nodded. "You are the only true person in my life."

"I am true to you. I tried, but nothing else works for me."

She burst out laughing. "You tried?"

"Jack and I, we were cruising. Well, I told you I saw you at that Nicolo place and I just died inside."

"You poor baby. And I was having such a miserable time with those fake farts of frumentation."

"What?"

"Oh nevermind. They were university people. I have to play the game. Or I did. I think I do." She looked confused. Then she reached out with one hand, keeping the other on the wheel. She squeezed his hand. "We are a couple. In this moment, we are married. There is only us."

In the moment. Yes. That will have to do.

They entered the small, picturesque commune or town Les Loges-en-Josas, neighboring Versailles, in the Yvelines Department, Île-de-France.

"One moment at a time," he said and squeezed her hand in return. "As long as we can make it work. A million heartbeats."

She swooned. "That's it, the love of a lifetime. A million moments, a million heartbeats. Paris—"

"If only," he said. "A million ifs and onlys, one for every heartbeat."

She pulled his hand over her chest. "Feel my heart beating for you."

"Don't hit a tree."

She snickered. "I'll try not to. You'll laugh, but I belong to a hundred different do-good clubs including one that says do no harm to trees."

"I love trees," he said.

"Me too. I hug one at every opportunity."

"They need our love."

"They cry out for affection. And plant food."

So, joking and ribbing, they rolled into the driveway of a tree-crowned estate on the western side of Versailles, in Les Loges-en-Josas.

"There it is," Emma said.

Chapter 25.

The sign read *Hotel des Amis*, flanked by two coach lamps next to a garage door and one more such amber, wrough-iron lamp next to a wooden door. Several windows, among hedges, sported blue wooden blinds overlooking flowerboxes overflowing with greens and colors.

Marc carried two bright, happy looking handbags, both hers. One contained her toiletries and delicates for a few days, the other his own necessaries that he'd brought in a scruffy blue gym bag. She'd stopped at a shopping center and bought him the outfit in which she wanted to see him. When he protested, back at the department store, she'd put a finger over his lips to hush him, and she'd said: "It's a candy wrapper for later, so I can unwrap you and eat you."

Signing in at the Amis was a brief matter at a counter glowing with yellowish light, with an older man graying and in a fuzzy wood-colored sweater. Clearly no formalities. No questions.

Emma, beautiful down to earth swaying Emma walked ahead in her light pink dress, color of blood in a butterfly wing, so delicate. Marc followed, devouring with his eyes her long tanned legs, and flowing buttery hair. They walked along narrow, silent corridors carpeted and very hotel-like, with room numbers in espresso dark brown on café-au-lait ellipses. The place had a faint tang of carpet cleaner, stagnating coffee—and fresh, fragrant flowers from open windows.

"I smell freshly laundered sheets," Emma said approvingly.

* * * *

Their room was simple, with a large double bed covered in dark blue durable hotel-grade nuclear-proof quilting. Otherwise, the atmosphere was hushed, with plain wheat curtains and light-beige wooden fixtures. They had a desk, a little setup of two chairs a lamp and a little round table in a corner, and a sliding glass door leading onto a tiny balcon. This little balcon, overlooking a green-choked garden, had two chairs and a tiny coffee table.

"For two!" Emma whispered delightedly, rubbing his back.

"Everything for two," he said, taking her slender form in his arm.

They held each other, looking together at a cascade of flowers and hedges and trees (plum, mirabel, cherry, apple) around and below them.

She whirled and faced him brightly. "We are alone."

He took her in his arms, relishing the slenderness of her back, the lovely curvature of her waist, and the softness of her rear and thighs as she pressed eagerly against him. Her grip felt strong on his back as his lips sought hers.

As they staggered drunkenly (with love) toward the bed, not even peeling back the coverlet, she whispered in his ear: "I want to kiss your cigar."

"I told you it's a carrot."

She chortled, nipping his earlobe. "I'm going to bite your carrot, you bad bunny."

"I'm a good bunny," he said, raising her dress and crawling up against her within her spread legs.

"You are a nice bunny," she said. "Take off your pants."

"You first."

And so it went, to the train's passionate derailment in the tunnel of love, drowning in the liquids of desire, moaning and sighing while stroking each other's bare skin. For a while the room sounded as if it contained a washing machine throbbing and soapy in its hard, steady rhythms.

* * * *

She waited to hold his cigar, and he shared it in a totality of love. It was one thing she best understood and cherished—so her eyes and fingers told him across the differences.

If only... *Si seulement...*

* * * *

They went for a walk, ate a dinner of stew and soup at a little restaurant with red lanterns on a tiny street of white buildings.

"I knew it would rain," he said holding her hand as they ran back up the street to their hotel

"My tummy is full," she said.

"We'll slow down," he said wisely. "Better to be wet then sick."

So they walked together, arm in arm, while the first delicate crystal lines of rain multiplied around them. Their hair grew sopping, and they sputtered with their lips. They laughed and laughed, doubling over while their clothes grew soppy.

No harm done. Just pure, cleansing water.

Lightning flashed, and thunder smashed. Hail pounded on an exposed patio as Marc held open the entrance door to the hotel.

Nobody saw them, and they saw nobody. *Discretion. So nice.*

Up in the room, they showered together.

Emma, slender and poised and vanilla, bent over to soap her ankles.

Marc felt an overwhelming hunger and turned her rear to him. She let him while he entered and slapped her to mutual orgasm. Afterward, they stood wet and warm and steamy, kissing deeply. He gently fondled her small, firm breasts. She put her hands over his and guided him to fondle more. She aggressively tongued him, standing tiptoe on her firm young legs.

He leaned her against the shower wall and kissed her deeply, while pushing the edge of his hand between her legs. She discovered the pleasure of this, and slowly, rising and falling, bicycled on his hand until her bud hardened and she came in uncontrollable gasps, weakening finally and nearly falling over in the splashing water. He knelt before her and sought that bud with his tongue and lips until she squealed and held her hands over it, crying "I'm so tender I can't take any more."

"We'll give it a rest," he said. "Now you do me."

And so she willingly and happily went down on him in the hot water, creating for him an agony of pleasure so total that he had to brace himself with both palms against the wall while his face transformed into shock as she handled and devoured him.

* * * *

They slept well that night. Deeply. Only when lightning flashed and thunder slammed, they woke to explore again. Two or three more orgasms, love, holding the arms out spread with fingers entwined, taking turns being on top and thrusting away, and the weather drowned out the noise of their joyous union.

* * * *

By morning, the storm was past. But not their love. They lay in bed, eye to eye, adoring each other. Why say anything?

We could stay like this forever.

He stroked her hair, and she looked worshipfully up at him.

A million heartbeats.

Moments...

* * * *

They ate a light brunch of coffee and croissants with jambon et fromage, ham and cheese, followed by butter and strawberry compote.

The grounds were spacious for a small, privately owned hotel. Marc did not want to see the bill, which he understood she was paying effortlessly through a network of banks connected to all sorts of nodes including her family's properties in the city, and in other parts of the nation.

"Feels more like spring than autumn," he said holding his fingers flat in the back pocket of her short demim skirt. She wore a sort of loud, happy, yet classy lollypop wool tunic with alternating broad horizontal apple-red and cream-of-wheat stripes. It had just little epaulets instead of sleeves, and a plain V-neck. He wanted so much to slip his hand down and hold one of her precious breasts, but dammit people might be looking. That hotel room, with the door locked, was their garden of eden. She stopped and rubbed his belly, looking down demurely. Clearly, she was full of thoughts.

"You are such a girl," he said.

"I love being a girl. Your girl." The palm of her hand rubbed all the more firmly, circles.

He took her hand and kissed her palm fervently.

"You are my man," she said in a voice so delicate it nearly had a lisp.

Autumn leaves fell, no plunged, around them rapidly and many, yellows and reds and dying browns. The air was crisp, with a faint aura of wood smoke.

"Someone has a fireplace?" he said as they walked again, linked with swinging hands, interlocked fingers.

"I wish we did," she said. *That faint lisp again.*

"Maybe we will soon."

"I'd love that." She laughed. "I would never let you go out."

"I would climb out through the window."

"I would catch you by one leg and pull you back inside."

"Why, my love?"

"To have sex with you, more and more."

Her eyes looked up, blue and raptured.

* * * *

That evening, they began to pack for the trip back to Paris.

He watched as she knelt before the bags, wearing only a plain white cotton shift, nothing underneath.

She sorted through soda cans, plus a slender red wine bottle for later.

"Very domestic," he said.

"You like that," she said.

"Yeah. This could be eternity and we'd be in heaven."

"I could dig that." She added, "With you."

"You are so perfect."

"I wish. For you."

"And you?"

"I could hold your cigar."

"If I had one."

"You will."

"How do you know?"

"Because I love you."

"I adore you. So there."

She said: "I'm just a secretary—smart, but not brilliant like you or Jérôme. I was going to be on a calendar of beautiful beach girls once, but he wouldn't let me."

"When?"

"Ten years ago."

"Why?"

"He needs to control."

Marc rolled his eyes up. "You go right now and be in that calendar." His heart ached for her lost chances.

She made a sweet, wistful face and said in a forlorn tone, "Too old. They want girls your age or younger."

"I would keep you forever."

"I'd love to be." She added, "Kept by you."

"Problem is I don't have a cigar and I have nothing to give you."

"You already are, you do, you have...so so so much."

"No, I mean, as a man, to protect you, to shelter you, to build you a place out of mammoth tusks and keep out the sabertooth cats and other predators, including insecure faculty bullies."

"Worse yet," she said, "greasy little wannabes."

"We are safe here," he said, looking aroung their brief nest.

"From the world," she whispered. "I love being your wife."

It rained again during the night, a gentle falling during which they stroked each other, nuzzled, kissed, made passionate moisture inside while outside nature drizzled and lisped and leaves fell, slapping in windy gusts against the shut (but not shuttered) window.

Mercurial rain drops encased them, sealing their time and space off like an aquarium.

* * * *

Late in the evening, after the news on the television, she gathered things about her. It was a nest-building, like that of a swallow, *une hirondelle*, graceful and ready for winter.

She had thrown on her plain white cotton shift, while Marc lounged about wearing only underpants and t-shirt in the privacy and intimacy of their love nest.

As she worked, Marc sat in a big plush chair near the slightly ajar balcony door. He savored quenching coolness, a fruity fresh breeze that ruffled stagnant curtains, in the room gone stale with their sweat and other moistures. He breathed an atmosphere of upholstery, carpets, cleaning agents—pretenses and hopes—while she fussed with food and drink things inside the glowing refrigerator. In a dim moonlight leaking from outside, the soft refrigerator light x-rayed her white skirt. His eyes traced the tan contours of her thighs. With dangling hair and twisted knees and waggling elbows, she concentrated on her work, preparing for the journey back to reality.

The only snake in this garden is time. The apple is the pleasure we eat of each other.

"Do you really think he doesn't suspect?" His voice quavered.

She closed the refrigerator, shutting off his voyeuristic movie, and came to sit on the armrest of his chair. He felt her knees against his leg and rested his hand on a round, firm buttock. As he did so he wondered if there was a mathematical equation which could render that curve, from the wealth of thigh through the amplitude of buttock to the abrupt hip bone and the frail waist where blood pounded under downy skin. Probably something like that fabled golden ratio in music and architecture and yes in poetry and verse flowing like saxophone jazz music pouring out in the sluices of the soul…

"No," she said intimately.

No, what? No bananas today, no show, no he doesn't.

"But he wouldn't care. He's fucking every kangaroo in Australia. He's forgotten me."

Marc was astonished. "The man who married you. Who made all kinds of promises. And you held his cigar."

"It was an exploding cigar. He was full of itching powder and made me sneeze."

"I care," Marc said meaning he cared about her. "About you and only you."

"I don't care anymore." She bent down to press a kiss on his nose and her hands were cupped around his jaws. "Are you afraid?" She stroked his hair.

"No, I love you too much to care. Yes I am afraid. Of losing you."

She looked down, away, into an abyss. He wasn't sure she could see the truth there, but he sure couldn't. Only in his heart there was a faint tearing, autumnal, perilous, tempestuous melancholy, like the ache of an old burn, or the itch of an unhealed scar.

We are one soul. I want to cry—not for losing you, but to have you, keep you, cherish is the word like in the ancient song.

She whispered, "This is our little space. Just you and me. You can keep me and be nice to me."

"I will."

She murmured. "Promise you will be sweet to me."

"I love you."

She lowered her voice to a broken whisper. "Promise you'll be tender and take care of me."

So she implored, helplessly, as she sat on his lap and stroked his hair until they kissed and he gently urged her onto her back. With her hands, she pulled on his shoulder blades to bring him down upon her. She was already breathing hard. Her eyes were half closed in a delirium of taking and letting go. He fell into her galaxy and it was wondrous like a ride among suns. This was their hour, their time, their candy bar of the million moments and heartbeats, so savor and never forget, cut off from all external worldly thoughts, people, and worries.

Just you and me.

It rained again at dawn but they did walk in the garden next morning, just one more time, before saying goodbye to that shadowy room of love with no clock.

They had a quickie in the brightly sunny room.

She laughed delightedly as he tickled her neck and nibbled behind her ear.

She retaliated by blowing up a big fart noise with her lips on his neck.

So they rolled around, dressed and ready to go, but he got his carrot into the damp whatsit between her pantie and her thigh. Which she held open for him, the wannabe calendar girl.

You are so on my calendar.

Chapter 26.

Close to autumn equinox.

Marc closed his eyes and lay back on the couch of the living room of Emma's secret apartment on the Boulevard Saint-Germain. It was evening, dark out early, almost two weeks after their wonderful trip to Versailles.

Emma was in the kitchen, a wife, domestically rattling and shoving things about. All the ordinaries of life, including vegetables (carrots), a pudding, a meat dish, bottles (wine, water), bread. She snapped the faucet on, water ran, then off, and water stopped running. He heard all this, did not get up to look. The sounds were universal, just as his sitting on the couch was probably universal as well. He was tired from eight hours of driving a bulky late-model black Mercedes through city traffic, dealing with people, getting in and out to open doors, handle luggage.

He'd been driving the taxi now for several weeks and felt ready for the next stage in life. This couldn't continue. He thought of those big shiny glass buildings around Issy-les-Moulineux. Time to think about adding computers or accounting or the like to his poetic resume.

* * * *

Autumn equinox: night equals day for one turn of the earth on its axis. Then the nights grow longer, the days shorter, light less, hope brighter.

He enjoyed inhaling mixed essences of lemon and skin cream, of damp air outside, of leaves soaking in the last drizzle of their lives. Equinox meant equilibrium, balance, when the scales of fate cancel each other in their fullness; harvest time since Stone Ages long ago. Time to harvest and lay in for winter, toiling under a full dark cheese moon bloodied on its rind; rich with time and truths that nobody can ever avoid.

He was thinking seriously now of returning to school, but not for literature or poetry or even history. Not for the things that were his passions. Think of it this way: to love one woman, but to marry and make your life with another. A practical arrangement instead of a passionate one. Just as all kitchen noises are universal and can be deduced from their sounds and smells alone, so the world contains about as many women as men. It is the great evolutionary coin toss.

The more often you toss the coin, the closer your result will trend toward fifty-fifty. At the same time, each life is unique. So this woman in her kitchen, making something to eat for both of them— she was the one who commanded his passion. He knew of people who had married the wrong person, and all their lives wondered and ached, thinking of the unknown love they had forfeited by selling out to practicality, the moment, the better option, whatever.

Life is full of surprises. Maybe I'll wind up with the woman I love and a career not in poetry but in bean-counting for some corporation in a glass building.

Emma swept into the room carrying two wine glasses. She wore an apron, but otherwise was dressed almost formally. Meaning dark slacks, dressy gray leather flats, a richly thick dark blue wool sweater with red, white, and beige patterns that blended enticingly.

"Honey, are you restless?" Emma said as if he were her husband and she his wife.

"Just thinking," he said.

"About what?" she said gently, handing him a glass of Chardonnay and plopping down beside him on the couch with her own glass at ready.

He stared heavily toward the tree crowns outside the window. "I was just thinking about school. I have to start getting real."

"You are real, baby." She sighed. Thoughtfully, she folded her hands on her belly as if to tell him something. She started to—then paused, had second thoughts—and stretched silently instead. "You really have to get away from that taxi-driving job," she told him. "I worry about you getting hurt. And do something more executive." She wrinkled her eyes calmly and lovingly. "You've got the stuff."

He stared sidelong down the side of his nose. "I could start by kissing you."

"Not now, sweetheart. I am cooking *ragout* for us. Did you bring home a loaf of bread like I asked?"

"Yes, dear." He felt very much married. It wasn't a bad feeling. Sort of like owning very stiff new shoes, but you knew they were going to break in and be a swell ride.

She bounced up. "Gotta go check the pot."

"What's in it?"

She stopped and swayed her wine glass in the air. "I like mine with pork. Very easy. Cook long, cook slow. Carrots, potatoes, peas, onion, a shred of garlic, a bit of beef base. Braise pork loin, cut it up, add to the stew. A little butter, a bit of red wine…all my own concoction."

"Sounds wonderful." He sniffed. "Smells even better."

"I hope you like it." She strode off into the kitchen.

* * * *

After a late dinner, they rested together watching a variety program she liked, with jokes and dancing and singing. The dishwasher in the kitchen was doing its robotic chore. After their meal settled, they went for a walk outside.

The air was crisp, and filled with the sound of leaves rushing like ocean waves. Definitely a change in the air. They walked down to the Seine and stood on the Quai de la Tournelle, looking along the Pont de l'Archevêché or Archbishop's Bridge, toward the eastern end of the Île-de-la-Cité, the end where the memorial of the Deportation Martyres lies behind the apse of the Notre Dame de Paris cathedral.

They walked leisurely, with linked arms, like so many Parisian couples. As always, they drew some envious looks because they looked quite young and professional and well-off. Strangely, he was beginning to enjoy this feeling. He was so used to being the outsider, the rebel, the poet and artist, that he had never quite considered what it would be like to give in a bit. "And grow up," she told him at one point, during a discussion about these things, while giving his arm a yank as if he were a little boy. Not tonight, though; he had already grown into the idea because it was so logical, and the idea of strutting a little money never hurt.

* * * *

He lay awake into the early morning hours, savoring a glass of sweet brandy with a nice bite to it. She did snore, lightly, in the moonlight beside him. He touched her golden hair lovingly without disturbing her. Her hair looked unruly and tousled, making a sort of pretzel shape above the bedclothes pulled up to her ears.

I am so lost in you.

He was thinking of how well he knew the grooves and smooth planes of her body. She was like a long-playing music track. He could play her endlessly, quietly, like a jazz anthology, in the dark while resting his head in her arm and lying beside her. They could breathe the same air and grow drowsy together. Not tonight; he had a restless energy, a disturbance like that in the air and leaves outside.

He ached for every curve and every pore of her. Yet he was not happy. Desperately, Léopold Montblé—who could not compose in half-truths—yearned to find independence and a more perfect union.

He had not written a poem since he'd spotted her melancholic smile in the dusty, bookish university lounge. She was nearly thirty and it made him want to vault over the porch, to leave her and seek the true tan flesh which would spell hope to his demanding sense of—oh Léopold Montblé, you would not die of old age without once more partaking more permanently of young skin wet with aspiration. In other words, you will want to seek a younger chick. Such moments came and went—a song played on both their gramophones at once, to use an ancient metaphor, and they each knew it. The brevity of their wonder together made it all the more wonderful.

The phone under the rubber palm rang stridently, and she slowly moved her lithe body to answer. He rose and stepped away, knowing only one person would be so rude as to call at this hour.

As she half-woke, half-sat up tangled in sheets, and spoke in short breaths, still half snoring, he backed away to give them space.

He regarded the moon, so far and cold and alien, while hearing the bitter and matter-of-fact sound of her voice in the bedroom.

He was still a bit preoccupied with the feeling of Léopold Montblé, that maybe there was yet a different life, a different train, not yet arrived on the platform of his life.

When she called him tiredly to the bedroom, he felt a sinking sensation occasioned by her downcast eyes.

"That was Jérôme," she said, settling back into the bedclothes, her nest, now ruffled.

Marc sat in a chair beside the bed, and tried to fathom her worried facial lines in silver light.

She said, "He is coming home on leave. For a month. He is going to ask for a divorce."

Marc settled back in the chair. "You going to fight it?"

Her fine face, irradiated with acceptance, was clever and weary and lined. "No, I won't," she said almost absently or maybe defeatedly.

"Not on account of me," he said.

She looked pained. "Of course not." She smiled at her lover the poet Léopold Montblé. He regarded her anxiously.

She held out her hand to Marc. "Don't worry."

He crawled into bed beside her, feeling helpless. This was not the life of a tyrant, a cigar-chewer.

She said, "Oh, Marc. I know you are looking."

He lay back, hands folded on his flat stomach, pretending ignorance.

"I know you aren't looking just now, but you will be looking for someone your own age."

He felt pained. "Do you know how beautiful you are?"

She said sadly, "I'm not the love you are looking for."

He sat up in denial, knowing he was lying. "I could hold on to you as long as I live."

She reclined. Her breasts, in their diminutive sheath, puckered. She said, "I wish."

"It's all about wishing, and hoping, like in the song." He slid close beside her. He lifted her hand to his mouth, noting how carefully her fingernails were trimmed and how fragrant were her knuckles.

She looked up at him. "I won't be able to see you the whole month he is here."

"That makes no sense." He kissed her hand, drawing her to him. She cuddled, girlish and graceful, firm in that mature, intriguing, ripe way, forbidden fruit.

He rose and visited the bathroom.

Rather than wait in the bed, she padded after him and knelt on the tiles, pulling his shorts down. She cupped his aftercheeks in her hands, then kissed each after inspecting it. "Nice ass."

"Thanks. Not so bad yourself." He turned, took her by the hand, and led her back to the bedroom. There he kissed her, pressing her panties down along her thighs as he pressed his mouth to hers and her tongue stabbed around wetly seeking his tongue.

And here was the thing. The more threatened their delicate arrangement was, the more they desired each other. She let him do what he wanted. He was sweet and passionate and gentle but strong. Letting him was part of the beauty of it. Submitting, radiant as the moon, lying with her arms spread as if she were flying, and he groaning about her fundament, her lower body, bringer of life and perpetuity. *Sacred vessel.*

As he grew more passioate yet, she let out a cry—unable to restrain herself any longer—and helped eagerly, welcoming his firm command of her. She gave herself to him, pleading with her eyes and expression to take her, and take her more, anything at all.

Afterward, when they lay in the sweaty, ripped bed together, she pressed her thighs against his. She whispered, "Tell me again. Do you really think I am beautiful?" She curled up in a fetal position by his side. Her hair obscured his view of her eyes, revealing only the horizon of her forehead as he looked down and pulled her close.

He was naked; his hair was plastered to his forehead, and he moved lazily in the cooling night. His answer was exhausted, heavy, and truthful. "You are the most beautiful woman in the world."

He embraced her like the friend and love she was, and she snuggled like a kitten against him.

"You called me a girl."

"You are a girl. My girl."

"I love that," she said with a wriggle of the shoulders and a happy face.

They rubbed noses and talked in little pretty noises, cooing and coaxing and laughing together to bring each other yet more pleasure and love. Her eyes glowed, seeking his with her gaze, while she framed his face between her hands.

He planted a little kiss slowly moving across her forehead. She murmured or mewled with her eyes closed, burrowing closer to him; and pressed her face to his chest.

And so they changed the subject.

Chapter 27.

On a quiet afternoon, when they strolled through a museum gallery dedicated to European Medieval art, Marc remembered he'd had a one-semester infatuation with all things Parzival, Condwiramurs, courtly love, all the formalities and holy grail hunting of many centuries ago.

He remembered in the late sunlight to show her at his desk in the garret the poetry he had written, along with the illustrations in the textbook of that class period. The poem was a double: #91: Parzival and #92: Beautiful Words, My Love.

She stood, face awed and washed in late autumn and late day sunlight, as she read along with him while he intoned in his steady, pleasing voice.

"That could be us, except for the dying deer buck animal thing."

"It's a metaphor for how love slays us, but we are reborn."

"Oh Marc, you are so," she ran out of words. "You intoxicate me. I'm drunk with you. I don't know if it's the poetry or the attitude or the freedom or what, but I want to spend the rest of my life with you. Will you promise to keep writing stuff like this?"

"Easy," he said. "It's my only passion in life. Besides you. And because of you, Paris."

"We've both been rediscovering our city."

City of Light, the tourist brochures called it. *Why not?*

"Remind me about Parzival."

"Sure." He gave her a brief summary on the courtly literature that had shaped so much of the medieval world before the Renaissance, before Europe conquered the world, before there were modern nations like France or Italy or Germany or England and all the rest. It was just a patchwork of feudal domains connected by fading, ancient Roman post roads. The Roman roads were so well built out of stone that they withstood century after century of weather, wagons, and hooves.

Religion connected the thousand violently warring puzzle pieces of little fiefs. Earls and barons and counts and dukes and the like swore oaths of loyalty (fides, hence feudal, fief, and the like). The biggest commercial activity was relic hunting and pilgrimage to visit the holy relics thus acquired. Faith was rife. You believed that some little sliver in Prague or Budapest came from the True Cross. You believed that a hair came from Jesus' beard. You believed that a certain shroud had once been the burial sheet of Jesus, and just getting near it alone in the proper state of contrition would heal you from leprosy or measles or syphilis. And the most romantic activities consisted of adventuring into distant lands to seek after the most fabulous treasure of all, the cup of the Last Supper, that final Passover meal in Jerusalem before the Crucifixion.

Parzival, along with Gawain and King Arthur, and so many medieval superheroes, moves in a constant adventure of knightly combats, driving off infidels. Parzival and Gawain and their sort wooed an endless series of the world's most beautiful women from Condwiramurs to Sigune to Herzeloyde. At the same time, they moved in a fantasy world combining the best of ancient Celtic and Germanic lore (like the mermaid Melusine, or the Fisher King Anfortas, and assorted figures from Druid and other ancient lore). All this goes on like a fabulous modern fantasy series of the most imaginative sort, combining the wise men of Scriptures with those of Greek and Roman epic lore and, well, Marc ran out of breath trying to recite it all for Emma.

"You are sort of a hero," Emma told him as they embraced by his opening window on a sunny day, with curtains blowing around them.

"Who?"

"Parzival, the superhero knight who rides out into the world in search of the Holy Grail, and along the way rights wrongs and saves damsels and helps rightful princes gain the thrones of their kingdoms."

91. PARZIVAL

The words are spoken from our finger tips,
love, you are best to be with,
Helen, marbled Dardan, black Troy;
Shubiluliuma, Hatshepsut;
Antony, Cleopatra; Tristan, Ysolt;
Parzival, Condwiramurs, <u>Condwiramurs</u>!

You are swift in piercing, Love:
My heart seeks you out.

Pictures, portraits, statues,
lutes, pergaments, porcelain;
White stag bleeding on rocks,
Two lances broken in his side.

92. BEAUTIFUL WORDS, MY LOVE

The words are beautiful, my love,
spoken from our fingertips.
you are so good to be with.

Marble of Greece, red of Carthage,
Shubiluliuma, Hatshepsut,
Antony, Cleopatra,
Romeo, Juliet,
Yellow, Cathay, Indigo, Brasilia
Hymen, Hymen, Hymenaiee

Blue sea
you drown our secret words
Sun, shine, sun shine,
take our hearts to the cliffs
Two lances broken in his side
A thousand deaths in her belly.

"And you are my Condwiramurs. He married her."

"I wonder if we have so much imagination anymore today."

"You and I are living proof that Romance is not dead."

"Does it always end Happy Ever After?"

"Not always in the heavy literature. King Arthur trusted his knight, Sir Lancelot, to behave like a gentleman around Arthur's wife Guinevere. Lancelot ends up having an affair with her that ends tragically. There are kidnapings, murders, poison, wizards (Merlin chief among them), and every imaginable fantasy beast from dragons to unicorns, from fairies to goblins."

"I've read some of it, seen the movies," she said. "Sounds like one gigantic soap opera."

"Yes, and it went on for centuries. Troubadors went from castle to castle, telling those stories and embroidering them. Once you get past the ancient Celtic and Frankish names, it all sounds like something you'd watch on the television today."

"But you don't plan to write a huge romance like that," Emma probed.

He shook his head. "I think I'm more like a street corner musician, improvising as I go along, small pieces. But then again, it all hangs together. Arthur and Parzival met at some point, the same way Batman and Superman meet for adventures. Asterix knows them all by their first names."

"I have a story too," Emma said. "I love the music of Erik Satie from the 1890s or 1900s around the Montparnasse and the Moulin Rouge area."

"Ah, those slow, soulful Gnosiennes and Gymnopaedies."

Emma said: "There is a story that if you listen to them closely, you'll see that there are regular changes of a beat. That's because, after Satie became famous and was able to afford an apartment across town, he would walk the whole way at night. And every so often, as he hummed to himself and had ideas, just like you do with your random inspirations, he would stop under a street lamp and write down the notes. So the whole of his work has the sound of a slow walk by starlight across Paris."

"I have one more for you. More of a celebration."

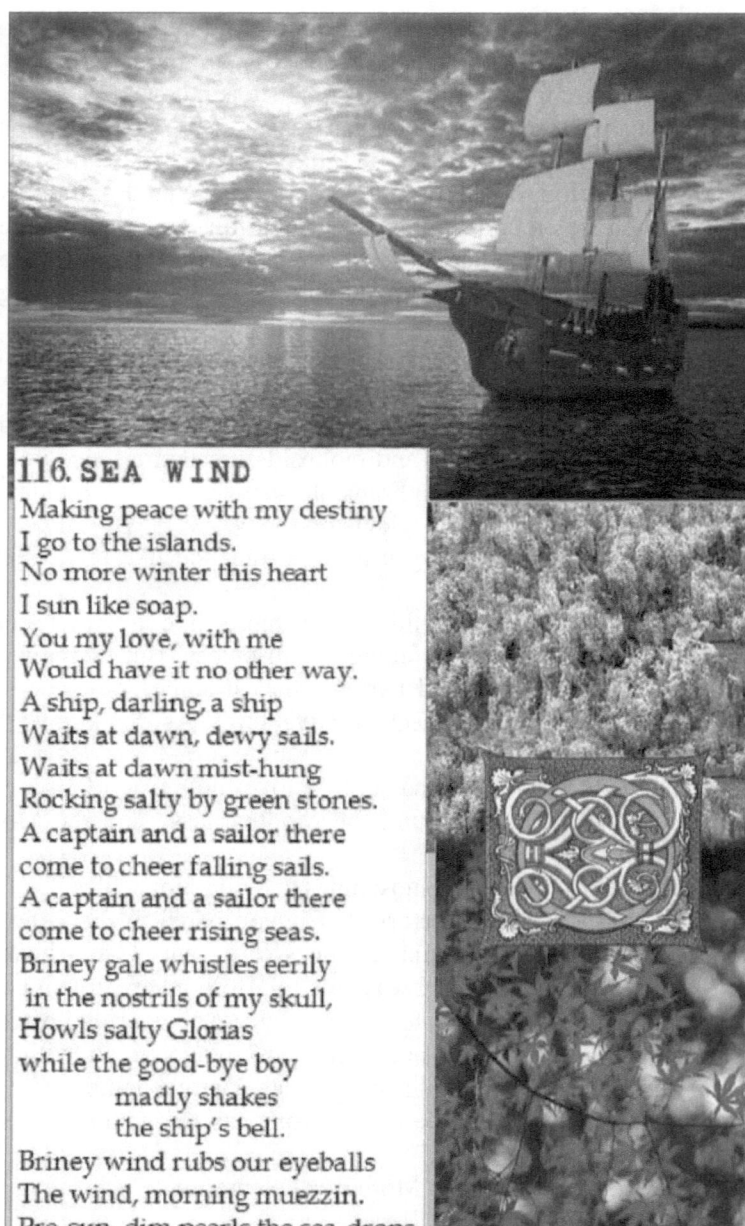

116. SEA WIND

Making peace with my destiny
I go to the islands.
No more winter this heart
I sun like soap.
You my love, with me
Would have it no other way.
A ship, darling, a ship
Waits at dawn, dewy sails.
Waits at dawn mist-hung
Rocking salty by green stones.
A captain and a sailor there
come to cheer falling sails.
A captain and a sailor there
come to cheer rising seas.
Briney gale whistles eerily
 in the nostrils of my skull,
Howls salty Glorias
while the good-bye boy
            madly shakes
            the ship's bell.
Briney wind rubs our eyeballs
The wind, morning muezzin.
Pre-sun, dim pearls the sea-drops
The wind, rubbing our backs.

Chapter 28.

Autumn: Vincennes Park: A magnificent bequest to the city and the people of Paris by a long dead monarch and tyrant; but no dogs or ball-playing allowed. Léopold Montblé wandered the grounds with pen and notebook in his pocket, seeking to distill poesy or pick poesies or play with words as butterflies danced in a late, burnishedsunlight.

Late-afternoon haze of a final hot day in fall oozed through the blown grass of the many-acred park. It had faux rivers and forests, the Medici Fountain with its hidden surprises (figure tableaux hidden within other figure arrangements). It had ponds, paths, workers scurrying about with wheeled trashcans and brooms.

Here was the general region where Emma had sacrifice her precious heirloom to the Celtic or Druid underwater and underworld spirits in eternal memory of their love affair, she and Marc forever commemorated. They'd made love there, as they did everywhere they went, impulsive as children.

Post-summer heat crawled around the trees amid air filled with twirling, dying yellow leaves that were radiant with the last sunshine of their days.

Marc had driven the damn taxi all day and was ready for a change of pace. Where was Emma? He wandered around the paths and fountains where she had asked him to be for her.

Oblivious of laws, a golden-maned spaniel fetched sticks on the estate's rolling lawns. A grinning man on a bicycle pedaled furiously on a crumbling carriage path.

It's life, and life must go on until it doesn't, and by turns glorious and terrifying (like lightning flashes) while it does; but that is the wonder and the thunder of it.

He paced on rustling gravel walks, mindful in a dim way that once pompadoured men and women had ambled here—the men with their culottes. Not far from here had been a massacre of Communards in the 1870s, and the storming of the Bastille in the 1780s.

Time covers all things.

Emma had apparently been here a little while already. He found her sitting on a bench in the graying atmosphere amid a closure of pine trees in a corner of the great estate.

Something is wrong. Something is different.

Pale of face, very sober, she looked at him as he approached, as if seeing him for the first time. She wore a short, black cotton dress. Her hands were curled together over her groin. Her tan neck was down-turned, almost swan-like. Her blonde hair was bound up in a bun, and her fine nose, blue eyes, and elegant tannin-ruddy cheeks had a bronzed look, even against a backdrop of earth, grass, and browned pine needles. He ran toward her, bounding over compressed moss and pine needles. Trucks roared on distant highways as he took her in his arms.

"I am so glad to see you."

"Is something wrong?"

She did not answer immediately. They walked arm in arm on a hard clay path where birds warbled wetly and crickets shrilled amid poison ivy and unkempt grass.

"I came as soon as I got your message," he said.

She clung to his arm. "It's true, what I was afraid of."

He sat down with her on a bench, stricken, and took her arm in his fist.

"I'm pregnant."

Like a hammering fist, guilt and shame and defeat pounded down on his head. The if-only and had-I-buts multiplied like swarming bees as he fought off a bout of giddiness.

She placed a hand on his cheek.

He stared at her in helpless anguish.

She said, "Let me take care of it. You didn't know. I should have taken precautions. Don't let me cloud your life with my stupidity. I don't want you to remember me with pain."

He thrust his hands in his pockets. "I can't run from this."

"Nobody is asking you. This is not your situation. Not really. Is it? If he were a real husband?" She smiled through her tears. "What would you do? Marry me? I'm still married to Jérôme. He's been back for three days. He has no idea. Would you make some promise to me so that I should get a divorce in order to marry you?" She shook her head. "I love you too much to do something like that to you. You are young and single and have your whole life ahead of you."

He buried his toe in the pine needles, moss, and black soil. "It was my doing too."

She shook her head, face glistening. "I've made my decision." She looked far into the distance, filled with hard calculations. "If he divorces me, I'll want something for my best years that I gave him. I can't let his lawyers trot you out and make me look like Downskate."

He stared at her dully. "I missed the boat somehow."

She shook her head, placed her fingertip on his lips. "No, don't. It's my life, my body, my decision. I made my decision to hold his cigar when you were still in grammar school. Shake yourself loose, moody guy." She spoke warmly to him amid such cold calculations.

"It hurts me," he said. She must be holding up several fronts right now, managing many pots cooking all at once. "Whatever I must do, I am there fore you."

She drew him into the late shade inside a grove of mixed pines and wild-growing ferns. "My hero. Just hearing that makes it all so much better already."

They walked slowly, arm in arm, to her car, until she lunged forward, towing him along by his wrist. "Stay with me a bit."

At the car, she embraced him tightly. Her wet face and warm lips ravaged his face. He felt the familiar stirring in his loins. He grasped her close, feeling the firmnesses of her breasts and hips against him.

Feeling his hands roving over her, she shrank back with desire as if magnetically pulling him to her. "I need a quickie." She amended, seeing his expression, "We need a quickie."

Tears dazed her face, like raindrops spattering on the windshield of a speeding car.

"Come," she said. "I have another apartment nearby."

She drove a few blocks from the Bois de Vincennes on the Avenue Daumesnil and then to the smaller Avenue Sainte-Marie in Saint-Mandé. This was a high-end little town of exquisitely clean, well-kept apartments and houses. Emma (how many secrets did this woman have?) waved a garage opening wand. Slowing down, she pulled into a tight little townhome driveway. As the garage door rose open, she drove into the one-car garage and parked. They got out, as the door rattled shut.

"The tenants just moved out," she said. "I hope it's been cleaned."

Upstairs in the empty home just vacated, whose kitchen still smelled vaguely of old food, but the rest of the place of cleaning fluids, she said: "Ah, good. The cleaners came and went."

She towed him into a bedroom. "I hope you don't mind."

He grabbed her by the buttocks. "Slow down."

She ceased her frantic motions, and sort of went limp while he embraced her and began working devout and sincere kisses around her neck and shoulders. She let him turn her, and submitted as he took her face in his hands and kissed her.

Everything was different somehow, in ways he could not explain. The bubble of time had popped. Things were more urgent, frantic, desperate now. Reality leaked in. The movie was over. And yet here she was, wrapping her arms hungry and needy around his waist.

"I wish I were a better person," she said.

"My love, you are the best."

"I love you so much," she said, kissing his cheek in friendship and appreciation.

How many more times will I have the liberty of her body and soul?

Her fingers brushed against his belt buckle, a hint.

Marc and Emma melted back and down onto a freshly made bed with a wine-red coverlet, almost as if they were again in Versailles, only this time the walls had clocks on them, the dials were turning as he watched, and the ticking grew louder.

She knelt before him, supplicating herself. "Let me adore you. You will let me?"

"Of course. Have we ever said no to each other?"

She undid and dropped his pants, and took him like a chalice to her mouth, holding him with both hands while she tenderly licked him.

Chapter 29.

Marc did not see Emma for a week, then two weeks, and time went on. If she wanted to call him, he knew that she would. He would have spent every moment with her. He would have driven her crazy with phone calls and emails. He would have sent flowers. He would have driven the damn taxi past her house (or all of them) and honked the horn.

Devastated as he was, he made himself do something hard. He studied the catalogs of various colleges and found one that would transfer his credits so he could start business school. An advisor, a sympathetic little Tunisian-Parisian with dark skin who spoke flawless third-generation French, counseled him that his writing skills would be very useful in business and management. Not only that, but he could count on at least some sort of modest internship within about two years. Also, he could work at some low-paying but safe job like filing papers or assisting at the library. It seemed like a positive direction, and Marc signed up for the spring term, which would begin in three months. Until then, he could write poetry, drive a cab or tend bar or whatever, and sort out his love life if anything was still left.

* * * *

And of course that opened new possibilities. Wondrous leaves crinkled in a late breeze, for it was now October. Jack had met a young girl, his own age at 23, from a private art college. She was a painter, an artist, who always had some yellow ochre or red oil or blue streaks on her loose-fitting jeans. She was post-Gothic, with a few tattoos of fantasy dragons on her caramel skin. Her name was Aurora. She was a petite, intense young woman with emotional dark-green eyes and a wild froth of curly hair like Medusa coils on her head.

Jack had been a little jealous of Marc and that gorgeous, exotic blonde who seemed to have walked right out of the pages of a top-echelon modeling catalog, complete with expensive clothes and cars and apartments. But now Marc was in a pickle, and Jack hoped he could fix Marc up with somebody, a friend of Aurora maybe. Time would tell. Life marches on.

* * * *

Léopold Montblé, resigned to memories of a summer fatuation with a married woman seven years and many tears his senior, busied himself transcribing memories of lost romance on his typewriter in the moth-filled garret.

He had never written so much material in a waterfall of feeling.

Marc Fontbleu still drove a taxi, conscious that Emma Delors moved around the orbit of his immediate memory, but she did not call and he did not try to contact her. He was afraid to cause trouble for her with the Kangaroo guy. He knew she was in pain, and he did not want to make it worse in any way. He would let her carry the ball in the game.

He was happy to see his old friend Jack finally in a relationship that seemed to have meaning and promise. She clung dutifully to him, while Jack now lavished embraces on her dark-haired, shapely presence. They seemed to be falling passionately in love. Jack had never looked happier, and Aurora with them.

How things changed. Before, Jack had hung at the periphery, looking lost and hungry. Now Jack was too busy to spend much time except an occasional coffee on the run, at some bistro. He was impressed with Aurora and thought she might be good for Jack. Aurora seemed honest and very devoted to Jack. It was obvious she liked him a lot, although she had none of the depth or intensity of a more mature woman like Emma. Aurora was kind, and true, and straight-forward, and it was clear she expected the same from Jack. For his part, Jack seemed transformed. He seemed to have more purpose and zeal in life. In some strange way, Marc thought, Jack (who only dabbled at playing bass guitar sometimes in local bar-bands) had latched up with an artist, thus almost replacing the poet who had been his friend. Of course it was a different thing altogether, since his new artist was a woman and his lover.

So in more than one way, Marc felt a sharp loss in his life. He knew that, if he truly cared for these two persons (Emma and Jack) he would stand back and let them have their freedoms. That sense of rightness was the only good thing in a life that had become several degrees colder, darker, lonelier as autumn swung toward winter.

He did manage to hang on to his garret on the Rue Monge, since he was able to pay the bills again. And he eagerly awaited some word about his university application, since he could then immerse himself in campus life—eating, living, sleeping, studying, and meeting new people.

* * * *

This was the turning of autumn toward winter. Days were short, skies over Paris gray by day, twinkling with frosty lights at night.

A gray quality about the heat told him it was past the opportunity for summer love. He drove his taxi in the poor parts of town, conscious of the loves and hates of strangers. Robberies and muggings were on the rise, and he resolved he would soon have to find another occupation.

At least once every shift, women (strangers) he drove about offered him invitations to stolen love, sinister sex, secret rendez-vous or rendez-fous...

One was a teenage nursing student, another a woman slightly older than Emma who was divorced and worked at a suburban library (lonely). To the attractive ones he said yes, to the desperate and unappealing ones he gently said no. What they all had in common was that none saw him twice. Partly he didn't want to, and partly their interest in him had been brief, shallow, and transient like a sunny morning during a cloudy week. It was all right with him; he needed the contact, but couldn't manage a relationship longer than a few hours at most.

To one such tender he did consent. Madrigal was South American, his own age, but mature beyond his years. She had run from some oppression and lived with a dozen family members in a house on the edge of Goatville. She was elegant and insisted he be gentle. She was divorced, she said. She had two children and her breasts were soft with milk, her nipples were loose, her hips bore stretch marks, and his taxi was her only means of escape from cloying, desperate, jealous, angry men in her family.

Madrigal took a taxi home once a week from her English lessons. She said she would feel safer, knowing him, so he agreed to wait each Monday night outside a certain public school. She was hungry for passion, and took him twice a week in his back seat on a dead-silent, lonely back street—a common spot for rows of cars with steamed-up windows, including passenger sedans, the occasional taxi or upholstery van, and at times an airport limo. Madrigal was a small, lively woman with coal-black eyes. She was secretive and fervent, responding to his kisses with honesty. Her husband had stayed behind in their Andean city, evidently in charge of an action grupa of some rightist party she despised. The whispered liaisons of Marc and Madrigal were quick, like snacks, but Madrigal was always thankful. It was far less than love, but far more than a casual thank-you. She was genuinely grateful.

As a taxi driver, Marc was captain of a ship, and for some reason or for many and varied reasons, some women looked to him for solutions, refreshment, adoration, who knows what they sought in him. He avoided them all, stepping into the danger zone only with little Madrigal. He prayed there was no sombrero and bandolier wearing gaucho with heavy beard-shadow, who would come with his action *grupa* and search for Marc and Madrigal amid the Parisian sprawl of encrusted city lights.

After a few weeks, Marc found the curb empty. Madrigal had moved on, to parts unknown. Marc was suddenly grateful for his release, and never tried calling. Too much heaviness there. He was alone again.

* * * *

In early October, to his surprise, he found a letter in his mailbox. He took it inside, poured himself a glass of wine since he was done driving for the day and it was already night out. The letter was from Monsieur Arthur Mézières of Livres Charleville, the Strasbourg arts publisher. typed in halting Pica. The small note read:

Please pick up your manuscript. Lovely stuff. Have you published anywhere else? I'd enjoy speaking with you.

—*A. Mézières*

Someone else (Chalmers?) had signed it in inked cursive over Arthur Mézières' name.

Irradiated, Marc let out a whoop.

Duly, his neighbor pounded on the wall for him to keep quiet. The two Sorbonne students had moved out, replaced by a Sorbonne grad student with no sense of humor, given to collecting moths when not memorizing long lists of entomological names. Lately a guitar student had moved in, and then out again, when the graduate student threatened to have him arrested for making noise while practicing arpeggios and plucking sonatinas late in the night.

Marc pounded back on the wall, and the grad student gave up their combat.

Marc Fontbleu seated himself at the keyboard, and Léopold Montblé originated a brief poem in the shape of a classical vase with two round, hinged handles, one on either fluted side. When it was done, and printed, he sketched flowers pouring from the thick ceramic lip on top, and then even watercolored the flowers and green leaves lightly. Not his usual repertoire, but he was ecstatic.

Finishing another glass of wine, he sat on his bed with his back to the bathroom wall. He dreamed of seeing his book at last in binderies and bookstores. He read and reread that Strasbourg letter a dozen times, each time sensing some added nuance in its terse and ambiguous text. He fell asleep, while moths crept through the holes in the screen. He dreamed of Léopold Montblé's brilliant future. He forgot about Emma for the first time in weeks, or months counting their feverish time together. He woke up with a dream that Emma was shaking him gently, saying his name urgently, but he had no idea what her shade was trying to tell him.

* * * *

The next morning, he called the taxi company early. He said he was sick. He'd take a day off without pay—a sacrifice *por la causa*. Madrigal was already gone from his life, but he'd taken away a few words of Spanish.

No experience in vain, nothing ever lost.

Gray dawn had not yet turned into warm daylight as he had a breakfast of sausage and eggs to soothe his queasy stomach. Slightly hung over, he gulped coffee, which only made him jittery. He took the Métro and then RER home to Créteil to pick up his car, which was parked safely near his parents' home. He had enough to fill the tank and buy a snack at the petrol station nearby.

* * * *

Once again, he found himself on that numbing drive, almost five hours, almost in Germany (or actually in Germany, depending on which war you were nearest to in the past century or more).

He rolled into Strasbourg, with its half-French and half-German place names, and parked again at the train station. This time the path to his destination was no mystery, and it seemed he walked there in a fraction of the time.

In old Strasbourg, he wandered amid tingling humanity. He was full of wonder already, and did not pause to gape at anything along the way. Nothing could distract him from his urgent and impassioned mission. He considered dedicating his first book to the relaxed editors at Livres Charleville.

As before, he made his way past the downstairs receptionist—a chubby young redhead in a flowery yellow blouse, who admitted Marc's existence with an utter lack of excitement, contrasting with the knots in Marc's stomach.

Upstairs, the young male receptionist at Charleville shrugged, glanced at the letter Marc showed him with trembling hands, and spoke briefly on the intercom.

An elderly woman in a gray sweater, with a pencil through her gray hair, stepped out of the inner offices.

Are you not going to invite me in?

"I'm sorry, Mr. Mézières is not in," said the *grise* lady.

But I drove all these hours from Paris, Marc thought with pleading eyes. He stood suddenly amid the crumbling ruins once again of his life.

The universe played tricks. There had been a sea change. The pretty young woman receptionist of summer, Jess of the violet eyes and beautiful smile, had vanished, or changed into this librarian of disapproval and stormy gray looks. "If you are a writer, you are not allowed here without an appointment." She rifled through her calendar. "I have nothing blocked in for you."

Marc Fontbleu's knees knocked together as his legs trembled.

Léopold Montblé paused at the crossroad of his career. He said with sinking heart, "My manuscript is waiting for me." He showed her the letter.

"Oh really?" she said, while he supported himself against the counter for fear of collapsing. No nuns today. No old ladies in shorts. No young secretary in purple, with white teeth and violet eyes. The woman searched amid a pile on her desk. She extracted a manila envelope. "You are Mr. Montblé?"

He nodded, taking back the very same folder with the little fleurs-de-lis decorative pattern that he had brought one sweaty day in the early middle of a promising summer. He hastily opened it, finding his manuscript and clippings intact. After a brief search he located the note. It was a rejection slip printed on a common format. Underneath were penned the lines:

Sorry. Maybe another time. Power and beauty, but not for us. Better luck next time. C.

"Is that all?" breathed Léopold Montblé.

The secretary regarded him with dismissive eyes.

"Who is this C or Chalmers?"

"I am Madame Chalmers," she said frostily.

"Is Mr. Mézières in?" he asked.

She recited, "Mr. Mézières is taking a two-week vacation. Can I take a message?"

He shook his head. "No thank you."

She pointed toward the door. The young male receptionist had one eye on her and the other eye (and his hand) on the telephone, as if ready to call the police if this Montblé started a ruckus. One never knew with this sort who barged in, thinking their stinking verse was worthy of anyone's time.

* * * *

Drunk with shock and fatigue, and smashed with anger and disappointment, he strode through this atmosphere of suddenly *faux* books and synthetic carpeting toward the elevator. It would be a long and heart-broken ride back to Paris. Even more so than on that summer day, he was eager to never see Strasbourg again. But that time he'd been filled with hope, as well as longing for Emma.

Now he could only hope to find solace in the familiarity of his little home. Maybe if he banged on the wall, his neighbor would respond with banging. It was, in its own way, a relationship.

Was this karma, revenge, Jérôme, fickle finger of fate, greasy faculty conspirators whose reach had no limit, like that disgusting little creature driving the Renault and coming on to Emma (she had told him long after the fact, for fear of Marc's protective male reaction).

The long drive was a blur of endless concrete roadways and shimmering signs he could barely read for raindrops in his eyes. The eminent publication of Léopold Montblé was sunk like the Titanic. He had been skewered not by meaningful discussion and repair, but by a casual and offhand and coldly cruel rejection.

Numbly, he perceived that he was back at square zero, born again, fresh as a baby, diapered in endless swaddling of possibilities. Everything was once again as remote and intoxicating as a hopeless dream. The ever-optimist was reborn from the dashed amniotic fluids of failure.

Evening descended with a clear blue brush stroke over the ocean skyline as the car speeded toward the skyline of Paris. The Eiffel Tower beckoned with its lights and monstrously beautiful imposition on the senses. Léopold Montblé longed to return to his garret, carrying a bottle of wine, as an especially intense and poignant poem was making its lines felt under Léopold Montblé's half-closed eyes as Marc Fontbleu's gaunt, grieving features were reflected in the hard, cold auto windshield.

Cruel, senseless world.

Chapter 30.

Wind murmured suspensefully, fresh as Creation. Dry, early leaves pressed up against the humming screen overlooking Emma's timeless porch.

Marc Fontbleu lay in Emma's bed, feeling exhausted and feverish. Jérôme was gone, back to Australia. Emma, in her evening robe, brought a steaming bowl of tea and brushed his forehead tenderly. It was the week just when the cold front swept down from Arctic Finland or Russia someplace, and leaves died by the gadzillion in bloody glowing lanterns and overflowing honey. In another week the sky would be leaden, and leaves just rustling husks blowing in circles on restless sidewalks.

Léopold Montblé's heart died and was reborn in a bloodied and honeyed agony after his odyssey to the gatekeepers of mediocrity in the city that never weeps. His very soul intimed the approach of winter in a visceral, car crash sort of violent, stunned manner.

Emma bent her long, elegant face over him and he, wracked with the trauma of an early cold, looked with resignation and rebellion upon the young/old lines around her eyes and mouth. In the press and density of November, Léopold Montblé had suddenly neared exhaustion and needed nourishment. She in turn needed the same. Her warm, dry hand brushed lovingly over his forehead. He coughed rackingly and sat up in bed to accept the tangy steaming tea she brought from crocks and jars secrete.

"Poor Léopold Montblé," she said softly. "All broken. I feel the same, so close to you. Drink, my poor love."

He ran a hand over the curve of her waist and hip. Under the night coat, her small, firm breasts dangled willingly—offerings near his cheek. Her thighs were smooth and rich to his touch. He coughed as he sat up to accept a steaming cup from her ministering hands.

"I missed you so much."

She went back into the kitchen. He sat upright with his back to a pillow and wall. He cradled steaming cup and saucer amid twilight. Far away, a lonely carillon of bells from long-ago centuries and dead souls clattered slowly and wistfully across evening air. The tune sounded almost like Strawberry Fields by the Beatles. Its tentative, halting notes—much like a sweet woman's lisping whisper—seemed to say: *Nothing has changed. Why be upset? Time rolls on forever and ever.* Nothing to be upset about. And look at us, we are here, back together, in love. Nothing else matters.

He felt smothered and loved in the aura of her caring. Jérôme had left, too quickly to consummate a divorce; the papers were pending in the hands of Parisian lawyers.

Marc had a new feeling, finally, of belonging within the youngness and oldness of her apartment. His life was taking on that same timeless, experienced, tired resignation he heard in the caresses of that distant carillon. Those bells were there long before he was born, and they would be there long after he was gone; he and Emma and Jérôme and the hierophants of mediocrity in publishing and macadamia and all the rest of the world's nuts.

What really matters? Love, probably, and only.

As he sipped his tea, he could not separate her wifeliness from her motherliness. It was a fatal dichotomy. He put the tea aside and stared with disquiet at the leaves blowing up against the screen window. No, he realized, he was not about to marry; it would all be a game of pretend until some reappearance of Jérôme or some other spectre of reality. In him, too, Léopold Montblé—rogue and poet, mower of lawns, taxi captain and puffer at cigars (not)—remonstrated at this all too easy passing of summer. He patted his stomach, pressing starchy sheets close, and reflected that she, like himself, had only just had a deflating trip to her own private Strasbourg.

She'd gone from his life for a short while, during which she had visited a clinic in Poland and (whatever; Marc Fontbleu's imagination shut down). Marc had not been consulted and she reassured him (as had Danielle and Jack) it was for the best.

Marriage was so far beyond his horizon that it, too, was in the ethereal zone. He might marry her and there could be children. But when he was thirty-three (which seemed to him a very old age) she would be nearing forty. Léopold Montblé cried out against this termination or smothering of the hunting and pecking instinct. He wasn't done hunting yet. Or if he was, he didn't know it.

Emma finished her work in the kitchen. She returned smiling, with a tray of cookies.

"How is my brave man doing?"

"My thoughts are like a blender. I'd like to turn it off, but it's making a strawberry parfait."

"I'll get the whipped cream for you then," she said metaphorically. "Cookies for you."

"You smile like a calendar girl," he told her as she sat down on the bed.

Her blue eyes glistened. Her lips crinkled around white teeth. "That was so long ago," she whispered in a gentle voice, holding out her hand. She amended, "Could have been so long ago."

Never was. Oh well. Life is filled with never was, so love that which is.

He took her hand and kissed it.

You are at the ripest point of all best things. You are beautiful with young skin and wise eyes. You are at your perfect moment.

Her lips were perfectly vulnerable when he moved close, as he captured her in his net because she let him, because she needed him, because they loved each other. She rolled over like a cub when he played with her. They held each other a long time.

Chapter 31.

Léopold Montblé, alias Marc Fontbleu, stood knee-deep in a pile of autumn leaves and improvised a swirling solo, punctuated by high, wheezing notes and basso comments while Emma clapped delightedly sitting on a bench under stripped, skeleton trees.

To emphasize his seriousness, he loosened his belt and let his pants drop down around his ankles. Thus he stood on the open hillside, echoing with leaves and trees, growling Coltrane-esque on an imaginary saxophone air horn, overlooking the 19th Arrondissement from a forested, leafy cove atop the Cliffs or Buttes de Chaumont.

He paused to look at Emma. She sat rapt on the chilly bench in that late brown-gold light, her hands folded child-like on her lap. Her narrow, fashion-model glowing face with sensuous lips and dark blue eyes was framed in golden hair. She patiently and delightedly noted his every gesture.

Seditious autumn air crawled like blood plasma around sweet-smelling tree trunks, raising essences of stored nuts and decaying leaves from around gray, knotted roots. Wind blew through his boxer shorts, and he abruptly let the air-sax evaporate from his open grasp. He bent to pull up his pants.

"Why can't we live forever?" he asked. The autumn forest could not answer, nor could she. Emma raised her thumbs in an Upskate, go-pilot gesture. She dropped her hands back into her lap, demurely, and glowed with smiles.

He offered a hand. She rose, and he led her along an old promenade amid strewn leaves.

"Jerry Lewis did that once, you know," he told her.

"Did what?" she asked calmly. As she walked, she regarded crumbling asphalt before her feet on the long-closed road. He found it strangely post-world, apocalyptic, this street that had once carried traffic. One day, when the human race ceased to exist, the whole world would be covered with dead roads like this.

She wore a newly bought olive-drab, military-looking ski parka. She'd thrust her hands in its pragmatic pockets, while her long brown skirt rustled around her softly muscled calves. She easily paced his sauntering stride.

"Stood in his underwear on a balcony in Manhattan and played the saxophone."

"Why did he do that?"

"To call attention to himself. It's how he started to become famous. Made the morning newspaper headlines. Got out of jail and immediately found gigs around the city. I should be so bold and so lucky."

She laughed. She tossed her head and her long blonde hair shimmered, imprisoned in her collar. "I'll never forget you back there, dropping your pants."

"My own brand of fame."

She extracted a hand from her parka pocket to twine her arm around his elbow. The smell of autumn was everywhere. It was a leafy smell, reminding of ink, of chlorine, of airy freshness.

She pressed a soft, warm hip against his muscular leg. "Someone will write a biography of you," she said.

He stopped, pulling her short. "When Léopold Montblé wins prizes, it won't matter. No photos please." He rubbed noses with her as she looked modestly agreeable. "Except of you."

"Please, that's the last thing I need, a married woman having an affair."

They walked on. He stubbed through the leaves covering the road, uncovering with his toe a serpentine, barklessly smooth branch which he kicked sailing through the air.

He stopped and put his foot on a rock. "This reminds me of school."

"How's that?" She had put her hands in her pockets and was staring over the city, her face insular, her eyes probing far. She was about to tell him something. He sensed it coming and tried to talk and talk to stop her from saying whatever it was. Léopold Montblé had been devastated. Now it was Marc Fontbleu's turn.

She said: "This smell in the air. We graduated from pencils to pens. Schoolgirls took to writing with laundry markers. They'd put their heads together over their homework and make big magic marker circles over their i's. Teachers protested. Later came felt-tip pens. I preferred fountain pens. I made a lot of mistakes and has to erase often. You could buy an ink eradicator in a little bottle; it smelled like bleach and it turned the ink gold and then white on the page. That's what autumn smells like."

"It's a lovely smell," she said and inhaled deeply—a sigh from the heart. Her face was set and sad. "Jérôme and I will be moving at the end of the month."

"Where to?" Chills moved up and down his weakened legs. His breath caught short in his throat.

"He's returning from Australia. He'll have a teaching job in Vancouver, on the Canadian west coast."

Marc tried to recall his geography. "How far is that?" His heart already knew the answer.

Too far.

"Thousands of miles, Marc."

A lifetime at least.

"We'll never see each other again."

"It's for the best."

"Anything is possible." he said bravely. "We'll find some way. Even if we have to make love in the snow."

She shook her head—no—but laughed thinly and kissed him.

What had the great poet Rilke written: *"Herr, es ist Zeit. Der Sommer war sehr gross..."*

Lord, it is time. Summer overwhelmed.
Drop your shadow over the sundials,
And let your winds loose in doorways.

Force the final fruits to ripen,
Give them yet two sunny days,
Press them to their ripest ending, and drive
A fullest sweetness into the heavy wine.

Who by now has no house will build himself none.
Who now is alone will remain in solitude,
Will lie awake, read, write long letters,
On the boulevards he'll wander without rest,
as leaves rustle in circles around him.

Chapter 32.

Marc and Emma enjoyed yet a few weeks together, as if time had shut off, as if the clocks lost their dials, as if bell towers grew silent and planes stopped thundering out of Orly where Jack's family had moved from Créteil.

Marc had a taste of what married life would be like with the perfect woman. That was during the early December weeks, before the return of Jérôme Delors. With her, it was wonderful. Because it was a lovely golden doomed time, it was perfect. They both knew that nothing so perfect had happened to either of them before, nor ever again would happen. Her apartment was sunny and safe even though it might be raining and windy outside. At times the late autumn sun broke through, while smooth rock tunes warmed the air inside.

Sometimes he and she would dance slowly together, pressed shoulder to shoulder while the oak floorboards made perfect speaker amplifiers, throbbing sexually under their feet and up their legs.

She still kept her little secretarial job, which she had taken to not be so lonely while Mr. Kangaroo was on the other side of the world and on the flip side of the seasons. She walked to work each morning through sifting leaves (like Rilke's driving leaves in Prague or Vienna, wherever it was, a century ago or more), and it seemed to Marc, watching from a window, that she hummed to herself with contentment. She'd stride away under stripped trees, among old 1800s Belle Epoque mansarded houses, on her way to that office in Pantheon-Sorbonne, amid gray, forlorn shades of coming winter. That was ironically where Emma and Marc had met nearly a year ago, and here the story was near its final chapter.

He moved in with her, giving up his garret on Rue Monge. He was tired anyway of the surly grad student banging on the wall too often, every time Marc made a sound to many. *Good riddance.* His computer now sat on a sewing table in her living room on the street of owl-eyed windows, awaiting the talented fingertips of Léopold Montblé.

This was a time longer and more perfect (superlative upon superlative) than their weekend marriage in that Hotel des Amis in Versailles.

Time stood still, and they shared perfection. Every second in this brief parenthesis must be made to count, must be turned into a golden hour.

* * * *

At some point, they read together out loud in English the poem of Thomas Carew five centuries ago to a courtly lover who might have been a delicate few years older but all the more beautiful:

> Ask me no more where Jove bestows,
> When June is past, the fading rose;
> For in your beauty's orient deep
> These flowers, as in their causes, sleep.
>
> Ask me no more whither do stray
> The golden atoms of the day;
> For in pure love heaven did prepare
> Those powders to enrich your hair.
>
> Ask me no more whither doth haste
> The nightingale, when May is past;
> For in your sweet dividing throat
> She winters, and keeps warm her note....

The poem continued for another two stanzas, but by then both Emma and Marc were too broken up to form the words well anymore. So their recitation faded into silence while outside cars swished by in a gentle rain, and the last leaves tumbled to earth through coffee-dark air.

* * * *

They made love long and searchingly every night. In the mornings, after she left for work, he would go for a long walk to prepare for a day's writing. Later, he'd put in a half shift at the taxi job, but his heart wasn't in it. He could not bring himself to face the future just yet, but after she and Jérôme left forever to land in far Vancouver, on the other side of the world, he would begin a new future for himself. He had no idea how or what. He might even leave Paris, and start graduate school someplace. Anywhere other than Paris or Strasbourg. Those avenues seemed closed.

He would go for a jog in gray dawn light. His shoes crushed through parchment leaves like a million discarded poems. Were any of them by Léopold Montblé? Had any of them been thrown from the high stories of glass buildings, to flutter twirling down shafts of city canyon air? He had an image now of some goon who never read poetry standing at a high-up window while Léopold Montblé's poems twirled in the air, and screaming in frustration for his money. It was all about money—nothing more, nothing less, and Marc Fontbleu must earn his crust (and Léopold Montblé's) by the sweat of his brow after the gates of paradise closed behind him forever.

As he ran, his breath steamed in chill morning air. He was reborn. He saw the world anew. He was at one with a milkman, a stray cat, a ten-year-old walking to school, a thick-jacketed woman raking leaves in chilly air. It was good to be alive.

Each of these golden atoms of the day is worth the ticket to this crazy show.

Each day, he'd pick Emma up to walk home together from work. They made a good husband and wife. They'd go out to eat, to a museum, to an art gallery, to a lecture about nematodes or papyri or codpieces. Anything is possible in a great university town. There were carillon bells to hear, organ concerts, violins, symphonies, jazz and rock concerts, Renaissance lutes, or warbling operatists. Especially poignant was a recital of ancient Ovid, accompanied by wistfully clanking *kythara* or melancholic soughing *hydraulis* water organ of two thousand years ago. There was no end to magic. They would speed home and make passionate love as if each day was their last; which was close, because soon only days remained.

His walks took him along the Seine quais, where he would gently finger used volumes of poetry in bookstalls, and marvel that this Rilke or that Rimbaud, this Anna Akhmatova or that HD, or an Apollinaire with his head bandaged from World War I, had found their way into print and eternity, when that doorway was closed to a Léopold Montblé.

How absurd it now seemed that when Emma had innocently asked why he insisted on hiding behind a pseudonym, he had replied that he did not want to have his fountain of inspiration tainted by fame or applause. He wanted to remain anonymous to preserve the purity of his vision. Now it was clearly a vision whose eyeglasses had been torn off by zoo monkeys and their shattered lenses stomped on by hippos and camels.

He'd walk for hours on the city's streets and boulevards. He would sift impressions, filter memories, wondering what to take home with him to type out into reality. The days became shorter, leaves deeper, porch lights yellower. Each day, Emma would bring her special aura of patience and refreshing humor as Léopold Montblé sat at his typewriter.

At any moment, she was ready for love, and wet, but she would sigh. He could have her any time, and he did often. Sometimes she would come behind him as he typed, and slide her hands into his pants and massage him to passion.

They had the perfect life together, man and woman, for that brief moment.

And then again, not so much.

* * * *

"No novel yet?" she asked one rainy afternoon as she came home from work. She seemed wounded and grouchy.

"Dammit, no," he said, staring at a commercial. She left her raincoat by the door and stamped off into the kitchen. "I have ideas, but I can't get the juice flowing. The keys are ready but the fingers are not." He rose and followed her. "I'm sorry. That's not your fault."

She moved tiredly, putting a pan on for mixed vegetables. She barely grunted in reply.

"I'm going to take a drive tonight," he said. "Jack Poncelet called. We're going to kick around some ideas about starting a business."

"Oh? That's nice." She moved about, dropping the empty vegetable pouch in the trash and stirring her near-boiling water. "What kind of business?"

He said, "Anything other than creative arts. Certainly not publishing. Maybe we'd manufacture lawn dwarves or something."

She laughed. "Oh my god. That I would like to see." It was clear she wouldn't.

He enthused, "No telling how far we could go. No matter what the product is. Books, lawn ornaments, poison arrows, calendars. Anything you can sell in a store that people will pay money for."

She stirred her vegetables, checking the quality of the gas underneath. "You're not doing much writing lately."

He said, "Emma, I try and try. It just isn't working."

She cast a dark glance in his direction, as if he were implying she was to blame. He put his hands in his pockets and returned to the living room. Settling before the TV, he said "Thus, no cigar for you."

She came into the living room, slammed two plates on the table, and returned to the kitchen.

Minutes of silence later, he drifted into the kitchen to apologize once again. While she stood with her back turned, and he was about to cough to gain her attention, he noticed a slip of paper under a refrigerator magnet. On it was written *Jérôme* followed by a day, date, and time at Charles DeGaulle International Airport.

20. UMBRELLAS / REFLECTIONS

umbrellas
in sunshine
rain drops twinkle
on my toes

when I

look down

I see two people

smiling

in the puddle

Part Four: Winter

Chapter 33.

"Jack," Marc said, "I wonder if you'd like to drive to Norway with me?" They sat in a cool back table area of the Kino Korner Bar. It being a weeknight, the bar was quiet and half-empty. A young bartendress hunched over her counter, washing out beer mugs with a face full of concentration. She seemed to shiver in her sweater against the cold seeping in. The radio was tuned to a local college station playing cool jazz from the 1950s. Radiators banged and sighed anciently in corners. A tousled Sorbonne student in corduroy sat reading at a table with a beer bottle and ashtray filled with bent and twisted filters. Two lovelorn women held hands while they murmured in a far corner with their faces close.

"Norway," Jack repeated as if Marc had said the moon or Mars. "Why the hell Norway?"

"Somewhere far away, that we've never been to."

Jack shook his head slowly and looked into his beer mug. "I'm doing okay with Aurora."

"I forgot. Of course. More power to you. I thought you always wanted to take one last crazy journey in your youth," Marc said.

Jack squirmed. "Yes, but. Well, not now. I've got to save some money to go to grad school next year. I'm also in love with Aurora."

Marc rubbed himself on the cheeks. He combed fingers through wavy hair.

Jack looked up. "Say, you're not trying to run away, are you?"

"What do you mean?"

Jack toyed diplomatically with a match book. "Well look. I've been waiting for weeks to ever get a call from you."

"You've been busy with your girl."

"I know. She keeps asking to meet you."

"I'm about to have a lot of time on my hands."

"Oh." Jack looked sympathetic.

"Yeah. Emma and her lawn dwarf are moving to Far Gibrue out beyond where whales migrate and whatnot."

"Sorry to hear it. You haven't been the same since you met her."

"You haven't changed in the past year," Marc said in a voice freighted with irony.

Jack shrugged. "Danielle says the same thing."

"She's an authority."

"She is an objective observer. She's been worried about you getting shotgunned by the crazed husband."

"I slipped into a thing."

"Sideways," Jack said. "Head over heels. You have been out to lunch. I don't think you've even been to see your parents in a month. You're shacked up and whacked out over there. Are you doing any writing?"

Marc made a fist. "That's part of it. I can't seem to even look at a blank page without nausea anymore. Even the thought of grad school fills me with fright. I don't know what to do anymore!"

Jack cleared his throat carefully. "Say, uh, maybe you already know the answer and won't admit it."

"What do you mean?" Marc regarded him warily.

Jack gestured. "Well, uh,...you're getting laid regularly, aren't you? I mean, is there more to it? Or are you just so damn comfortable in your existence that you hate it, and her, and yourself?" Jack, having made his point, sat back.

Marc studied the whiteness of his curled knuckles. He said softly, "You've been my friend for many years." He stared at his knuckles. "I think you may be right." He looked up, feeling a strange mixture of fear, elation, and relief. "It's over now. She's leaving me."

"For her husband," he said in a voice weighted by the lead of irony.

"I know. It's crazy. I'm being dumped for her husband by a married woman." When he thought of Emma, he felt as if someone had cut a hole in the sidewalk before him a million miles deep, and he was about to step into it and fall forever—a new meaning to falling for her. The thought of her in bed with him was possessive and obsessive. He felt a wrenching sense of loss. She was a drug he could not kick.

"C'mon, let's go for a walk," Jack suggested.

They walked under coldly bluish streetlights. Shadows danced where light fell between stripped branches. Rustling sidewalks seemed to roil with electricity as lights and shadows played nervously over the concrete.

Eternal night distantly echoed with highways and factories. It felt intimate but without compassion. In that clarity lay truth. Marc walked with his hands in his pockets and silent tears streaming down his cheeks.

Jack shuffled patiently along, blowing steam, patting him briefly on the back.

"Futz," Marc said as he wiped tears away and loved the night.

"Futz what?" Jack inquired.

Marc burst into a grin. "Just, futz. Aw, futz."

Jack nodded. "Yeah—what the futz." He added, "You're welcome to stay with me and Aurora for a while. You can sleep on the couch."

"Thanks. I think it may come to that."

"We'll leave a key under the mat for you."

"What is Danielle doing these days?"

Jack seemed startled. "She asks me about you every time I see her. I have a feeling she might have a crush on you."

"No." He pictured Dani, and realized that she might just be the other woman in his life.

"Give her a call. Just don't cry on her shoulder."

"What do you mean?"

"She was going out with this fool. I couldn't stand the guy. A real dick. And thank god he dumped her for some other chick. She didn't even cry. Strange thing. Danielle. Been my sister all my life, and sometimes I think I hardly know her."

"I'll figure out an excuse to drop by," Marc said, and filed that whole thought away for a time when he could think straight. They walked a long way. Jack puffed from exertion. Marc was thankful to him. The city murmured heavily around them, as always, a vast animal with lungs as big as clouds and darkness in its soul, along with a million or more living humans and their pets and house plants. A chill, soughing wind—aromatic with dead leaves, irradiated with moonlight—was playful like an old friend. Dim gray house walls and scraping empty tree limbs portended infinite and rejuvenated liquid syllables and revelations for Léopold Montblé.

"I think I'll go home and write a poem," he told Jack.

Instead, he took a long walk—back to Emma's apartment.

Chapter 34.

It was the night before the morning when Jérôme's flight was due in from Australia.

Emma's apartment, when he arrived there at two in the morning, was in a shambles—very uncharacteristic of Emma. Stacked clothes, towels, books, utensils, were everywhere.

Fresh from his revelation, Marc clumped up the stairs and found Emma sitting on a suitcase in the middle of the living room, crying. She did not immediately see him.

He stayed in the doorway, hands in his jacket pockets, wondering where to start.

"What are you doing?" he finally said.

She looked up with red eyes.

He walked in and said, "You're picking him up at the airport?"

She nodded. "At ten. I have to leave at seven. I'm a wreck." She shook her head, blew her nose, and dried her tears, while he fetched two brimming glasses of cold tea. "I've made arrangements for friends to come put my things in storage. We're going to rent this place out, my family and I."

"Here." He offered her the tea.

"Thanks," she nodded, sniffling, as she accepted the tea. "I was crying because I didn't know if I'd see you again."

He sat down on the couch, hands folded peacefully and urgently between his knees. "How are we going to do this?"

"Do what?"

"Never see each other again. Live here with memories of you, while you fly off to the other side of the world."

Renewed tears flowed from her eyes, and it wasn't the old contradictory Emma in that moment, taught to laugh and cry at the same time to drain her of all emotions.

He was just as hollowed out. "You realize that when it's day here it's night there. When it's night there, it's day here. Something like that. The sun will never shine on both of us again at the same time. Whenever you look up at the moon, I won't be able to see it over here."

She understood. "I know it's a lot."

"What?"

"Giving you up. Going back with him."

He could say nothing, so they stared at each other.

"I was going to let you have the apartment. My family wouldn't catch on for months."

"Thanks, but I would die here, knowing we made love and I could never have you again."

She nodded and sobbed.

"Do you want to do this? Go there with him?"

She shook her head.

He waited.

She said: "I want everything to stay like it has been. We get along so well."

"Yes? And?" He stood with his arms apart, hands open, expecting a change of heart, some logic, anything.

She did not answer. Her stolid, distant look said, *It's a done deal—me and Jérôme, you and me—all of it was fate long ago decided and so we all move on.*

He watched her hands, and thought of holding them, but there was a barrier now. "I'm tearing myself apart inside over losing you."

She kneaded a couple of wet, wadded, ragged tissues in her fingers. Part of it was the shreds were hard to get a grip on, and part was she was so nervous. "Jérôme called from Hawai'i on his way here. He was crying. He wants to pack it all in and come back to me for real."

"And you?"

She stared at him with trapped eyes. "What else can I do? I was born and raised to be a powerful, wealthy man's calendar girl and hold his cigar."

"It's not a joke anymore," Marc said.

"It's for real," she said. She cried some more. "There is a whole history there between me and him that you don't know about. It's life. Don't understand it. Just live it."

"Like you're doing."

She stared blankly, looking swollen.

"Like your life is a runaway train and you have no idea where it's going."

"I made my choice."

"Yes."

"You'll find someone young and beautiful. You deserve a nice young girl."

"We could be married. I can see it."

She shook her head. "I'm not meant for you."

"So I'm not meant for you," he said. "*Très bien.* What can I do? Nothing. I accept this fate."

She nodded. "We leave for Vancouver straight from JFK. I won't be back." She cried unrestrainedly.

He sat beside her, took her in his arms, and found her stiff and cool toward him. She was no longer his. She no longer wanted him either. She belonged with Jérôme—holding his cigar in that commercial showing off his golf stroke, his hard smile and businesslike eyes, his winning fist on a cocked hip.

Don't mess with Jérôme the Man.

She rose and paced away, with her arms folded defensively before her like a fortress rampart, off limits to him.

"I was going to pack everything and go to Australia."

"What?"

She nodded miserably. "I was going to beg him to take me back."

So that's how it is.

Léopold Montblé sorrowfully patted Marc Fontbleu on the back in a flickering old blue and black and gray movie.

She paced up and down. "But why? I sort of won, didn't I? He's coming back here."

Marc rose and rubbed his hands together briskly. "I'm going to grab my things."

"I already packed your bag for you. It's by the door," she said as if he were a taxi driver who'd come to collect her heart for a ride to the airport and then *finis.*

She put her iced tea aside and rose unsteadily. He suspected she had had a drink. She put her hands on his shoulders and he smelled a faint tang of gin, but she was entirely lucid. Her eyes glowed—a little sad, and deeply grateful in an entirely summary sort of way.

Are you going to hand me a dollar tip too?

Marc resolved to end this in a graceful way. He'd fall apart later, but that was then and this was now. "Good luck."

She gave him an awkward hug. "You too, Marc Léopold Montblé Fontbleu. Write a lot of painful, passionate love poetry. You know I don't even read much." She eyed him compassionately. "It was swell. This was the most wonderful time of my life."

He touched her elbows but did not offer to embrace her. "I think it's for the best. Léopold Montblé wasn't doing so well. Neither were you, I guess."

"I'll never need to have another affair. You've given me everything I'll ever need. I'll never forget you." She burst into tears and pressed her face against his chest. Her tears were hot and salty, as true tears of relief from anguish should be.

He embraced her, tasting her ocean salt on his own lips.

She pulled away, composed herself, sat on the couch. She blew her nose and wiped her eyes with a hankie.

Already, he stood at the door, holding his grip bag.

"Look," she said, "it's snowing outside."

"Oh geez." Sure enough, through the uncurtained windows, he saw thick gobs of snowflakes plummeting suddenly in the early hours of a blizzard. How was this possible?

"Where are you going?" she asked.

"Home to Créteil. I don't have an apartment in the city any more."

"How will you get there?"

He shook his head. "Walk? The trains don't run as far as the Lake this hour. Can you believe this merde?" He walked across the room and looked out a window overlooking the street below. Cars outside were covered in the first flakes of virginal snow, which glittered under street lamps obscured by more flakes dropping like silent rocks. "It's a damn blizzard."

"You're leaving?" she asked in a thin, high voice.

Absurd question.

"What else am I going to do? We just split up, remember?"

"We didn't split up. We will love each other forever." She rose and glided close. She put her hands flat against his chest as if they were dancing. "Where will you stay?"

"With Jack and Aurora out in Créteil for a while until I get on my feet. He invited me. I'll make it brief, not to be a burden. Back to square one. At least I'm not moving back with mom and dad."

"Honey." She laid her cheek against him. "Please. Stay the night. I'll be driving to the airport. Three in the morning is not time to bust in on your friends."

"I can't. I have to get out of here." This was the past. He was ready for the future. Every moment he spent here, tearing away, was another rip in the fabric of his heart and soul. Time and fate were taking the book of Léopold Montblé and ripping it apart, page by torn page, letting the papers flutter like confetti to the winds.

"I'll tell you what," she said. She patted him resolutely on the chest with one palm. "I have the Porsche outside. I'll drive you to your friends' house on my way to the airport."

"Tonight?"

"Now," she said. "I'll get an early start. It's like oh-dark-thirty now, and half-past-late."

Marc helped her carry a few things down to the car.

"Everything will be taken care of by my family. All I need is to carry a few bags. The car will be picked up at the airport and taken to one of our homes."

They dressed warmly. She made sure the gas stove was off, and everything shipshape before she locked the door and slipped the key under the mat on the upstairs landing.

Holding hands, they skipped down the stairs together, out the front door, down the snowy steps where sweet air like fresh bread filled their nostrils.

"You look so cute," he said. "I didn't know you looked so cute in mittens."

She smiled like a sixth-grader as she waggled her wheat-speckled knitted porpoise fin mittens before gripping the steering wheel. "I like to look cute for you, my poet." She wore a knitted cap, the military ski jacket, corduroy pants, and suede boots with fake fur trip around the top.

She started the car and gripped the wheel.

"You think you can drive on snow?"

"Watch me," she said. The tip of her tongue stuck out of one corner of her mouth as she turned the wheel. Looking all around, she navigated into the snowy street. "I won't scare you too much."

"I'm not scared at all," he said. He put his arm around her, and laid a hand on her thigh as she drove down the street. She headed toward the Seine, from where she'd navigate with GPS until she reached Charles de Gaulle International Airport—after a quick detour to Créteil. Odd that Jack had chosen to relocate to their old home town, when his parents and sister had moved to Thiais.

"You are making me wet," she said, and patted Marc's hand lovingly with her thick woollen mitten. Snow fell thickly as they crawled along the Peripheral Boulevard that circled central Paris. Heavy fists of snow flew against the window. It was cold, dry snow. She had the windshield heater blowing, and the hot air kept the glass warm so that the snow melted as it hit. The windshield wipers worked steadily, beating a rhythm, left and right, pushing the white stuff out of the way. The rubber blades kept cutting wet, melting little splatters of water away to either side.

Not long after, they came to a familiar exit in Créteil. She sailed slowly and carefully down the ramp, curving around, to reach the wet, glistening street below. Snow plowing trucks had already made one pass here, and the street was lightly fuzzed over between tall banks of piled snow.

"You'll have to give me directions."

"Just go the way you're going."

"I want a nice kiss goodnight when I drop you off."

He said, "I'd take the ride for just one stolen kiss goodbye."

She smiled. "I was hoping you would care. Because I care. Léopold Montblé—I want to be sure you're going to be all right."

He held held her slender waist in both hands. "One last time."

She seemed suddenly shy. "Really?"

He kissed her earlobe. In a short time, it would be over. He'd never see her again. It was best not to say anything out loud.

"You know," she said mysteriously. "I could use a quickie."

"Here in the car?"

She shook her head. "Too many snow plows and cops on the road. I'd hate to think someone would check on us to see if we're in trouble and find us, you know—*derelicto.*"

"In flagrante," he said. "*Mucho erecto.*"

"Look in the back seat."

"Huh?" He twisted around and pawed in the dark with both hands. "Suitcases. A pack."

"No pack. Open it."

He did. A sleeping bag popped out and unrolled. "Wow, that looks warm."

"It's down, made for mountain climbing. Nobody will notice if we duck behind the house for a short while, if we stay quiet."

"And you don't yell or moan," he said.

She laughed excitedly. "Just stuff my briefs in my mouth."

"We'll suck on them together," he said. "We'll salivate like two dogs as we pull them apart."

"Wow-wow-wow!" she barked. Then she said very softly, "Touch me. Get me ready."

"After all—" he started to say. After all, they were still lovers until the last melancholy wink of red tail lights when she drove away on his street, and that would be the definitive end.

After all.

He touched her, and she let him, eagerly. He felt as though a hundred years of discarded history had just risen in a glad and merciful resurgence, begging binding like some final and overdue book of poems by Léopold Montblé.

ONE YEAR AFTER THEY MET

Le Fin au Debut

End at the Beginning

Chapter 35.

Marc Fontbleu and Emma Delors made love in the snow. The bluish light of the street lamps illumined spreading fans of glacial snow currying among suburban houses. His friends slept inside, blissfully unaware, as did the neighbors in their houses. This was a quiet suburban street where nothing much ever happened, aside from births, marriages, more births, and eventually deaths, in an ongoing cycle that had no beginning or end.

Together in her sleeping bag, they snuffled and giggled, moaned and cried together. He pounded her and she pulled him down for more. She bit his shoulder to stifle her cries. He shouted into her breasts before enjoying them with his mouth. She offered him her nipples and he sucked like a puppy while his hot dog relished her bun.

Afterward, they chased exhilarated over the snow fields, throwing snowballs and chasing each other on the slopes around the Lac de Créteil.

They stashed her sleeping bag in the car. He fetched steaming coffees from a diner near the highway—the road that would now take Emma forever away to climes far out west, where the Pacific Ocean glowed long after dark with the setting sun; where Jérôme Delors could teach and write about his discoveries in prehistory; where Emma could hold his cigar and look stunning at faculty parties, as she had been born and bred to do.

Sipping gingerly at their hot coffees, they leaned on a railing near a factory-loading ramp. The world was coated white. Their whispers and giggles were muffled by the white coating.

"I hope you'll be happy together," he said tenderly.

"We'll make a go of it—a whole new start." She held her coffee as they stood shoulder to shoulder, looking over passing cars. One second you saw white headlights, then you saw red taillights, and then each car vanished forever, not to be seen again in his life.

There must be no regrets. Only memories.

"I'll do the same here." He tried to stay upbeat. "That's life. A love affair, and we move on."

She shrugged, laughing. "Jérôme is still trying to shed his winter coat. That is, he isn't so sure of himself. That is something I discovered. Our problems won't be over in a heartbeat. That's why I wanted to exchange this little going-away present with you. To tell you how much I love you, I'll cherish you forever, and I'll never forget you."

"I will never forget you."

"I will try to help him. It will take time. He was hurt badly in Australia. Some broad named Lemony or Melancholy grabbed his cigar and ran away with it."

"Emma, while there is still time—just once more—I could never love anyone in my life, in my future, as I love you."

"Shush. I love you too. We shared so much."

Every moment, every gesture, was important. Marc and Emma stacked their styro cups steaming, buried them cup-in-cup in the intimate but merciless snow. Then they walked back arm in arm through the snowfields.

They walked back to the car. She drove him to Jack's place. He'd sleep on the couch until something better came along. Emma parked a block away, pointing the car at the highway entrance. "I'll walk you home," she said.

They walked arm in arm, trudging in the deepening snow. A plow rattled past. Its front blade scraped the street and threw walls of whiteness to the side.

Cars whispered on the distant highway. The night was filled with stars, with sounds of fog horns, with the familiar and loving sounds of a close and unencumbered wind. Her hair flew, rimed with frost. Her smile was white, her cheeks were red, and her eyes glowed as if she'd spent hours skiing.

"Are you going to make it?" Marc asked.

She squeezed his elbow. "Yes. I promise. Don't worry about me. And don't forget me. But move on."

They hugged long and hard. She cried again. He sobbed, touching her drippy blue lips. It was cold, but they hardly noticed.

They parted at the top of a rise.

After one final long, tender kiss, and a last failing grasp of two hands reaching for each other but pulling apart—she hurried off, leaving her lone, solitary track in the wasteland of snow.

He watched as she ran to that familiar dark plum Porsche.

He waved after her once more.

She was a tiny figure under a bluish streetlight.

He blew her a kiss.

She stood under that bluish streetlight, waving. She blew him a kiss from far away.

He waited until she got into the car and started its engine.

Moments later, she tooted the car's horn. Then, on sturdy snow tires, the Porsche moved strongly away amid the feathery snowdrifts. All that remained of this love story begun in the Latin Quarter was memory—and a gold bracelet sunk forever in green water.

That's it.

The suburbs were quiet save for a distant humming of tires on the highway.

Forever.

Wind sighed among sleepy suburban houses. Fog horns muttered in forlorn, haunting groans across the water.

She's gone.

240. Piano

My thoughts played piano
long and softly from your eyes.
I could have put your apples in a jar
but there were places to stay
(while you chafed to go)
and you left
(you said you would)
me in poetic triumph

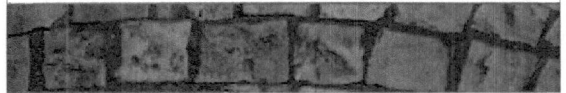

Chapter 36.

Days, weeks later...

Call it fate, fortune, luck, whatever—one day, while Marc was working part-time in a stationery store near Montmartre, a bearded intellectual in a black suit and brown motoring cap came strolling in and asked about journals.

The store was one of those with a small front on a side street, in a tiresomely, unoriginally ornate stone building, with a tiny Belle Époque shop window. This was in the Seventh Arrondissement, off the Avenue Duquesne. Inside, the store was narrow, but ran deep into the guts of the building to a small cobblestone courtyard surrounded by high windows and stone walls. The store was dry and bright, but in the courtyard the atmosphere was mossy and damp, since little sunlight ever penetrated there—a fitting metaphor for Marc Fontbleu's soul these days. Dominating the courtyard was a dark blue steel dumpster, next to a pile of debris including discarded empty boxes. Marc made many trips out there while accepting incoming shipments from a small gray panel truck that backed in nearly every day with deliveries. It was a new venture, something safer than taxi driving or bartending, and more sheltered from the elements than lawn mowing. *Progress.*

"What sorts of journals?" Marc asked while straining to move boxes of printer paper around.

The man, whose early patches of graying hair (not gray, but graying) had Marc put him at about forty, affected a dreamy, desperate look. "It's the tactile thing. I write poetry, and need just the right tools—good pen, good notebook—to make the art work."

Marc felt a knot in his stomach. "Are you a published poet?"

"I edit a poetry review," said the man. "So yeah, I'm a published poet."

"I've been a struggling poet all my life," Marc said, continuing to shift heavy boxes around.

"Ah, then you understand." The man had gray eyes and a sincere face.

Suddenly roused from indolence by thoughts of jazzy, smoky word riffs, Marc set a box down. "I can show you some." It was going beyond the call of duty. He was stock boy, not sales clerk. For that, you had two ladies who wore gray lab coats and radiated expertise.

Marc was glad not to be driving a cab out on slick winter streets, in drizzle, fighting traffic, dealing with unreasonable fares. So he didn't mind working in the cramped shoebox of a store whose origins, like so many nooks and crannies of central Paris, still had a foothold in the 1800s. It was downright dreary, unless you considered the alternatives, and thus the optimist in Marc was fully employed. "This way," he told the motoring-cap.

They threaded their way down the long intestines of the store, climbing around stacked papers and colorful but dusty displays, always under an overly bright strip of luminescent ceiling lights that made the shadows and corners underneath excessively dark by contrast. They passed the awkwardly, jealously smiling (not smiling; just teeth) two ladies, one of whom was relatively young and dark, the other older and gray. "Here we are." Mark extended a pointing hand toward a display of writing journals propped up against a far back wall.

"Oh my god," said the beard. "I'm in heaven."

"Let me know if you need anything else."

"You've been a great help." The hat paused. "I think I'll be a customer here forever." His eyes glistened as he took in the rows of delicious, artsy looking leather and cloth bound books.

"Those are my favorites," Marc said. "Check out the ones that look like ledgers. You know, green, official looking, but they are simply ruled for a tranquil mind."

"My name is Alain Bouvier, my friend. And you?"

"Marc Fontbleu."

Bouvier extended a sincere paw. "Thank you."

"My pleasure."

"You should come visit us at the magazine sometime."

Marc shrugged. "Sure. What is it?" He asked half-heartedly. He would have been thrilled, even three or four months ago. After the incidents in Strasbourg, not to mention a lifetime of rejection in Paris, he had become cautious, like a wounded animal, or a feral cat. And the pall of his loss lay upon him, that last aching month or so, memory of the woman whom he had fallen in love with. *Emma.*

"Here, I'll show you." There was a small book stand against a nearby wall, and Alain climbed with light-brown leather shoes under gray trousers (what a mismatch, Marc thought) toward the stand. The upper section held a rack of books, while the lower section was a magazine stand. In-between was a row of quarterlies bound in softly colored cardstock. Among these journals was his, titled *Le Pingouin*

Urbain (City Penguin). The cover motif included a neo-absurdist penguin looking out across city lights at night, maybe doing the puffin bar scene.

Alain clambered back to the other side of the narrow store to fawn over the many beautiful journals. Marc, meanwhile, picked up a copy of *LPU* and idly flipped through its slick, glossy pages.

Moments later, Marc's blood froze in his veins. He could not believe what he saw. There was a poem of about sixteen lines tucked in between a scathing review of some romantic novel and a commercial for (no, not cigarillos). The poem resonated in Marc's head, and he liked its familiar rhythms, until he realized with pounding heart and sick stomach that it was one he had written. How was this possible? He sat down hard on a box of stationery and held the magazine open with both hands.

Alain was darting from one side of the rack to the other, deciding whether to pick the ledger style journal with gray cover and faintly green interior, or a merlot-red leather bound with speckled interior pages.

Marc could barely speak, so tightly he gritted his teeth. "You pick these?"

"I'm the editor, yes."

"And they are submitted to you?"

"Yes."

"But you pick them?"

Alain, sensing Marc's fury, stopped. "Well, no. They are chosen by a committee. That way we keep the process honest and objective."

Marc shook the magazine so it rattled, as if that would cause the truth to tumble out in puzzle pieces. "This poem titled *Philosopher King.*"

"Yes?"

"I wrote it."

Alain laughed uncomprehendingly, as if Marc had made a joke. "You aren't Denis Resnil, are you?"

Marc shook his head. "No, I am Marc Fontbleu, the guy who drove to Strasbourg to deliver his book of poems to the gatekeepers of mediocrity."

Alain became huffy. "Look here, friend."

Marc felt a tear of rage in each eye, as if he had been mugged on the street, and now the cops thought he was at fault. *Punish the victim again?*

Alain stood before him, clutching his choice (the merlot) under one elbow-patch jacketed arm. "You are stating that you wrote a poem we published?"

"Yes. This is—"

"Excuse me, I don't have time for this." Irately, Alain Bouvier stormed past Marc.

Marc watched in shocked, almost disabled fury as the editor strode in a huff down the long, narrow aisle toward the front of the store. There, Bouvier threw the journal on the elevated glass counter, behind which the store owner (old Gautier, a balding man in his eighties, with a high weak voice and hanging jowls) sat waiting. Bouvier hopped around, extracting his wallet from a rear pocket, while staring daggers in Marc's direction.

Chapter 37.

Marc had a long, bitter walk home that evening through dark streets crying with rain. Slivers of rain streaked through city neon like icicles, making silent comet impacts in quicksilver puddles. Marc wore his rain slicker hood up and marched with his hands in his pockets, wanting to strangle someone. Or throw himself off a bridge. Or leave Paris with its injustices, never to return. Maybe hitch-hike across Europe and find work in Poland or Slovakia, tending old castles or polishing war cannons in a museum. Anything but continue in this cruel, mocking existence.

These days, he'd found a tiny room let by an elderly widow by Montparnasse. This was in a pleasant alley off the Rue Boissonade, in a brick apartment building with many young professionals and couples working at the Croix Rouge or other concerns in the neighborhood.

He lay on his cot in the tiny room (which had no window, unlike his upper story dove's nest in the Rue Monge, now history along with the rest of his past (Emma). The package of poems had come back via slow mail from Livres Charleville in Strasbourg. Now, nursing a bottle of red wine from which he took short, angry, cutting sips at intervals, he studied the manuscript. He still had the wrapper (in the trash; he retrieved it; luckily he rarely emptied the can). There were the notes about—what was it?—genuine and classical and sincere, that fool had scribbled in his preposterous and pompous style. *Careful. Must not leap to conclusions.*

Was the thief Monsieur Mézières? Or Madame Chalmers? Or some lurk-a-clerk? Or a night-shift cleaning lady who wrote free verse and smoked pot in art classes? Anything was possible.

Where did you go about stolen poems? The police? Did they have an office of poetry detectives? Was it poecide, across the hall from homicide?

Marc almost threw the manuscript across the room, but changed his mind. He hugged it to him and cried softly, with tears rolling down his cheeks. It was like hugging someone he loved, who had been hurt, or killed, or suffered a tragedy. Swigging from the bottle, he stroked his book to comfort it, and himself.

* * * *

The offices of *Pingouin Urbain* lay in a nice part of the city. Everything about the neighborhood, the building, and the offices had that urban chic about it. This was something other than students. It wasn't strictly about fashion, or money, or glitz, so what was it? It was about a certain way of living, was the only thing he could figure as he rode the elevator up to the eighth floor. There, he emerged with pounding heart and cold hands, clutching his manuscript.

The lobby was small but plush, with thick carpeting. And it smelled faintly of carpeting, cleaners, light perfume, and maybe a tinge of bouillon or something. Marc was so nervous that the smell made him nauseous.

A circle of greenish-milky glass screens atop an elliptical half wall shielded *Lou*'s offices from the lobby. He entered through a double door and found himself at a receptionist's desk.

"Monsieur?" asked the busy young African-Parisian woman, very dark, very pretty, with a black woolly sheath provocatively rounded over a pert rear sitting in her typist chair.

"I've come to see Alain Bouvier. My name is Argle Glavadier." He was afraid to say his real name for fear that Bouvier would not see him. Or if he were bold and said he was Denis Resnil, would that lead to unforeseen complications including maybe being led out in handcuffs? Better to improvise.

"What is your name, Sir?" She paused, one hand on the phone.

"Argle Glavadier. I write reflatier domalicains."

She frowned in puzzlement. "I'm sorry."

"Reflatier domalicains," Marc repeated stolidly, giving his manuscript a shake under one elbow while he kept both hands shoved deep in his pockets.

The young woman, still frowning, spoke on the phone while sitting back, arching her back. "Alain, there is a gentleman here to see you named R. Gargle or something." *Pause.* "Yes, he says he writes blap-something *Americains*." *Pause.* "Very well, I'll tell him." She placed the receiver on the switchhook, and looked up at Marc. "Monsieur Bouvier says he'll be out in a moment."

She resumed her typing, while Marc stood by feeling sick. He must go through with this.

A door opened with a squeak somewhere, followed by the sound of soft footsteps.

Alain Bouvier, minus the hat and jacket, stood stiffly in a doorway, regarding Marc with fury. "Of all the nerve."

Marc held up his manuscript. "Evidence."

"What?"

"Evidence. I can prove my case."

Alain looked white and sick. His gray eyes refracted disbelief. He looked at Marc the way Marc felt about whoever had stolen his poem. "What if I call the police?" he said in a small voice.

"Good. Then maybe someone there will listen with an open mind."

Alain's eyes filled with calculations as he regarded the folder in Marc's hands.

"I can prove my case."

Alain licked his lips. "It's happened before. Come on in and show me."

Marc followed him down a narrow, dusky hallway lined with photos of plants.

They entered a modest office with a small desk, surrounded by towering bookshelves. "Show me." Alain left the door open, as if he might need to call for help in case Marc turned out to be a violent madman.

Bouvier extracted a pair of thick, dark reading glasses from his pocket and put them on.

Feeling from Bouvier continued walls of hostility and disbelief, alternating with moments of sorrow, Marc laid his book on the desk and explained. "I have been writing since I was a kid. I keep a journal, often decorating my poems with clippings or drawings or whatever. Here is the book I submitted last summer at Charleville in Strasbourg. Here are the comments written by two or three of the editors there. And here is the poem *Philosopher King* in my book."

Marc waited as Bouvier examined these things.

"My god." Bouvier whipped his glasses off and looked at Marc. "The poems came from Strasbourg."

"I am not lying," Marc said.

Bouvier walked around his desk and began digging in a wastepaper basket. After a moment or two, he held high a manila envelope covered with franked stamps. "Denis Resnil gives an address in Oberhausbergen, a suburb of Strasbourg."

As Bouvier stared at him with trembling lip and distraught eyes, Marc said: "You might want to check what town Chalmers or Mézières live in. They are two of the editorial staff I saw there. Which is not to say—I lay awake all night thinking about this— maybe some copy boy or delivery man stole my work. Anything is possible."

"Sit down." Bouvier himself sat down heavily, with a long sigh. "I have a feeling you are telling the truth. I am sorry I was rude."

"Find the truth and I won't hold it against you."

Bouvier nodded. "I owe you as much. I mean, why would anyone lie about a poem? We pay twenty Euros. It's not worth the energy wasted."

"I give my life, writing this stuff. It's my energy, my passion, my life." He added: "It is worth everything to me."

Bouvier nodded. "It's about the prestige. I've had two other instances of this. I can almost feel the symptoms." Suddenly he popped up like a cork in water. "Wait a minute." While Marc watched, full of stomach knots, Bouvier rushed to a table in a corner that was piled high with documents. "The mail," Bouvier said. "I remember seeing something." He shuffled through stacks and rows and lines of envelopes and folders. "Here it is. I knew I'd seen this." He grabbed a buff envelope and carried it to his desk. It was already open, so he easily extracted the folded sheet inside. He muttered as he looked through several sheets of paper: "This arrived yesterday. Cover letter... poem... poem..." He looked suddenly and sharply up at Marc and said: "In your book there, do you happen to have a poem titled *Café Macho*?"

"Two of them," Marc said.

Bouvier read out loud: "Your string has fallen, pharaonic dancing girl, I see you tan skin in the flute music..."

Marc found the page and joined him, so they read together: "...in the liquor, the dusky lounge, the air-conditioned dance place..."

Bouvier stopped reading, and Marc continued while Bouvier silently stared at the submitted poem before him: "...with women to pick from, pastiche of loves that might have been were it not for..."

Marc looked up, stopped, and Bouvier picked up the reading from Marc: "What tender celebration if you were you and I were I but here we are all the should be, the would be, and may be..."

Then they read together in one voice: "She walks out to accept this dance,, her eyes are black and fierce, her beauty is terrible, ringing, like an army with banners flying... She deigns to accept his embrace from the ninety-ninth shadow of the man she gave her soul..."

Bouvier slapped his hand down on the paper before him, as if commanding silence. The poem continued, but they were both silent, looking at each other. "I believe you," said Alain Bouvier. "How can I make this up to you?"

Marc stared at him, feeling frozen. He wanted to say *publish my work, give me credit,* but no words came from his mouth. Of all the moments to be paralyzed.

"I am so sorry," Alain Bouvier said quietly. "I can imagine the pain you feel."

Yes. O god yes.

Bouvier continued in a small, steely voice. "I once had a short story stolen. I had given it to a teacher to read in my first year of college in Créteil. That teacher told me he had lost it. Then, months later, it showed up in a literary magazine in Toul of all places. It was submitted by a fellow teacher, who had stolen it from my teacher, and submitted it to a magazine when he transferred to Toul, never thinking it would find its way back to Paris."

"What did you do?" Marc asked in a suffocating voice.

"I thought about driving to Toul and beating him to death with a club in the parking lot. Then I gained my senses and wrote a letter to the dean at his college. I got a reply back from the dean's office, saying to me that 'there is a special place in hell for liars and thieves like you.'"

"That must have hurt."

"It did."

"Then what did you do?"

"There was nothing I could do."

"You just let it go?"

"I learned that the man who stole my short story committed suicide a short time later. He threw himself under a train. Must have been a gory mess."

"Why?"

Bouvier shook his head, with glazed eyes looking into the past. "I think he hated himself."

"So he was already in that place in hell."

Bouvier nodded. "I placed that same story in a niche specialty magazine in Marseille under a different title. Circulation was about 500, I believe." He laughed. "Big deal, huh?"

"Not enough to kill one's self over."

"Nothing is." Bouvier sat back and steepled his fingers. "Would you like to work for me?"

"What?"

"Yeah. Work for me, as an editor. You are a very talented young guy."

"Oh my god." Marc felt like kneeling on the floor.

"I can pay you a little more than they do at the stationery shop."

"Yes. Yes. Yes."

"And I will publish your poetry."

"Oh my god."

"You deserve a break, after what these people have done to you."

"Who is the thief?"

"Mézières lives at that address in Oberhausbergen. That tells me enough."

Marc thought about it. "If we were poetry detectives, we'd be sure we have a case."

"A very convincing case," Bouvier said. He rose and extended a hand. "Will you please forgive me?"

Marc rose and accepted. "I am honored." *And still hurt, but I'll get over it.*

"I am starving. Have you had lunch?"

"No, but I have to hurry back to the stationer's."

Bouvier made a dismissive gesture. "I'll call old Gautier and tell him you are doing some work for me. I've known him for years. He'll take my word for it that you are in good hands."

"Wow, thanks."

"I owe you. Let me buy you lunch."

"I am honored," Marc whispered, and it was all that he was able to stammer forth.

Alain laughed as he clapped Marc on the shoulder on the way out. "They say imitation is the highest form of flattery, but I'd say stealing your poetry is even higher."

Marc laughed along but couldn't help adding: "Yeah, while they tell you they have no use for your poetry. It's genuine and classical and sincere, but there is no market for it, and who would ever want to read material from an unknown like me?"

Chapter 38.

One spring day, Marc took a long lunch break and walked along the Boulevard Saint-Michel in the direction of the Seine. It was the first real sunny, warm day of the season, and he was in the mood for a long flânerie, an aimless stroll in the real Parisian tradition. He was also a little bit hungry, and entertained a half dozen possibilities to stop for a quick bite.

He came to the intersection where everything was named Saint-Michel, and crossed from the Place over the Quai (wharf) to the Pont (bridge). Staying on the Left Bank with the Seine at his left, he walked briskly eastward on the Quai du Saint-Michel, toward the Petit Pont (Little Bridge) where it turns into Quai du Montebello, across the street from the little Rue de la Bûcherie and the famous Shakespeare & Company English-language bookstore. At the intersection were some of the usual bookstalls attached to the railings, overlooking the green flowing river with spring blossoms floating on it.

There, amid a light crowd of tourists and locals, he saw a tall, striking dark-haired youthful woman standing by one of the quai-side bookstalls, looking at a magazine she held open with both hands while cradling a black leather purse under one elbow. She wore a navy blue business suit, whose sheath skirt came to just above the knees. Her legs were her most striking feature—long, perfect scissors in modest night-sky blue nylons that revealed a shimmer of pale skin. She stood on medium matte-black heels, and wore her glossy dark hair in smooth bunches like shiny purple-black plums clustered on a tree. Every time she moved her slim neck, her curls bounced. And there were small beaten-silver earrings hidden in that thicket. Her face was slightly averted, and looking down at the magazine with poised, elegant attentiveness.

Every man in the area noticed her, as did a lot of jealous (and a few admiring, even attracted) women. She was who every woman wanted to be—that statue come to life, like those that stand around the city in Classical poses, an Athena holding apples in one hand and a warrior's spear in the other.

Marc could not take her eyes off of her (she was about his height) as he walked past her, about eight meters away. Where had he seen that woman before? He was just about to enter the Petit Pont to cross over onto the Île-de-la-Cité (City Island) with its Notre Dame Cathedral and other landmarks. His head was twisted around, and he bumped into someone who was also staring at this woman; he and the other man mumbled *excusez-mois* while circling around each other without taking their eyes off of her.

More than one hoot or whistle could be heard, rudely slicing the air, including a cowboy cattle call from a passing car full of drunken young French soldiers.

As he passed by, Marc took one last look and thought: *she looks familiar.*

The girl with the magazine was Danielle Poncelet.

Chapter 39.

Marc did a ninety degree twist and sauntered toward her. "Hey."

She glanced up from her magazine, just as another cat-call sounded. "Save me."

He rushed to her side and offered his arm.

She slipped her strong, thin arm through his and pulled at him with surprising energy. "Where did you come from?" she asked.

"I could ask you the same question. You are look different somehow."

She laughed, old Dani, those wry lips darkened with a deep red, almost chocolate lip gloss. "Yeah, I brushed my teeth this morning. Does it show when I smile?"

"You ate spinach. It's all over your teeth. That's why everyone is yelling."

"Oh stop it. I did not." She gave his arm a yank, and at the same time ran two fingers over her teeth to check for spinach. "You are terrible, Marc Fontbleu."

He gave her a rough tug in turn, jock that she was, with a smile like the sun. "Where have you been the past few months?"

"Busy, same as you." By now, they clung together, arm in arm, walking toward the square in front of Notre Dame Cathedral. The bells up in the twin Gothic towers were just starting to clear their throats and tinkle, in preparation for a noon-time *Ave Maria* and carollade. In the center of the parvis or walking zone before the cathedral is a point-zero marker on which all roads across France are calibrated. They sought a bench to sit on along the rim of the square, with the Gothic façade looming nearby.

"So why are you different? You are dressed like a fashion model."

"I am a fashion model."

"No."

"Yes. I am getting a few gigs here and there. But today I was interviewing for a teaching job."

"I've been so out of touch. You finished your degree?"

"And my teaching credential. I will be starting to teach gymnastics at the high school in Thiais."

"I am so proud of you."

"Things are going well," she said without total conviction. A cloud passed over her gleaming eyes. "And you?" There was something missing; her eyes looked strongly needy, actually imploring. He put an arm around her, feeling her warmth, the strength yet softness of that long, finely tooled body. He inhaled an opiate whiff of her faint perfume, which seemed almost tropical amid this breezy, sunny spring day.

"Long story. Can I buy you a little drink or something?"

"A coffee would be just perfect. How about you?" He thought of a restaurant back in the Latin Quarter.

"Coffee with you would be perfect."

She clung tightly to his arm. As he started to rise, she pulled back on him.

"What is it?" He regarded her with concern.

She seemed to be struggling for words. Her lips quivered and her face had an urgent cast, but the words would not come out. Her eyes were dark and huge. Her heart lay open before him.

He got the message, deep in his soul, before she could say a word.

She looked terrified.

The great and medium and small bells of Notre Dame did the talking. Rocking and pounding on their anchors, they thundered forth a wondrous music that shook the sky and the earth around Marc and Dani. Their power was such that the sidewalk seemed to roll, like in an earthquake. Relentlessly, the bells clamored in a single river to drown out all rational thought. That was their purpose—to sing to heaven. Sound, golden sound, poured around them in a flood like their emotions.

What happened seemed to be in slow motion—two bees floating toward each other underwater in a jar of sunlit honey. That is how slowly time seemed to move in that pounding sound all around. Dani's features were a motion picture of honesty and sincerity. Words came from her sweet lips, in that soft, narrow *gamine* face, touched up with light makeup and cherry-dark chocolate lipstick. Her eyes overflowed with emotion. She held his arm in a death grip—and she was one girl who had the strength to arm-wrestle a man if she wanted to.

"I am so happy to have found you," Marc yelled.

She looked into his eyes, shaking her head, and yelled back: "I am not going to let you go."

"Please don't," he yelled back. "Here, let me help." He took her into his arms, and she flowed toward him eagerly, rising upward to blend into him. They were like the Marne and the Seine, flowing together near Bercy. They had known each other since childhood, but this was the first time they had ever really kissed, much less even thought about it.

They were not who they had been even a few months ago. He was a man, and she was a woman. They had found each other at point-zero, starting point of all roads.

Paris is famous for the sight of a young man and woman kissing obliviously and passionately in springtime, on a bench, in the square before Notre Dame Cathedral, or along the river walks under the bridges where barges pass with a whisper of water and a faint loudspeaker voice talking to rapt passengers about the sights and the scenery (including lovers).

As they sat on the bench, most passers-by barely took notice of them, while a few admiring faces shone toward them in the sunlight, and a few eyes blinked at something special—a handsome young man in a business suit, and a gorgeous young woman so elegantly dressed and so poised—there was no doubt that it was springtime in Paris.

She turned out to be a lush, lively kisser, with a warm tongue that filled his mouth and made love with his tongue. He was assertive, but she gave as much as she took. She pressed home with body language to help her tongue. This girl, no woman, could wear a man out. But he was a poet and he was strong. He held her to him and could not get enough of her, while the bells made the sidewalk and the bench and the air around them rock with divine and deafening music.

As the bells grew tired and reached the end of their hymn, so did Marc and Dani.

* * * *

"I'm embarrassed," Dani said as they strolled back across the Pont au Double foot bridge.

"Why?" He felt languid, almost ready for a nap, after all that warm honey. He was still filled with her warmth and love and affection. They kept their arms between them tightly locked.

"Because I spilled my soul. I never do that. I let everything loose."

"Me too, you goose."

"I was terrified that you might not understand."

"I feel like I just woke up from a thousand year sleep, and I see the sun for the first time."

"Am I the sun?"

"You are. And the moon, and the stars."

They walked in silence a few moments along the shade in the winding little Rue du Fouarre.

She shook her head, never letting go of him. "Who are we?"

"Adam and Eve."

"Yes. You are such a poet. Will you love me?"

"Forever."

"Honest?"

"On my heart and soul. Would you like me to kneel before you?"

She gave him a shake. "I don't want you getting your nice pants dirty."

He stopped with one of the biggest sighs ever sighed, and held her to him in both arms. She put her strong arms around the small of his back, and clung to him with her cheek pressed against his chest. They didn't need to say anything, but held each other for several minutes.

An eternity.

Chapter 40.

He took her to George & Harry's Restaurant, with its old oak-paneled walls and leaded glass windows, a few of which had secular stained glass motifs. The tables were heavy oak benches, but the seats were wooden with arm rests and comfortable. There was no rain riveting down the windows outside (ancient history, another planet). Instead, spring blossoms sighed in a sweet wind.

They sat closely together, so their thighs touched, and toyed with their coffees. He took her wrist, and turned it over to examine her long fingers, her lightly caramel skin, her dark merlot fingernail gloss that closely matched her lipstick.

She rested her cheek on his shoulder. "I feel as if I have known you all my life."

"You have," he said with a comradely grin.

She raised a hand and gripped his shoulder, beside her cheek, as if trying him on for size. "So I have. But not."

"What do you mean?"

"We are strangers, meeting for the first time."

He understood exactly what she meant, and could not agree more. And yet he teased: "What about the times we played in the back yard at your parents' house. How old were we?"

She kept her cheek on his shoulder. "Four. I think. Or three? You're the older man in my life." He was a year older, same age as her brother.

"Yes, and you were so proud of your little tea service."

"I think I served you guys sand." *Marc and her brother Jack.*

"Every kid had a sand pile, that fine powdery sand from the Créteil quarries left after they hauled gravel away."

So many memories: Kindergarten, grammar school, high school...

"I don't want to live in the past, Marc."

"No, I don't either. It's just—."

She straightened up, stirred her coffee, *ding-ding-ding*. "It's just so beautiful that we have been friends a whole lifetime, and now what?"

"I am in love with you, Dani."

"I am in love with you too, Marc. I think I have been for a long time."

"You were there the whole time, and I didn't see you."

"You were a real nuisance too."

"I know. I'm sorry."

"I forgive you." She pecked a kiss on his cheek. "Can I do that more often?"

"Oh would you please?" He took both her hands in his and looked deeply into her eyes. "I think I have to take you everywhere I go."

"I know what you mean, but we have our lives to live." She grinned. "We can't be glued together. Although I'm in a mood to be glued." She slipped an arm around him. "Glued to you, baby. Watch out."

"Tell me about your fashion modeling."

"Sure." She looked so poised and mature, and he was so proud of her. "I wasn't looking for anything. I was window-shopping at a store in the Passage Vivienne, and they had a sign asking for living mannequins. So I thought that was cool and went inside. I got a four-hour gig, standing perfectly still in the store window."

"With a few breaks, I hope."

"Fifteen minutes on, fifteen minutes off. But still—man, my feet hurt, and I had to soak in the tub that evening. Never again. But an agency called, and they said they needed a tall, thin forest-dark brunette with legs and all that. I was embarrassed because I'm not really, you know." She made voluptuousness motions with both cupped hands, dropping them from her chest.

"But they took you."

"Yes. They seem to like me. They keep asking me back for more photo shoots."

"They made a wise choice. I want to ask you back also."

She touched his nose with her fingertip, looking momentarily cross-eyed. "You call, I come. I am yours."

"And I am yours. You say, I do." He cleared his throat. "Within limits, of course."

"We'll split the housework. I hate doing dishes."

"I'll wash, you dry."

"Deal."

"So we are finally *fiancé* and *fiancée*, like you told the lady in the green stripes in the bakery."

"You noticed."

"I nearly dropped the cake."

"I'm surprised you didn't run away down the road."

He tried to recall. "Oh, I was aching about—."

"Miss Cigar."

"You know."

"Jack told me. We were both worried about you. A married woman, no less."

"I have had my adventure in life. No more."

"Me too."

"What do you mean?'

She looked rueful. "A married man."

"No."

"Yes. He's movie-star handsome, wealthy, and in love with himself."

"Not with you?"

She shrugged lightly, looking ruefully back into her recent past. "I met him at a dinner with some friends. He was like wow. Older man. Sweep me off my rockers. We made eye contact, and the rest was like going down the water slide at Paris Disney."

"I know the ride. I nearly fell off when I was about ten."

"You were always climbing outside the structure. It's a wonder you haven't fallen off the Eiffel Tower."

"Don't knock it. I'm exploring the insides of things for their secret meanings. I'm not just climbing around. I am a poet and an intellectual."

"I want you to read poetry to me while I soak in a hot tub."

"I want to be in the tub with you."

"My tub is your tub."

"Let's get together this evening."

"Absolutely. Come on," she said. "I have to get home and change for a photo shoot this afternoon. Then I'll be free."

They rose and walked together, almost one person so close were they, outside and several short blocks to where her little sports car was parked.

"You drive," she said, handing him the keys.

"I'll take that on many levels."

"I mean it on every level." Her look was transparent, clear, courageous, forceful, honest.

At a loss for words, choking with emotion, he held the passenger door open for her. She moved graciously, a living poem in her elegant suit. He closed the door gently, not to hurt her in any way.

Driving was funny. He laughed. "Hey."

"What?" she sat in the passenger seat, with her purse on her lap in both hands. She had the seat way back to allow room for her long body.

"The seat," he said. "I have to move it, sorry."

"Go ahead." She shrugged. "Why?"

"I just realized. You have longer legs than I do, but I am taller on top. So I have to pull the seat closer to the wheel, or my feet won't quite reach the pedals below. But I have to turn the mirror up, because you're sitting there looking upward more. When you drive, you'll have to shove the seat back so your legs will fit, and turn the mirror down so you can see behind you."

"We are a matching pair." She put her long arm over his shoulders, so that he delighted in seeing dark-red nail polish by his left ear. She scratched his cheek gently, lovingly, with her long nails. Thus they drove southeast toward Orly and Thiais, a familiar drive.

"You haven't told me much about why you are wearing a suit."

"My turn. Okay, I was working in a stationery shop not long ago."

"I'm so glad you stopped driving taxis and tending bar."

"And mowing lawns, but that's over with. I got tired of hassling with nasty taxi fares and traffic and all that. While I was in the bookstore, I met this man named Alain Bouvier, who runs a magazine." He didn't bother telling her that Alain had persuaded Mézières to resign from any positions of responsibility, like his editorship at Charleville, and his position as a judge in several important literary competitions; that, or face prosecution. Marc continued straightforward: "Long story short, Alain hired me as an assistant editor. They are going to issue a volume of my poetry next year, in a limited edition."

"I am so happy for you."

"Thanks. Me too. So I doubled my salary, not that it was much, and I have my own little office with a desk and books and all that."

"And a secretary?"

"Not yet."

"What do you do there every day?" She sounded honestly interested.

"I read submissions. I am a good line editor, so I help with grammar and spelling and usage before each month's issue goes to bed." To press, that meant. "I do whatever is needed to keep the show going, and I feel very much appreciated for the first time."

"I know *Le Pingouin Urbain*," she said. "I'm in it."

"No."

"Yes."

"No."

She nuzzled close with puckered lips and dramatic face. "I'm the slinky brunette with long legs in the little black dress, holding the guy's martini glass on page thirty of next month's issue while we're pretending to stand at a bar in Zanzibar or something. You can imagine why he's grinning and it's not about the drink."

"You're kidding me." *Holding the cigar?*

She laughed. "His name is Pierre, and he's a young pipsqueak studying medicine, premed. The glass had water in it, not vodka, and I poured it over his head when we were done. He chased me around the studio, and I punched him on the jaw."

"Not hard. I mean, you didn't k.o. him, did you?"

"Nah. It was all in fun. I wouldn't let him grab me either. That's for you and you alone."

"Seriously, I want to take you home and grab you."

"Eyes on the road. Truck coming."

"I see it."

"No, you're looking at my knees."

"I am. I can multi-process. I see the truck and the knees."

"Rhymes with trees, *mon cher. Attention.* So how did you manage to get the attention of this Monsieur—?"

"Bouvier. Actually, I have two poems being published in the next issue. We're kind of close together again, huh?"

"Everywhere we go, there we are." She gazed at him as if he were chocolate. "Oh Marc, I am so in love with you."

He wanted to say the same, but he choked up and bit his lip. He gave her a teary look and squeezed her hand; pulled it close (she let him, urged him) and he kissed her fingers, one by one. "How long did you know?"

"All my life," she said with total clarity. "I just didn't know that I knew."

He pulled up in the driveway at her parents' house in Thiais. Jack stood by a hedge, watering the lawn. Nearby sat his squeeze, Aurora. They waved. "I wonder if Jack is going to be surprised."

"No," she said. "I told him already."

"You knew."

She sat in the passenger seat, facing him, with one shoulder on the back of her seat, and her hands linked as if she were making a proposition (or a proposal). "Like I said."

Marc turned off the engine and sat back as if he'd been knocked out. "It's all clear now. At last. And this is forever."

"If you want it to be."

"I do."

"Then I'm yours."

"I'll take you."

She raised one hand, palm up, like policewoman stopping traffic. "Don't say it. Not yet. Save it for when you buy me a ring, Mr. Poet and Editor. My Prince Charming."

"I will need time to save money for it. I want to get you a nice diamond."

"We have time, baby. I'll wait. I'll be there for you." She added with a twinkle and a smile: "I'll hold your martini."

Come Visit The Author's Webplex

Read Free or Buy: www.galleycity.com
Main: www.johntcullen.com
Books About Paris: www.booksaboutparis.com
(a.k.a. Paris Bookshop)

❧ Thank you, *merçi*, and many more pleasant reads! *❧*

www.ingramcontent.com/pod-product-compliance
Lightning Source LLC
Chambersburg PA
CBHW020800250626
47155CB00003B/1166